are you Kitten me

Quinn Anderson

RIPTIDE PUBLISHING

Riptide Publishing
PO Box 1537
Burnsville, NC 28714
www.riptidepublishing.com

Are You Kitten Me

Cover art: L.C. Chase, lcchase.com
Editors: Veronica Vega, Carole-ann Galloway
Layout: L.C. Chase, lcchase.com

ISBN: 978-1-62649-971-3

First edition
December, 2022

Also available in ebook:
ISBN: 978-1-62649-970-6

are You
Kitten
me

Quinn Anderson

RIPTIDE
PUBLISHING

For the real-life Meatball. Thank you for adopting me.

table of Contents

chapter one

Afternoon sunlight splashed through curtained windows and pooled on a small kitchen table. The wood warmed under Shane's hand as he thumbed a thin scratch he'd swear hadn't been there a week ago. Cardboard boxes of various sizes dotted the tile floors, waiting to be unpacked.

Much of the furniture—from the oversized sofa to the overstuffed bookshelves—looked secondhand. Mostly because it was, but according to the home-decorating magazines stacked on the coffee table, that made it "eclectic." Nothing matching meant everything went together. Who knew?

Shane perched on the counter by the sink and surveyed his one-bedroom apartment. Not bad, all in all. A little on the small side, but it was cozy enough, with a fresh coat of blue paint and potted herbs growing in the windowsill. Their earthy smell mingled with the scent of lemon dish soap and old cookbooks. Once he'd gotten a couple of paychecks and had recuperated his moving expenses, he'd pick out "real" furniture. Like an *adult*.

More important than Shane's evaluation was the smile on his father's face as he milled around the space, toeing the well-trodden rugs.

"Better than my first post-college apartment, that's for sure." Dad paused at an end table by the sofa and inspected an array of photos. Sandy hair fell across his lined brow—same as Shane's, though gray swarmed at his temples. Faces beamed from the frames: Shane's parents, friends from school, and a grape-like cluster of people wearing identical aprons and tall white hats. Dad selected one and held it up. "Remember this?"

"Freshman year," Shane answered, swinging his long legs like a child. "My first real cooking competition. If only I'd taken victory as a sign, I could have saved you and Mom a lot of hassle."

He'd meant it, but Dad laughed. "It worked out in the end. At least you got the college experience, even if it was only for a year."

Shane glanced away to hide a wince. "Better than nothing, I guess."

Oblivious, Dad made his way to an armchair and plopped into it. "I give this place four dad jokes out of five."

"Only four?"

"Of course." Dad's face was dead serious. "The fifth one's free."

Shane groaned, but that only made Dad laugh harder. Remembering his manners, he hopped off the counter. "Can I get you something to drink?"

"Nah, I'm okay."

"Are you sure? I squeezed fresh orange juice this morning. Or I can make tea, or—"

"Will you relax, champ? Your place looks great, and seeing you settled is more than enough for me. Though I wouldn't say no to a light snack. Your ma is on another smoothie kick. I'm one overripe banana away from eating my own hand."

"Yikes. Coming right up." Shane plucked a loaded charcuterie board off the stovetop. It featured apricots he'd candied himself, an assortment of artisan cheeses diced into cubes, plump green olives, and salami slices rolled into rosebuds. He floated over and presented it to Dad with a flourish. In the maître d' voice he'd perfected over the years, he said, "May I offer you an amuse-bouche, my good sir?"

Dad selected a cube and popped it into his mouth. "Mm, delicious. What is that, cheddar? Almost tastes like ham."

"Smoked gouda." Shane smiled brightly. "I'm glad it's gouda."

"Maybe leave the dad jokes to me, son."

"Yeah, that was pretty bad. Try the apricots next. They're fresh from the local farmers' market. I just wish I'd had time to soak some pears in brandy and bake them."

Dad blinked at him.

"I'm doing too much again, aren't I?"

"Maybe a smidge. I'd think you'd be too exhausted from work to go to all this trouble."

"And miss an opportunity to show off for my dad? Perish the thought." Shane set the board on the coffee table within reach, snapped a quick photo for his Foodstagram, and collapsed onto the sofa. More like *into* it; springs creaked in agony as he sunk down three inches. "Anything new in your life?"

Dad shrugged. "Same shit, different toilet. Ma sends her love. She wants you to call her later."

"It'll have to be much later or tomorrow. I'm still on the dinner shift."

"Tomorrow it is. I'll let her know." Dad folded his hands over the little potbelly poking out from under his oil-stained shirt. "That cooking class you recommended is going well."

"Really? Mom said she had to drag you to it. Not so much kicking and screaming as swearing and bargaining with God."

"Okay, you got me. I was a bit reluctant at first. Didn't think my food was bad enough to warrant professional help."

"Your specialty was tuna casserole." Shane shuddered. "Hot out of the *microwave*."

"Yeah, yeah, everyone's a critic. I still don't see why you can't teach me."

Shane mimicked his father's earlier serious expression. "Dad, I love you. I would take a bullet for you. But if I have to show you how to use a stand mixer, one of us won't make it out alive."

Dad chuckled. "Fair enough. We're learning sauces right now. Here I thought your options were tomato or cheese, but it's a lot more complicated than that. And we've only covered the French ones."

Shane plucked a petal off a salami rose and palmed it into his mouth. Salt and spice exploded on his tongue, amplified by the juicy olive that followed. "Wait until you get to Italian cuisine. You'll learn there are *degrees* of tomato sauce. Shades. Hues, if you will."

"You know . . ." Dad fiddled with a stray thread sticking out of the arm of his chair in a way that was a bit too casual, "last week, our teacher broke us up into pairs, and I've been working with this real sweet lady."

"Ah, the buddy system." Shane nodded sagely. "Classic."

"Yup, she's around my age and grew up in the area too. She was also talked into taking the class by her malnourished family." He smiled at his own joke.

Shane narrowed his eyes. "Sounds like you have a lot in common. Should Mom and I be worried?"

Dad leaned over and gave Shane's arm a light smack. "What do you take me for? Anyway, we got chatting about our kids—or kid, in my case—and it turns out she has a son who's only a few years older than—"

Shane wailed like a dying animal. "For the love of God, no more blind dates. Why are you always trying to set me up? Are you secretly a Victorian widower with six eligible daughters? Does our future depend on me securing an advantageous marriage?"

"You read too many books. Your ma and I want you to know we support you and your . . . Is it totally cliché to say 'lifestyle'?"

"Afraid so, Dad."

"Well, her son sounds like a nice young man. He's got a steady job, and he loves animals."

Shane quirked a brow. "Funny, I don't remember putting 'must love dogs' in my Tinder bio. The dating bar is so low these days. He's employed and doesn't kick puppies for fun? That's it?"

"It's a green flag, okay? Animals can sense good people." Dad shoveled more cheese into his mouth. He was still chewing when he spoke next. "But all right, if you say so. No more blind dates."

"Ah, I see. The last dozen times you said that you were kidding. But now you mean it."

"Smartass. That brings me to my next point."

Shane stretched his back, stiff from hunching over the stove. "I'm really not in the mood to talk about my dearth of romantic prospects."

"I was going to ask about your apartment. How long is your lease?"

Shane bit back a pained wheeze. Like the prophet Cassandra, he'd seen this conversation coming and had been powerless to stop it. "You don't have to worry about me, I swear. I know I needed some help after I graduated, but things are different now. I'll never come crawling back home again."

Was it his imagination or had dark clouds billowed across the sky as soon as he'd said that aloud?

Dad crinkled his nose as if he'd smelled something foul. "Son, you could have stayed forever. Your ma cried for a week when you left for college. That's not the issue."

And yet, Shane lay awake at night regardless, thinking about what a burden he'd been on his folks. They were a good few years away from retirement. In his worst nightmares, they were still hustling in their golden years, providing for their deadbeat son who never got his shit together.

He dispelled the image with a quick shake of his head. "It's a twelve-month lease. Why?"

Dad cleared his throat of cheese debris. "If you're going to be here for a while, you should make it your own. This is a fine place, but it's missing something."

"Window treatments?"

"I don't know what that is, but I trust your taste. In my expert opinion as a professional dad, I think you could use someone else around the house."

Shane looked him up and down. "But this *isn't* about my love life?"

"No, it's about having a companion. Maybe a dog, or hell, cats are cute. Trust me, I lived the single life for a long time before I met your ma. It's comforting to have another heartbeat under your roof. And you'd always have an excuse to leave boring work functions. 'I gotta walk Spot' or whatever. It's perfect."

Huh, a dog. He'd begged his parents for a puppy a few birthdays in a row, but he was pretty sure most kids went through that phase. The closest he'd come to pet ownership was winning a carnival goldfish that'd gone belly-up within twenty-four hours. Not the most auspicious start.

"I don't know," Shane said, already drafting a pros-and-cons list in his head. "Dogs need a regular schedule, and my hours are all over the place."

And brutal. Twelve-hour shifts, fifty-plus hours a week. Minimum.

"Promise me you'll think about it. No need to make a decision today, but this complex is full of families. I bet one of your neighbors' kids would love to walk the dog while you're at work and earn some pocket money." Dad paused. "Or, you know, if you were to meet a man . . . say, an animal lover. Then he could—"

"That's it. I'm putting a moratorium on dating talk." Shane swirled words around in his mouth, trying to pick out the right ones by taste alone. "But I will think about it. I have to admit, it's been lonely going from a house filled with family to an empty apartment. I love having my own space, but last night I caught myself telling the ficus about my day." He gestured to a decorative shrub by the back door.

"Doesn't that help plants grow faster?"

"Not when they're plastic."

"Well, I hear dogs are fantastic listeners." Dad tugged at the loose thread again. "I may have called the local shelter on my way over here. You know, the one on Third and Main?"

"*Dad.*"

"It was for your ma, I promise. Since you left, she's been talking about getting a bird, of all things. To fill our empty nest, I suppose. Do shelters even have birds?" Dad shook his head. "Anyway, good news: the lady I spoke to says they don't do home inspections."

Shane's feathers ruffled despite himself. "Why shouldn't they inspect my apartment? What's wrong with it?"

"Nothing, but I figured you wouldn't want a bunch of strangers trampling through your new bachelor pad." Dad's phone beeped, and he dug it out of a frayed jean pocket. "It's the boys from the auto shop. I gotta get going. Let's do this again soon, okay? When we have more time, I'd love to pick your brain about something called a morning sauce."

Shane grinned. "You mean a Mornay sauce?"

"That's the one."

"They bumped you up from béchamel already? You must be the star pupil."

"Yeah, yeah. All this nutmeg and Gruyère and unsalted butter nonsense makes my head spin." Dad rose to his feet, knees creaking like boughs in a storm. "I'll get out of your hair. Or *chair*, rather." That earned another groan from Shane, which Dad blissfully ignored. "I've got tires that need rotating, and you have plenty of unpacking to do still."

True as that was, Shane's heart throbbed as he walked his father to the threshold and hugged him goodbye. If he held on a little tighter than usual, Dad didn't comment. After a final reminder to call Mom, Dad shuffled out into the bright spring sunshine, and Shane shut the door with a sigh.

He stood stock-still in the living room, head cocked toward the murmured voices soaking through the thin walls without really hearing them. His thoughts ticked like gears. A dog might be exactly what he needed. It'd be nice to come home and feel like someone was happy to see him. Someone had missed him. Someone had noticed he wasn't there.

Did he have time to drop by the shelter?

Shane consulted his phone. In an hour and a half, he'd be right on schedule, which Chef Antoine would view as outrageous tardiness. That could work in Shane's favor, though. Having a time constraint meant he couldn't make any impulsive decisions; he'd have to think about it like he'd promised.

A mixture of nerves and uncertainty gurgled in Shane's gut. He dressed prematurely for work, donning a crisp white shirt and black slacks. Under normal circumstances, he'd drive, but a light breeze whistled a siren song through the tree limbs outside his window. They tapped on the glass, loaded with tiny buds that would unfurl into emerald leaves in the coming months.

His running shoes lay neglected by the doorway, gazing dolefully up as if to ask what they'd done to deserve such treatment. Fucking night shifts. They always left Shane too bone-tired to stand, let alone jog. But a pre-shift walk—and a break from all the unpacking—would do him good.

He exited through the glass back door, which opened into a large courtyard in the center of his red-brick building. Most of the adults and children were at work or school, respectively, but a group of older women standing under a tree took a break from their gossip to wave at Shane as he passed. He winked back, inspiring a round of adorable giggling.

At least someone found him charming. Dad seemed to think there was a glut of single gay men secreted away somewhere in their seaside town, but Shane hadn't had much luck finding them. His complete lack of free time didn't help either.

A quick glance at his phone confirmed he still had over an hour left before work. Breaking into a light trot, he opened the iron gate at the mouth of the courtyard and sidled through right as his stomach gurgled. Damn, he'd burned through breakfast making that charcuterie board. He should've grabbed some salami for the road.

If he skipped the shelter and arrived early—or earlier than was demanded, at least—he could scarf down some of the leftovers the breakfast crew always stashed in the back. Same as the night shift did with any choice cuts of meat that were going to end up in a dumpster. It was a solidarity thing. And on the off chance they were busy on a Tuesday, it might be Shane's only shot at sustenance for hours.

His feet, however, seemed unconcerned by his stomach's plight. They wandered down the worn sidewalk in the general direction of his place of employment but with a decided slant toward "downtown": three quasi-large office buildings, none of which scraped the sky so much as glanced wistfully at it from a safe distance.

Back when he'd first started apartment-hunting, Mom had insisted on touring the neighborhood with him as if they hadn't lived nearby their entire lives. Playgrounds filled with chubby-cheeked toddlers? Check. Small shops with velvety succulents in the windows? Check. Nothing exciting happened ever? Check. It was a sleepy town all right.

Come to think of it, hadn't Mom casually pointed out the animal shelter on Third and Main as well? It was official: after thirty years of blissful matrimony, Shane's parents had become a hive mind. As their child, he was contractually obligated to find it embarrassing. Yucky, as five-year-old him would have said. But, truthfully, he envied them. He'd take the stability of married life over the "thrill" of being single any damn day.

Adulthood was supposed to be a big adventure that culminated in a fairy-tale ending. But in Shane's experience, it was more like a to-do list that gained two new tasks every time he crossed one off.

Uneventful weeks slid into monotonous months, and all Shane had to show for it was lower back pain.

His feet won the debate Shane hadn't realized they'd been having. He found himself standing in front of the shelter: a nondescript cinderblock building with a large fenced yard stretching around to the back. Muffled yips and thudding paws echoed down the quiet street.

A bubble of excitement expanded in his chest. If he was here anyway, he might as well go in. Just for a quick peek. He was *not* going to adopt the first dog he laid eyes on, and if his resolve wavered, the time constraint would keep his promise. Besides, Bring Your Pet to Work Day wasn't a thing in his industry. Health codes and such. Though customers were allowed to bring their dogs onto the patio . . .

No. Shane would stop in for five minutes, see what the adoption process was like, and then go straight to work. His apartment wasn't pet-ready anyway. There were shelves to put up, and dishes to clean, and—

The bubble popped like an overinflated balloon. A scenario played in his head: The shelter workers took one look at him before declaring, correctly, that he was in no position to care for another living creature. Then Shane was tarred, feathered, and chased out of town by a pitchfork-wielding mob, never to return.

He shook his head. The bell above the door jingled when he walked in, bringing apprehension with it. He stepped into a reception area that he could only describe as overwhelmingly beige.

The noise registered first. Not only barking dogs and meowing cats but a dozen or so people bustling around like they had somewhere important to be. An assorted bunch too—all ages, sizes, and shapes. Pets must be a universal language. Next came the aroma. It smelled like the park on an overcast day: grass trimmings with a splash of damp fur.

A long counter separated the employees from the . . . customers? Adopters? Rows of folding chairs were dotted with figures bent over clipboards. Probably filling out paperwork.

Before sensory overload could chase Shane right back out the door, a woman in a teal shirt with a white logo materialized before him. Her nametag read, *Taina*, in block letters. "Whatcha looking for, hun?"

What a coincidence. Shane would love to know the answer to that question.

"A dog." He scratched his nose, though it didn't itch. "Maybe a puppy."

Taina gave him a once-over, and Shane stiffened like dried glue. "You've come to the right place. Can I give you some advice?"

"Um, sure?"

"Go for a dog. And I'm not just saying that because everyone picks the cute babies over the adults. Puppies need a *lot* of attention."

Wow, Shane's apocalyptic vision hadn't been that far off. He must look as tired as he felt, and he still had a long shift ahead of him.

Shane shuffled his feet. "Sorry, a dog, then."

"No need to apologize, hun. I certainly don't want to discourage you from adopting. Kitten season is in full swing, and we're at capacity." She swiveled in place and pointed behind her. "The puppy kennels are down the hallway to the left. If you go out the double doors, you'll find the big dogs in their play area. Small dogs are next to that. And please keep an eye out when you're entering and exiting. Our many escape artists have been working overtime today."

Shane thanked her and scurried off in the direction she'd indicated. He passed several glass-doored rooms, which contained kittens that were too young to be adopted yet, judging by their shuttered eyes and vibrating limbs. He paused long enough to coo at a pint-sized black panther who was pawing blindly at the partition, before he rounded the corner.

As Taina had described, the kennels were up ahead, along with two sets of glass double doors. Through them, Shane could see a mulched yard covered in colorful playground equipment. Dogs of all breeds and hues wrestled with toys and chased each other around the fenced perimeter.

One Labrador ran the circuit over and over and over until Shane felt dizzy from watching. Did dogs ever run out of energy? Could Shane keep up? Anxiety gnawed on his bones. Fuck, this was the exact indecision that had led to him dating Joey "Smoker's Cough" Kunz for three weeks in high school.

A flash of movement drew his attention to the left. More wire cages had been stacked against the wall, lined with padded mats. A handful of people were perusing them: an old man holding a little girl's hand, another teal shirt, and a guy dressed in black with his back turned.

Shane squinted through the bars, and it became apparent why these cages had been separated from the puppies. They were packed with kittens. Not as young as the ones he'd passed earlier, but their big heads and triangle tails belied their age. The adults must have their own area somewhere else.

A wobbly tortoiseshell cat locked eyes with Shane and let out a plaintive *mew*.

"Aw, cutie," he said out loud without thinking.

To his abject horror, the black-clad man glanced over. And he was *hot*.

Balls.

Shane flapped a hand in the air. "Not you! The, uh, kittens."

The man blinked and turned wordlessly back around. Shane would've kicked himself if he could bend that way. He hadn't gotten a perfect view during their five-second exchange, but the mystery man was around Shane's age with dark hair and eyes. And he had some serious bone structure. Oh, the bone structure. Sharp as a knife.

Should he say something? Apologize? Would that make things worse? God, he'd been single for way too long. He'd completely forgotten how to flirt. Or act vaguely human.

He drifted over despite himself, but Hottie McCheekBones was engrossed in conversation with an employee. So much for that. Shane covered his blunder by pretending to study the cages. After a minute or so, he would casually head for the dogs as intended.

Bright eyes caught his attention. They stared at him from the second-to-last kennel on the right, poking out of a pile of sleeping babies. A beautiful orange—almost red like a fox—kitten extradited herself (himself?) from the throng and pawed at the door.

"Oh, you are *gorgeous*," Shane murmured as he hurried over. An information sheet pinned to the cage said the orange tabby was a nameless girl they'd gotten in the day before. Twelve weeks old, two pounds. The closer Shane leaned to the bars, the harder she pawed, eyes sparkling and whiskers wiggling. When he dangled his index finger in front of her face, she sniffed it before giving him a tiny sandpaper lick.

Shane's heart filled with confetti and then burst like a piñata.

"Ah, there you are." Taina had appeared as if by magic. "I wanted to make sure you didn't get lost, but it seems I shouldn't have worried. I know that face. Love at first sight?"

"No." The lie weighed on Shane's tongue. "I'm here for a dog. Right?"

Taina giggled. "Sometimes I wonder why I bother asking people what they're looking for. Would you like to hold her?"

"Yes, please." Shane sounded like a child who'd been offered ice cream.

Taina unlocked the cage, quickly extracted the kitten in question, and deposited her into Shane's trembling hands. He half expected to drop her, but she snuggled right into the dish he'd formed with his palms and then swiveled her angular head to stare at him.

Shane peered into her eyes for all of two seconds before his mouth formed the words his brain was screaming. "She's the one. This is my cat."

Holy shit, holy shit, *holy shit*, what was he doing? Sweat beaded on his brow, but the kitten was soft and warm and so damn *cute*. One more peek at her sweet little face and Shane was hers, no denying it.

"I had a feeling! Congratulations. She's a beauty." Taina moved to take her back. The kitten dug sharp claws into Shane's sleeve like she didn't want to leave. Thankfully, she got all fabric and no flesh. The second she was back in her cage, she yowled in such an affronted way, Shane laughed.

At the sound, the hot guy glanced over—long enough for Shane to catch his gaze—before snapping back around. Was it Shane's imagination, or had a couple of sparks flown when their eyes had met? The pure bliss flooding through Shane's system almost convinced him to waltz over and introduce himself after all.

But Taina clapped him on the back. "Let's get you an application. Assuming all the paperwork checks out, you can take her straight home and get settled."

Paperwork. Home. The words were loose marbles rolling around Shane's skull.

What time was it?

He waited for Taina to leave before whipping out his phone. Fifteen minutes had passed since he'd first arrived. How was that possible? The breath he'd been holding came out as a relieved whistle. A second later, he sucked it back in.

He had zero pet supplies, and he had to work soon. How was he going to get the kitten to the apartment, feed her nonexistent food, and make it to his shift in time? Would she be safe on her own for the next twelve hours? Did the shelter have a layaway program? Could he put a cat on hold?

A mantra of *Oh God, what now?* played in his head as bliss transformed into panic. Before he could work himself into a proper froth, a muted sound broke through the din. The kitten tapped at the wall of her cage with a teensy paw and gave an even teensier mew.

Shane's pulse quieted to a manageable staccato. Either he was a huge sap, or the kitten had magical soothing powers. Possibly both. He inhaled deeply, exhaled slowly. He'd figure this out, whatever it took. Calling out once wouldn't kill him. He'd say he had a cold and then hit up a pet store for whatever she needed. Everything was going to be fine, and for once, his inner voice sounded confident.

When his lungs were back in working order, Shane patted the kitten through the bars one more time before strolling over to the kennels. Excited puppies launched themselves at him, tails wagging so hard they blurred.

"I'm sorry I'm not adopting you." Shane pet velvet-soft ears wherever he could reach them. "I meant to, but my heart got stolen right out of my chest. Forgive me?"

The puppies gave no sign they understood, of course. Probably for the best, or Shane would be apologizing all day. He fidgeted with his phone, already dreading the call he had to make. Chef Antoine had a top-notch bullshit detector, and Shane could lie about as well as his dad could cook. Would he be fired if he blew off work an hour before his shift?

His stomach bounced around his torso like a tennis ball in a washing machine. He peeked at the kitten for comfort, but her cage was blocked by a familiar black-clad back. The other employee had disappeared, leaving the hot guy from before alone. He was hunched over, playing with Shane's kitten.

Perfect opener.

Shane took a fortifying breath, stuffed both hands into his pockets, and sauntered that way, pretending to look at other cats before stopping next to him. "Isn't she stunning? The red one, I mean."

"Yeah." The guy straightened up without looking away; he was a couple of inches taller than Shane. He smelled good too. Like musky cologne. "I wonder if her eyes will stay that blue."

"Time will tell." Shane chewed on his bottom lip, searching for something witty to say. He landed on a simple "I'm Shane, by the way."

"Damian." He finally glanced over. "Oh. It's you."

At least Shane had made an impression?

"Sorry about before. I, uh . . ." His mind blanked and then produced a colorful string of swear words.

"Sorry about what?" Damian blinked hazel eyes at him like he had no idea what Shane was prattling on about.

"Nothing. Forget about it."

Damian shrugged and leaned back down to make *pspspsp* sounds at Shane's kitten. And Shane couldn't blame him. She was rubbing her body against the bars in a way that cried, *Pet me, love me, give me your wallet.*

The cat was better at flirting than him. Excellent. Maybe she could give him some pointers. Or maybe he wouldn't need them. With an adorable baby animal waiting at home, he had the perfect excuse to invite over cute boys like Damian. Jackpot.

Before Shane could formulate a pickup line, Damian broke the silence. "This might be the friendliest cat I've ever met. You can tell she loves to be loved."

"I know, right?" Shane gave her ear as good of a scratch as he could manage. "So calm too. She's going to make a great pet."

"For sure. I can't wait to take her home."

Shane's heart stopped cold in his chest. "What?"

"This is my new kitten." Damian grinned so brightly that Shane was momentarily blinded. "I'm waiting for the application as we speak."

"You can't adopt her!" Shane blurted out. A frog had taken up residence in his throat.

Damian's thick eyebrows shot up to his hairline. "Why not?"

"Because *I'm* adopting her!"

"What? No way." Damian whirled around to face him. "You can't be—"

"And we're back." Taina reappeared by Shane's side with a clipboard in hand. "Fill these forms out, and we'll get you on your way."

Shane had never kissed a woman in his life, but he had half a mind to start now. He jabbed a thumb at her while glaring at Damian. "See?"

Damian's awful, not at all soft-looking lips popped open. "*What*?"

Taina's gaze darted between them. "Is something the matter?"

"Yes!" Damian cried, while at the same time, Shane shouted, "No!"

As the tension in the air went from a simmer to a boil, the employee who'd been talking to Damian strolled up with an identical clipboard in hand.

"Here are your adoption papers. Fill out the highlighted sections, and we'll review it." He was smiling, but when everyone stared at him in tense silence, the smile slipped off his face like it'd been soaped. "Did I miss something?"

"You and me both." Taina's brow furrowed. "It seems there's been a mix-up."

Chapter Two

"Let me get this straight." Damian pinched the bridge of his nose, a migraine jabbing him between the eyes. "We're both trying to adopt the exact same cat at the exact same time? Seriously?"

"I'm really sorry," said Tom, who Damian had learned was a volunteer from the local high school. He was practically shaking in his sneakers. Poor kid. "This almost never happens."

"This is ridic—" Damian stopped short and patted Tom lightly on the shoulder. "Sorry. We'll figure this out, okay? Don't worry about it."

Tom relaxed under Damian's fingers and shot him a grateful look. For three whole seconds.

"I'm worried about it!" cried the kitten thief. Shane, as he'd introduced himself. His protest turned Tom's limbs into wet noodles.

Damian glared at Shane. "Don't take this out on the shelter workers. It's not their fault."

Shane narrowed light green eyes right back. "Trust me, I blame you and you alone." He turned to the woman next to him. "This *almost* never happens, Taina? So, it's not unheard of?"

"Not entirely." Taina shrugged. "The puppies and kittens get a lot of attention. Sometimes multiple families show interest in the same day. But it's not usually the same *second*."

In true kitten-thief fashion, Shane declared, "I saw her first!"

Another tendril of pain sprouted above Damian's eye sockets. "You got here after me. Remember?"

If the soft pink that bloomed in Shane's cheeks was any indication, he recalled their initial exchange well. It had certainly been a learning experience for Damian. First impressions weren't everything after all. How had he ever thought this guy was cute?

Apparently, Shane was a stubborn thief. "You weren't looking at the kitten, though. You were standing over there, talking to Tom."

"Yeah." Damian crossed his arms. "About adopting the kitten."

"That doesn't prove anything, and Taina left to get my application first."

Taina waved her hands, clipboard and all. "No fighting, please, or we'll have to escort you from the premises. *Both* of you."

Damian, who'd been about to fire a hot retort, shut his mouth with an audible *click*. Shane rolled a muscled shoulder before staring down at his shoes. Sandy hair fell artfully over his smooth brow, and Damian's stomach flipped. He must be coming down with something.

Once they'd quieted, Taina blew out a breath. "Again, we apologize about this. Our adoption policy is first-come, first-serve. Normally, whatever party put in their paperwork first would get the animal. But neither of you have gotten to that stage yet, so we're at an impasse."

Shane's head popped up. His eyes—Damian had to shoo away thoughts of fresh mint whenever he looked at them—darted to the clipboard in Taina's hand.

For a second, Damian's mind was blank. Then, the dots connected and flashed red like warning lights. "Don't even think about it!"

"What?" Shane's hand was already creeping toward the clipboard.

Taina snatched it away, tutting. "Absolutely not. You two are not going to race to see who can fill one out the fastest and end up with a big pile of scribbles. Printer ink is expensive."

Shane's arm dropped. "How are we going to decide, then?"

A sly remark perched on the tip of Damian's tongue, but Shane was staring at the kitten, face pinched. She'd huddled in the back corner of her cage while the others slept on obliviously. The shouting had to be stressing her out.

Cold guilt drenched Damian, and he'd be willing to bet Shane felt the same. Sweet kitty. She didn't deserve this. Rationally, neither did Shane. He wasn't trying to *steal* the kitten, no matter how much

Damian's lizard brain screeched at him. It was a coincidence. An annoying one, but it wasn't like either of them had planned this. And, according to the fists clenched at Shane's sides, he had a dog in this fight, for lack of a more apropos phrase.

Damian's outrage ebbed. He cleared his throat and switched to the soothing customer-service tone he used with irate clients. "There's a compromise here somewhere if we can keep our cool and find it."

Shane peeked at him with wide doe-like eyes. "You mean it?"

Good to know Damian hadn't lost his touch. "I do. It'll be fine."

Tom piped up. "Maybe you two should fill out the applications. There might be something that makes one of you ineligible."

"I've adopted from this shelter before," Damian said. "Granted, it was a while ago, but if there was nothing wrong then, I doubt there will be now." He glanced at Shane for his response. Shane's face had *panic* stamped across it in bold capital letters.

Taina turned to Shane. "I hate to say it, but weren't you interested in a dog?"

"I changed my mind."

"Remember what I said about puppies, hun. Kittens are the same way. They need tons of time and energy. If not a dog, you might be better off with an adult cat."

"I don't want *a* cat. I want *this* cat." Shane reached through the bars, and the kitten abandoned her defensive position to rub against his hand.

Jealousy thumped Damian on the back. Hard. He shook it off. "I'd also like *this* cat, so what are our options?"

"I got it!" Shane stuck a finger in the air like he was about to shout *eureka*. "The shelter has security, right? I saw the cameras when I walked in."

"Yeah," Tom said. "Sometimes people try to steal puppies so they can sell them. Or worse."

Shane grimaced before picking up steam again. "Let's check the footage and see which of us asked for an application first. Whoever it was gets the cat."

Damian snorted before he could stop himself.

Shane rounded on him. "Problem?"

"No, he's right," Taina said. "We could technically do that, but Tom and I are on the clock. There are other pets that would love to get adopted today, and our security is ancient. We can't drop everything to review the feed like we're TV crime-solvers." She shook her head. "You're grown men. Can't you talk this out?"

Damian glanced at Shane, and Shane stared back. The friction was so tangible it might as well have been a shower of red sparks, but a silent agreement passed between them.

"Yes," they said at the same time.

"We'll leave you to it." Taina clapped a hand on Tom's shoulder and steered him away. "I'll be back to check on you in a few minutes. If a decision hasn't been made by then, I'm afraid neither of you can adopt the kitten."

Her words reverberated in the air long after she'd disappeared, ominous as tolling bells.

"Fuck," Damian muttered.

"I agree." Shane dragged a large hand through his hair. "What a mess."

"I already know the answer, but I'll ask anyway: Are you sure you can't just pick a different pet?"

Shane looked him dead in the eye. "Can you?"

Damn it.

"I would, really. I love all cats, from the Grumpy Gus to the Prissy Pants. But I've been searching for this one for a long time."

"What?"

"Well, obviously not this exact cat, but a ginger girl."

Shane blinked. "There isn't another one around here somewhere?"

Damian wrinkled his nose. "Um, no. There are plenty of orange cats, but females are extremely rare. I've been in and out of shelters for the past year looking for one. I did come across a couple, but they got adopted out from under me." He restrained himself from adding, *like what you're trying to do*.

"Huh. I didn't know that." Shane's eyes narrowed. "Wait, you only want the kitten because she's rare? Would you have been happy with any orange girl? I want this cat, specifically."

"Please don't insult my intentions. I haven't insulted yours." Not out loud, anyway. "My grandmother had one when I was growing up, and I adored her. She loved me too. Her name was Tabitha, and she'd always sleep with me when we spent the night. Right on top of my head like a fuzzy hat. She pretty much convinced me orange girls are the best and, considering this is my third attempt, I rest my case."

Truthfully, Damian didn't care what color she was. He'd fallen in love with her the second their eyes had met. But it was a good story and a convenient excuse.

"Can't argue with you there." Shane cleared his throat. "I mean, nice anecdote and all, but it doesn't mean you should get the kitten."

"All right." Damian crossed his arms over his chest. "Why should you? Won any Best Cat Dad medals recently?"

"Uh." Shane's eyes widened. "Actually, I've never adopted before."

Damian brushed that off. "Not a deal breaker. It only takes one to become a cat person for life, trust me. Which means we're at a stalemate, and we're running out of time."

"Time." At that, panic eclipsed Shane's face once more. "*Work.*" The way he said it made it sound like *Oh, shit.* He pulled a phone out of his pocket and paled when the screen lit up. "I gotta make a call."

"Are you late or something?"

Shane's hand shook so badly he almost dropped the phone. "I will be if I don't call out soon. Not that it matters much. My boss is going to be pissed regardless." He laughed, but it rang hollow. His earlier confidence had fled for parts unknown. It was almost enough to make Damian feel bad for him.

Almost. "You should get on that. I'll wait right here."

"Thanks." Shane started to walk away, but then he snapped around. "And if Taina comes back while I'm gone?"

Damn. So close. "Sorry, but it was worth a shot." Damian took a breath and tried to radiate calm. "Listen, there's no shame in getting in over your head. Maybe you should go to work and try again tomorrow."

"No way. My job can wait." Shane's face was set, but his voice wavered as if he were a kid telling a fib.

God, did Shane have to be so *cute?* It was making this unreasonably difficult. Damian shifted his weight. "I don't want to stress you out any more than you already are, but—"

"I'm not stressed!" As soon as he'd said it, Shane bit his lip hard enough to whiten the flesh. And draw Damian's eyes directly to his mouth, surprisingly pink against his tawny skin.

"Clearly." Damian rooted around for a question to distract Shane before he popped like warm champagne. "Are you from around here?"

Shane nodded. "Born and raised. I've got a place over at Windy Groves. The apartment complex? It's like fifteen minutes from here. Ten if I jog. I've clocked it before while on a run."

Huh, Damian wouldn't have pegged Shane as a cardio person. His big arms and muscular back suggested either physical labor or regular trips to the gym.

Damian dispelled that errant thought with a quick head shake. "Weird coincidence. That's where I live too."

How had they never bumped into each other? Damian would have remembered seeing a hottie hanging around.

Because he would have steered very, very clear.

"Really? How long have you lived there? Do you like it?" For a second, Shane's eyes were bright as spring grass. Then he frowned. "You're trying to distract me, aren't you?"

"Busted, though I was curious." Damian pursed his lips. "Any idea what we should do?"

"Hell if I know. Compare our credit scores?" Shane swept an arm at the room around them. "Taina could be back any minute, and we're no closer to deciding who gets the kitten."

Speaking of which, she'd been darting looks between them like a child watching her parents argue. Unwelcome memories barged into the forefront of Damian's mind. He shooed them away before they could dig in claws.

"Whatever we do, let's try not to give the kitty anxiety."

"At least we agree on one thing." Shane fell silent, and Damian could almost see gears ticking behind his eyes. "Rock, paper, scissors?"

"Please tell me you're joking."

"You got a better idea?"

"I guess not." Damian made a fist and then rested it on the open palm of his left hand. "On the count of three?"

Shane's hands formed a mirror image of Damian's. "Works for me."

They played, and Damian did his level best not to think about how silly they must look: two grown men using a children's game to decide the fate of a cat.

Any amusement he might have derived from the situation was quickly squashed. Damian's rock beat Shane's scissors, declaring him the victor. It was a game of chance, yet somehow he wasn't surprised.

When Shane proposed they go best two out of three, Damian agreed without protest. Inexplicable unease had draped itself over his shoulders. Damian won the next round as well. He should have been thrilled. He should have crowed with victory. But Shane's eyes were bloodshot. Tears? Shit.

"Best out of five?" Shane's hands were shaking again.

Damian chewed his lip. "Okay."

Shane won—scissors cut paper—and his expression brightened, but then Damian took round four. The unease became an anchor dragging Damian's whole body down.

"Best out of seven!"

"Enough." Damian's heart plummeted into his stomach. "I'm sorry. It's over."

"But I can't lose!"

"The game was your idea!" Damian flinched at his own raised voice. What was it about this guy that got under his skin?

"So, that's it, huh?" Shane's face scrunched, his eyes fixated on the kitten. "My first real pet, and I fucked it up before I even got out the door."

Damian reached out, hesitated, and then dropped his hand. "Are you all right?"

"Nope. Not in the slightest."

Did Shane have to sound so miserable? The migraine Damian had been ignoring punched him behind both eyeballs. "I don't know what to tell you. Fair is fair."

"You don't understand." Shane's voice lowered as if he were talking to himself. "The moment I saw her . . . I swear, *she* picked *me*."

On the contrary, Damian understood perfectly. Most pet owners did. The animals did the adopting, and their humans were along for the ride.

The kitten yowled and batted at the cage like she was trying to reach Shane. Another wave of jealousy crashed over Damian. Did she like Shane better? It hardly mattered anymore. Her tiny baby brain would forget him in a week or so. Somehow, the thought wasn't comforting.

Blowing out a breath, Damian settled on the one thing he could say that was at least genuine: "Shane, I'm so sorry."

"Yeah, right."

"I mean it." Damian had ripped Shane's heart out and stomped all over it. Good reason or not, it was far from his proudest moment. "What a shitty situation. I wish there was something I could do."

Shane considered him, a line etched between his brows. Damian stared back, and as seconds ticked by, his mouth went dry. Something crackled in the air around them. Damian had called it tension before, but now he wasn't so sure. He ordered himself to tear his eyes away, but they were glued to the handsome, heartbroken face in front of him.

Taina waltzed into the room, and the mood shattered like a pane of glass. "Everything okay in here?"

"Yes," Damian said.

Shane's shoulders slumped. "No."

"Have you come to a decision?"

"We have." Damian faltered for a fraction of a second before holding out a hand. "I'm adopting the kitten."

Shane sniffled but didn't protest, his eyes glued to the ground.

"I see." Taina patted Shane on the back. "Did you want to look at the other animals?"

Shane shook his head. "I've had enough for today."

"All right, then." Taina passed Damian a familiar clipboard. "Get these filled out, and bring them to the front desk when you're finished." With one last sympathetic glance at Shane, she left.

Damian shifted from one foot to the other. "Do you want to wait and see if my application gets accepted?"

"It will." Shane wiped his nose on the back of a hand. "You said you've adopted from here before. They probably have you on file or something."

"They do. My family's been coming here forever." Damian's breath snagged in his throat. "I . . . Um." He had no idea how to finish the sentence.

Shane's head popped up, eyes bright but not with tears this time. "Wait, I'm getting an idea."

A nonsensical flicker of hope kindled in Damian. "Oh?"

"We live in the same complex, right?"

"Uh, yeah?" After pausing for thought, Damian straightened. "If you want to visit her or something, I might be okay with that."

"That's it!" Shane clapped his hands together. "We'll adopt the cat together."

Had Damian been a cartoon character, steam would have billowed out of his ears. "*What*? How did you get that out of what I said?" Give a mouse a cookie . . .

"It's perfect! She'll belong to both of us, and we'll share custody." His confident act didn't match his pleading tone.

Share custody. Like divorcees with a latchkey child. That hit far too close to home, literally.

"We can't both adopt her."

"Maybe not on paper, but we're practically neighbors. We can make it work."

Damian huffed. "It'll never work."

"Why not? Taina said babies need constant care. I can keep an eye on her while you're busy and vice versa."

Busy? Damian? What a concept.

"Actually, I work from home, so I can watch her twenty-four hours a day if need be."

Shane whistled. "That sounds kinda nice."

"It is. I love my job. So long as I get everything done, they don't much care how or where I do it."

"Well, you have to sleep eventually, cushy job or not."

Damian squawked in indignation. His job wasn't *cushy*, thank you very much, but now wasn't the time to argue the point. "You're not thinking about the future, Shane. Assuming nothing tragic happens, this cat is going to live until I'm in my early forties. Do you know what your life is going to be like a year from now? A decade from now?"

Shane opened his mouth, but Damian cut him off. "And another thing: You're a complete stranger. An hour ago, I had no idea you existed, and now you want to adopt a cat together? For all I know, you're gonna disappear out of my life as quickly as you appeared."

"I won't." Shane clenched his hands into twin white balls. "Give me a chance, and I'll prove it."

Damian sighed. "You're not going to let this go, are you?"

In lieu of an answer, Shane folded his arms over his chest.

"Fine." Damian held out a hand before he could talk himself out of it. "Give me your number."

"Really?" Shane whipped out his phone so fast, Damian expected it to go flying across the room. "You'll share her with me?"

"No," Damian said point-blank. "But my grandmother is Italian, and if she found out I was rude to a neighbor, she'd hang me from a hook and make prosciutto. My first offer is still on the table. You can visit the kitten. If I have space in my schedule." Which he pretty much always did, but Shane didn't need to know that.

Why was Damian agreeing to this again? Ah yes, a hot guy pouted in his general direction. Damian's kryptonite.

To his surprise, Shane's face crumpled like a wadded-up sheet of foil. "Visit? That's all?"

"It's all I'm comfortable with right now. I don't know you."

"We could fix that."

Was Damian imagining the flirtatious tone? He must be. "You realize how bizarre this is, right? Most people wouldn't even consider it."

"Apparently neither of us are 'most people,'" Shane countered, and to Damian's horror, he found it charming.

Before that particular train of thought could flatten Damian, Shane held out his phone. "I want your number too. And please don't give me a fake. I've done that on enough bad first dates to know the signs."

There went Damian's last escape route, not that he'd planned on lying. Sighing, he tucked the clipboard under an arm and did as instructed. When Shane's number popped up on his own screen, he saved it under *Kitten Thief.* It scratched a certain petty itch.

"Satisfied?" Damian returned Shane's phone.

"One more thing. What's your apartment number?"

Damian took a step back. "Stranger danger, dude. What if you're a stalker? Or a murderer? Or someone who never uses their turn signal?"

Shane stared wordlessly at Damian while raising a single eyebrow.

"Okay, you're probably not. But why do you need to know where I live?"

"I'm mostly curious if we're in the same building but also for insurance. So you can't take the kitten and disappear on me. I swear I won't show up unannounced or anything weird."

Damian scoffed, but Shane's set expression never wavered. "Fine. I'm apartment 18A."

Shane perked up. "Oh hey, I'm 20A. We really are neighbors."

Two doors down from each other? And they'd never crossed paths before? Hm.

"Cool," Damian said aloud. "What a fun coincidence that definitely won't bite me in the ass later."

"There's no need for sarcasm."

"I don't *need* sarcasm. I want it."

With the exchange complete, they stood in silence, shifting from foot to foot like exactly what they were: strangers in a public place who should be politely ignoring one another.

After a beat, Shane tilted his head to the side. "Not to push my luck, but why did you say yes? You could have told me to fuck off."

"I don't know," Damian answered without pause. "You seem like a nice guy, and you looked so sad. I . . . didn't want to hurt you." He cringed at his own veracity.

The corners of Shane's lips twitched. "I appreciate it. You won't regret this, I promise. I'm a responsible cat dad in the making." He glanced at his phone and grimaced. "That being said, I'm so going to be late for work."

"You won't get in trouble, will you?"

Shane exploded into laughter, startling Damian back onto his heels. "If my boss is in a good mood, I'll get yelled at in front of my colleagues. If not, I'll be spatchcocked and made into *tourtière*."

Damian was about to ask what all those words meant, but Shane was bouncing on the balls of his feet like he was about to take off running. "You'd better get going, then."

Shane blurted out, "Do you promise too?"

Damian blinked. "Promise what?"

"You'll let me see her? You won't ghost me or keep rescheduling?"

"I said I would, didn't I? To the best of my ability, I'll let you *visit* the cat." Damian leaned closer to her, but she didn't seem to notice. She was attempting to snag Shane's sleeve with a claw.

"All right, I'll go." He paused long enough to pet as much of her as he could reach before turning hard eyes on Damian. "And I'll be in touch."

"Of that, I have no doubt."

Shane's response was a crooked smile followed by an excellent view of his broad back as he walked away.

Damian stared after him for what felt like an hour but was likely closer to a minute. Thoughts sloshed around in his head, predominantly curse words mixed with pleas for divine intervention.

An outraged mew shook him from his stupor. He turned to the kitten—*his* kitten—and rubbed her petal-soft ears. "Aw, did I stop paying attention to you for two whole seconds? I'm sorry, sweetheart. I'll be right back. Don't steal any hearts while I'm gone."

She meowed, and it sounded an awful lot like *Too late*.

Upon stepping outside, powerful afternoon sunlight left Damian blinking away spots. Thankfully, the temperature seemed to know summer was still a couple of months away. A mild breeze swept down the sidewalk, swirling papery leaves into miniature dervishes. It also blew his hair directly into his eyeballs. He made a mental note to take an aspirin the second he got back to the apartment.

The short walk home was spent calming the kitten as she circled her new carrier, avoiding nosy pedestrians, and replaying his entire interaction with Shane in technicolor detail. Watching a grown man almost cry over a cat was a tough image to shake. Shane was lucky Damian was such a damn softie.

"Stop it," he muttered under his breath. "Shane isn't another stray in need of adopting."

There was no sense in stressing about it. If their slapdash arrangement worked at all, it'd be a miracle. As soon as things got inconvenient—as was inevitable—Shane would give up. He'd bet money on it.

Why did his own mental voice sound uncertain?

Sighing, Damian directed his boisterous thoughts to the pile of work awaiting him. Thanks to the shelter mishap, he'd used up his lunch break and then some. The home office was bound to have emailed by now with questions about the coding Damian had submitted. Or hell, a paper jam that the older employees couldn't troubleshoot.

Ah, the exciting world of software development.

A park popped up on the left, along with the smell of blossoming flowers and hot asphalt. A dozen or so children clung like grapes to a plastic jungle gym, squealing and daring each other to touch a metal slide that might as well have been the surface of the sun. Beleaguered parents stood in clumps, clucking their tongues but otherwise letting the kids do their thing.

Right, he needed to call his mom. It'd been a couple of days, and for once, he had news. His phone was in hand and dialing by the time he reached Windy Grove's wrought-iron front gate.

She answered on the third ring. "I wasn't expecting to hear from you today. Lucky me."

"Hey, Mom. You got a minute?"

"For you? Always. What's up?"

"I found my ginger girl! She's the spitting image of Tabitha."

Mom hooted, and Damian pictured her dancing around her butter-yellow kitchen while her three cats darted underfoot. "How wonderful! You've been looking for a new feline friend *fur*-ever." She chuckled. "What's her name?"

"I haven't picked one yet. If you have any suggestions, I'm all ears."

"Food names are popular right now. Seems like every other cat I meet is Basil or Pancake or what have you. There's one on Instagram named Potato who has more followers than most of us humans."

Damian grimaced. "Too cliché. We can think on it and decide later. There's no rush."

"Is she an adult?"

"No, a kitten. But she's so cute, I don't mind."

Mom *tsk*ed. "Kittens are a handful, and you're not going to know what her personality is really like until she's grown."

"I know, I know. I would have preferred an adult too, but wait until you meet her before passing judgment. She's an absolute doll."

"I'm sure she's adorable. I just feel bad for all the older kitties who don't get as much love."

Damian ignored the gate in favor of circling around Building A, which was shaped like a big square with a cut-out center. The temptation to scope out 20A—a quick peek, nothing more—beckoned like a siren song, but he stopped at the concrete porch he shared with apartment 17. Instead of fumbling for keys, he sat down at a glass table he'd placed in his corner, setting the carrier on top.

"Me too, Mom. I'd adopt them all if I could. When can you meet your new grandcat?"

"Whenever you can pencil me in. I've been taking a class over at the community center that your sister talked me into, but otherwise, I'm free as a bird. Or cat, if you prefer." She paused. "Has your father heard the good news yet?"

"I'll tell him next." Damian kept his tone as insouciant as possible. "Have you talked to him recently? It's been a while on my end."

"Not since Valentine's Day, of all days. I think he might have been a little tipsy when he called."

"He was lonely, I'm sure." Damian glanced at his door, picturing the empty apartment beyond it. "Bachelor life isn't easy."

"Neither is being a single mom." She let out a short breath, and when she spoke next, her voice was cheerful again. "He'll be happy for you. Eventually. Do me a favor and, uh . . . you know."

"Don't invite him to see her at the same time as you."

"I'm sorry, kiddo."

"No worries. I get it." He held the speaker away from his mouth so she wouldn't hear his heavy exhale. "I'm afraid I have to cut this short. I gotta feed the kitten and get her settled. I love you very much."

"I love you too. Be sure to send me photos. Any other news before you go?"

Damian's tongue glued itself to the roof of his mouth, and it took him a second to figure out why. Shane. The shelter debacle. The co-adoption proposal. If he told her now, they'd be on the phone for an hour.

He pried his tongue loose. "Nothing I can't handle. Chat soon?"

"You got it. And don't forget. Pictures. Lots of them."

"Pinky promise."

After they hung up, Damian stared at his still-lit screen, debating. He pulled up his dad's contact info, but instead of calling, he composed a quick text.

Hey, Dad. I adopted a kitten! Not sure what I'm going to name her yet, but she's a beauty and very sweet.

He hit Send and then stood up, digging for his keys. By the time he got the door unlocked, his phone had pinged. Dad had replied.

If you ask me, you should have gotten a dog.

Damian groaned. "Which is why I didn't ask."

That was unkind, but why couldn't Dad say congrats and be done with it? He considered texting back, but the kitten was pacing around her plastic prison, meowing at maximum volume.

"I'm here, sweetheart." Damian picked up the carrier with one hand and pushed his door open with the other. "Welcome home."

chapter
three

"**O**uch!" Shane dropped the knife and gripped his left index finger. "*Fuck.*" The second the expletive left his mouth, he braced for impact.

"Maguire!" Chef Antoine's deafening baritone resounded across the bustling kitchen. "This is a family establishment!"

"Sorry, Chef," Shane shouted back at a more reasonable volume. He cradled his injured hand and trundled over to one of several double sinks. A saucier hefting a steaming pan dodged out of the way without breaking stride.

The water stung and pinkened as it washed over the shallow wound. Thank fuck. If he'd had to leave mid-shift to get stitches, Antoine would respond the same way he responded to every minor inconvenience: with murder.

Someone sidled up next to Shane, engulfing him in a cloud of sweet perfume. "You okay?"

"Yeah, I'm fine." Shane dried his hands and turned to face his coworker, Beatrix—an exceptionally tall woman with voluminous blonde curls covered by a flowery scarf. "Thanks for checking on me, B."

"Don't call me 'B' while we're working, *Maguire*." Beatrix winked to remove the venom from her admonishment. "What's up with you today?"

"Nothing," Shane lied. He hadn't cut himself while chopping in . . . God, years. Math-he-couldn't-do years.

"Uh-huh." Beatrix's smile was as sharp as the knives. "Don't let Chef see you acting all distracted, or he'll demote you back down to *chef de partie.*"

Shane grimaced. He'd sooner chop his finger clean off. He'd fought way too hard to make sous chef. "You raise an excellent and terrifying point. I'll get it together."

Beatrix wiped her hands on her pink apron, a stark contrast to the white ones worn by everyone else. "You'd better. If I have to work with nothing but meatheads again, I'm going to walk into the deep freezer and never walk out."

Shane chuckled as he bandaged the cut and covered it with one of the latex finger gloves they kept stocked for such occasions. "You can't. Then *I'll* be stuck with nothing but meatheads."

"That's a sacrifice I'm willing to make."

Shane surveyed the kitchen—dominated by gruff older men and fueled by tradition. In the six months since he'd started working at La Coccinelle, an upscale French restaurant, he'd learned a lot. Namely, he was too slow, too clumsy, not experienced enough, and *too slow*.

Beatrix followed his line of sight. "As Chef is always saying, 'If you want to make it, you have to be the best. If you want to survive, you have to be the toughest. And if you want a Michelin star . . .'"

"'You have to be both,'" Shane finished. "The first time I heard that I thought Antoine was trying to scare me. Turns out, he was just being honest."

The culinary industry chewed people up and declared them under-seasoned. Sometimes, Shane wondered why he hadn't picked a less stressful profession. Like lion-taming. But then he'd make a soufflé so light and airy it was like biting into a cloud made of cheese, and he'd remember what it was all for. If there was one surefire way to make the world a better place, it was to fill it with cheese clouds.

So long as Shane stayed off Chef Antoine's shit list, the job was tolerable. A stepping stone on the way to becoming a world-renowned cook. If nothing else, it'd gotten him out of his parents' house.

Shane had survived by being quiet, dutiful, and always willing to cover a shift. At this point, he'd paid enough dues to expect a membership card in the mail. A laminated one. Beatrix had chosen to swathe herself in femininity and radiate an air of *I can eat a grown man in two bites without smearing my lipstick*. Effective, but somehow Shane didn't think he could pull it off.

Beatrix bumped elbows with him, careful not to touch hands in case of contamination. "You want to grab a drink later and bitch?"

"Ah, our favorite after-work activity." Shane rolled a shoulder until the joint popped pleasantly. "Unfortunately, I can't. There's somewhere I have to be as soon as we're free."

"New boyfriend?"

"New mortal enemy, more like it."

"Sounds spicy. Do me a favor and count your fingers before you leave tonight. There are supposed to be ten of them."

"Yeah, yeah, very funny." Shane made a shooing motion. "You should hurry back. Chef's going to want his fish any second."

Beatrix shuddered. "God, I hate mackerel season. It lives rent-free in my nose."

"You could say we're *swimming* in it."

Beatrix's face pinched as if she'd taken a bite out of a lemon, and Shane shot her a thousand-watt smile.

Right on cue, Chef Antoine bellowed from somewhere by the grills, "*Where* is my *mackerel*?"

Beatrix slithered away like a pastel eel. Shane returned to the cutting boards, grabbed a fresh knife, and resumed slicing onions into paper-thin rings. Peace held dominion for about a minute. Then errant thoughts started banging pots and pans together in his head.

The kitten should have been Shane's. He'd totally seen her first. How had he let that distractingly handsome bastard snake her out from under him? Hours had passed, and he was still steamed about it. Mostly at himself, but he wasn't ready to admit that yet. It was far easier to point fingers at Damian.

Now that he'd absconded with the baby, Shane kept picturing horror scenario after horror scenario: the kitten abandoned on the side of the road somewhere, crying for help. Or bound to a train track by tiny chains while Damian cackled in the background, cartoon-villain style. Twirly mustache included. Which was ridiculous, of course—Damian was clearly a cat lover—but anxiety and an overactive imagination were one hell of a combination.

There was nothing Shane could do until he got off work, which could be well after midnight. Stupid adult responsibilities. Growling, he tossed the knife aside and wiped his sweaty brow with a sleeve.

He glanced down to discover he'd sliced a Julia-Child-sized pile of onions, easily three times what Chef had asked for. Shit.

Something inside him broke—the last straw, if he had to guess—and his phone was in hand before he'd registered yanking it out of his apron pocket. Facing the frosted glass that separated them from the restaurant proper, he typed a surreptitious message.

Is the kitten okay? Is she eating and drinking? Still has four paws and one tail? Please let me know she's all right.

He hit Send before he could question the wisdom of it. Was there any chance Damian would respond? Shane reread the two lines of text like he was going to be quizzed. He sounded neurotic. Accusatory. Or worse, stalkerish. Was this harassment? Could Damian get a restraining order?

Oh God, Shane was going to be sick. Panic trickled down his spine like a saline drip. If he—

His phone buzzed. Shane startled and almost dropped it. A notification had popped up, and he tapped it with screen-cracking eagerness.

It was a photo of his kitten sitting on a strawberry cat bed. Her big eyes sparkled with curiosity as she stared up at the camera. White whiskers glowed like hot embers in a stray beam of light. She looked relaxed and, more importantly, intact. Damian had captioned it: *She's all settled and adjusting well.*

Relief flooded through Shane. His fingers itched to type a reply, but the desire to not spook Damian was stronger. Once the phone was safely squirreled away, Shane leaned on a clean section of counter and breathed. In and out, until his pulse resembled a steady beat instead of a conga line.

A thought poked the back of his skull. Was this some sort of flex? Had Damian sent a photo so Shane could see how happy the kitten was without him? Perhaps the caption was really saying, *See? She belongs with me. Not you.*

Okay, he might be overreacting a bit. Damian could have ignored Shane, or given a one-word response, yet he'd gone out of his way to reassure him. That was a good sign, right?

What a mess. Maybe Shane should have picked a different cat after all. Or stuck to the dog plan. Or resigned himself to the fact that nothing in his life came easily. If the co-adoption worked—emphasis on *if*—Shane would have to tell his parents about it eventually. He already knew what they'd think: he'd gotten swept up by another wacky idea, like dropping out of college to go to culinary school. Ugh.

Before he could work himself up again, a memory of the kitten drifted into mind. When he'd held her for the first time, she'd purred as hard as an engine, eyes brimming with love he hadn't even earned yet. She'd nestled into his arms like she was meant to be there, a puzzle piece slotting into place. After twenty minutes with her, Shane had fallen more in love than he had with some past boyfriends.

No, he couldn't have picked another. He'd make this work. Whatever it took.

Something warm bumped his elbow. Shane continued his deep breathing. "I can't chat right now, Beatrix."

"You most certainly can."

At the gruff voice, Shane whirled around. Antoine. Fuck.

Shane blinked at the ruddy-faced man looming over him, reaching reflexively for the pocket where his phone was stashed. "Sorry, Chef. Didn't see you there."

"I'll bet. What do you think you're doing?"

Shane's eyes darted to the mountain of onions. "*Mise en place?*"

"Think you've *placed* enough *mise*?"

He flinched at both the butchered French and the accusation. "Yes, Chef."

Antoine shook his head, resembling a bear shaking off a long hibernation. "What's your problem, Maguire? You're holding up the line."

Too slow. Too slow. *Too slow.*

Hot blood roared in Shane's ears. He swallowed, grasping at composure, but it slipped through his hands like sand. "I cut myself. I'm fine, though."

"No one asked how you are, and you won't be fine if I serve a bloody plate of food. Show me your hand."

Shane submitted a twitching finger to inspection, anticipating a literal wrist-slapping.

After a moment, his boss grunted. "You followed sanitation procedure. That's more than I expected from you. Think I haven't noticed you slacking off all night?"

Shane fumbled for a response, and his brain produced a helpful surge of feedback.

Chef Antoine rolled his eyes. "Clean up your mess, and then get the hell out of my kitchen." Before Shane could have a heart attack on the spot, Antoine added, "Whatever's bothering you, get over it before tomorrow's shift. Or else." He lumbered away.

Jitters wobbled their way up Shane's limbs, turning them to jelly. He'd gotten his wish; he could leave early. And to think, he'd been worried about getting demoted. At this rate, he was going to get fired. Then he'd have to move back home. Again.

Shane packed up the onions and tidied his station in record time. After saying a quick goodbye to a flummoxed Beatrix, he hung up his apron and slipped out the back door.

The night air was pleasantly cool after the heat of the kitchen but thick with humidity. His shirt was clinging to his back within seconds. He stood in the parking lot for a solid minute, staring into empty space. Then he pulled up Damian's text. The kitten gazed back at him, as cute and sweet and perfect as ever. Before doubt could chew his nerves raw, he hit Call.

On the last ring, an irritated voice answered. "Do you have any idea what time it is?"

Shane checked the screen. Whoops. Early for him was still late for most people. "I'm sorry. Did I wake you?"

Damian grumbled under his breath. "No, I'm still up."

"Can't sleep?"

"It's not that."

When Damian failed to elaborate, Shane asked, "What were you doing?"

"Lying on the sofa, watching the kitten. She's been exploring her new home all day."

Home. The word stung as surely as if Shane had stumbled into a patch of nettles. He shoved it aside. "Can I drop by?" The thunderous silence that followed prompted him to add, "Just for a minute, I swear. I— I don't want her to forget me."

There was a long pause. Then Damian sighed. "You really want to see her? Tonight?"

Shane glared at the quiet parking lot, mentally superimposing Damian's face onto the pavement. "Of course I do."

Another pause. "Fine. But please make it snappy. If you're not here in the next fifteen minutes, I'm going to bed."

Shane's heart thudded against his rib cage. "Thank you. I'll be there in ten, tops."

"You remember the apartment number?"

"Kind of hard to forget, neighbor."

"Okay. See you soon."

Shane broke into a jog, cursing himself for not going back for his car after he'd left the shelter. He'd thought he was saving time, but it might cost him in the long run.

Speaking of running.

Shane sprinted to Windy Groves, beating his personal best. His shirt was drenched by the time he reached his building but not from humidity. Most of the first-floor apartments had two entrances: a front door around the perimeter and a back one that let out into the courtyard. Shane typically used the scenic route, but Damian struck him as the sort who expected guests to follow proper procedure.

Shane hurried to the left, toward his own apartment. Most of the outward-facing windows were dark, reflecting the light of the moon overhead like pale eyes. Not all, though. Apartment 18A was as aglow as a crackling hearth. Shane stopped in front of it, clenched both fists at his sides, and slowly unclenched them before knocking on the door.

Damian opened it a second later. "You're punctual. I'll give you that."

Normally, Shane would crack a joke, but he registered what Damian was wearing. Or not wearing, for that matter. "Uh, Damian?"

"What?" Damian blinked, apparently unaware that he was standing there in nothing but gray pajama pants. They hung off his hips, exposing a V-shaped cut of muscle above the waistband. And his torso was . . . perfect. Maybe not everyone's definition of the word, but certainly Shane's. No washboard abs or showy muscles: just a tight, lean swimmer's build.

In other words, trouble.

"You *were* expecting me, right?" Shane looked anywhere but at Damian's toned chest, his pulse racing for reasons he didn't want to acknowledge. As if his nerves weren't frayed enough.

"Yeah, sorry." Damian glanced down at himself. His dark hair was sticking up in places, and he rubbed both eyes with a large hand. When he peeked back up, his cheeks were conspicuously pink. "I went to put a shirt on, but I got distracted."

Shane's face grew hot to match. Was Damian gay too? Or bi? Into men in some capacity? Did it matter? Christ, Shane could play it straight if he needed to, but not with a hot half-naked guy standing in front of him. "By the kitten?" His voice cracked like a teenager's.

Damian nodded. "I answered your call on speaker out of habit, and I guess she thought someone else was here. She's zooming all over. Nearly broke my water glass." He opened the door wider and stepped back. "See for yourself. Quickly please, before she gets out."

Shane trotted into a neat one-bedroom apartment that was a mirror image of his own. The walls were standard white, except for the kitchen dead ahead, which had been painted buttercup yellow. The living room to the left featured sleek black furnishing that all matched, and a few abstract paintings dotted the walls.

It looked like a page out of a catalog. The only disarray came in the form of several potted ivies by the glass back door and a familiar strawberry cat bed in the corner. Feathery toys and food bowls were scattered next to a leather sofa.

Shane lingered in the entryway, trying not to act as awkward as he felt. "Where is she?"

Damian turned toward an open doorway in the far wall that Shane recognized as the bedroom. "Ginger?"

What?

"What?" Shane asked, eloquent as always.

Before Damian could answer, the kitten came racing into the room, almost tripping over her own paws.

"There she is." Damian made a labyrinthine attempt to grab her, but she snaked around him and went straight for Shane.

"Gorgeous girl!" Shane bent down and gently pet her triangle head as she batted at his fingers. "Did you miss me?"

She stretched her back into an arch—he was never going to get over how beautiful her deep red stripes were—and closed both eyes before opening them again.

"Oh hey, you got a slow blink." Damian smiled. "Lucky you."

"What's that?"

"It's like a cat's version of a kiss. Some say it means 'I love you' in feline, but it's more like a show of trust. Same if she rolls over and exposes her stomach to you."

As if she'd understood, the kitten flopped over and curled her white-tipped paws in the air.

"Oh my God, so cute!" Shane moved to rub her belly with his uninjured hand.

"Don't fall for it. It's a tr—"

Before Shane could react, the kitten whapped him with her claws extended.

"Ouch! Jesus." Shane inspected the digits. She hadn't drawn blood—thankfully, or he'd have matching wounds—but it still hurt. He sighed. "The cat newbie strikes again. She's strong for such a tiny thing."

"Ginger." Damian tutted. "That wasn't very nice. Sorry about that, Shane. I tried to warn you. When a cat rolls over, it doesn't mean the same thing as when a dog does it."

"Uh-huh, that's great. Why do you keep saying 'ginger'?"

Damian paused, inspecting the kitchen counter a bit too casually. "That's her name."

Shane's mouth popped open. "You named her—"

"I couldn't keep calling her 'the kitten' forever," Damian interrupted.

Shane huffed and tried again. "You named her *Ginger*?"

"What's wrong with that? She's ginger. It works."

"It most certainly does not!" Shane slapped his brow with the palm of a hand. "Do you want our cat to grow up to be a casino dealer?"

"*Our* cat?"

"Stay on topic! The name's all wrong. Ginger, while a sound ingredient, is spicy and abrasive when not cooked correctly. The opposite of this little sweetheart."

"She clawed you two seconds ago."

"That wasn't her fault!" Shane paused. "Because . . . of reasons."

"Uh-huh." Damian cocked his head to one side and then the other, seemingly considering him. "What were you going to name her?"

"Dorothy."

Shane's answer was met with dead silence.

"What?" He shrugged. "It's my mom's name."

"She's a kitten, not a Golden Girl."

"It's better than *Ginger*. Could you have been less creative? Why not call her Big Red?"

Damian chuckled. "Or Lucy."

It was Shane's turn to stare quietly at Damian.

"Oh God, please tell me I'm not that much older than you. *I Love Lucy*?"

"Ah, gotcha. After that masterful attack, I was thinking *Xena*, not Ricardo. I'm twenty-four, for the record. You?"

"Twenty-seven." Damian was blushing again. He slid both hands into his pajama pockets. "So yeah, here she is. Safe and sound."

"Um. Thanks. For taking care of her and all."

Awkwardness settled over them like morning dew, but colder. The kitten abandoned her supine position in favor of racing between Shane and the sofa. She tossed herself onto the cushions like gravity had no effect on her, circled around, and then sprinted back to sniff his feet before running the whole circuit again.

After her sixth lap, Damian seemed to find his tongue. "She's been doing that ever since you called."

"Sorry."

"Don't be. I think—" Damian cut himself off.

"What?"

"I think she recognized your voice."

Warmth enveloped Shane as if he'd stepped into a sauna. "Really?"

Damian's eyes were glued to the floor. "I mean, it's possible. You have that deep, gravelly thing going on. It's pretty distinctive."

Shane sucked in a breath he hoped wasn't audible. Did he detect a hint of flirting? Unable to stop himself, he darted a look up and down Damian's sinewy form. He easily could have grabbed a shirt by now.

But then Damian added, "The shelter was noisy, though. It's probably a coincidence."

Mixed signals. Delightful. "I see."

Damian groaned and rubbed his eyes again. "That came out meaner than I intended. I'm cranky because I need to sleep, 'cushy' job or not."

Shane glanced away before Damian could catch him peeking. "That reminds me: manners are a thing. Thanks for having me over. You have a nice place."

"Thank you, though it's not lost on me that our apartments are identical."

"Less so than you'd think." Shane rooted around for a polite way to phrase his thoughts. "Yours is a little lacking in personal touches, if you don't mind my unsolicited opinion."

"I did some painting—" Damian gestured to the kitchen "—but beyond that, I didn't see much point in decorating."

"Why not?"

"I . . . had to move out of my last place in a hurry. A lot of stuff got left behind. And it's not like I plan to live here forever either." Damian shifted his weight. "It's getting late."

"Hint, hint?"

"Unfortunately, yes."

The intriguing glimpse at Damian's past emboldened Shane. "If it's so unfortunate, can I stay for another few minutes?"

Damian opened his mouth only to shut it again. "I guess. Doesn't look like she's going to run out of steam any time soon."

The kitten had abandoned her circuit and was now striking the fear of God into Shane's shoelaces. Her paws made little *bap bap bap* noises as she pounced.

A metaphorical light bulb appeared over Shane's head. "You know, if you need a break, I could take her for the night."

To his surprise, Damian laughed. When Shane raised a brow in response, his eyes widened. "Oh, you're serious? Nah, no way."

"Wow. Don't give it too much thought or anything."

"If it's any consolation, it's not personal."

"What is it, then? You think I'm going to take her and never give her back?"

"You can't." Damian's voice was flat. "My name is on her adoption papers, and I'm not too proud to call a lawyer over a cat. Besides, if I thought you were a thief, I never would have let you into my home."

That last part smoothed Shane's ruffled feathers, but hearing Damian bluntly lay out the legality of their situation smarted. Shane was no law student, but there were only a few ways the cat could become his. At the moment, neither marriage nor Damian's death sounded appealing. Though if Damian kept giving him the run around, he might warm to the latter. "Are you going to answer my question or not?"

"Between the shelter and here, she's already been moved around a lot today. We can't transport her to a third unfamiliar location. It's confusing, and she won't understand what's happening. If only the lazy lump would learn to speak Human, we could explain." He chuckled, but when Shane failed to join him, he covered it with a cough. "My point is, she needs to acclimate before she goes anywhere else. Does that make sense?"

It did, but Shane had to bite his cheek to keep from asking if Damian was making this up. He could be counting on Shane not knowing any better.

"You promised you'd let me see her."

"And so you have. But it's been a very long day. I'm tired."

Irritating, but true at least. Damian's angular face was growing more drawn by the minute. Even Shane had a yawn building in the back of his throat, and Damian still wasn't wearing a fucking shirt. Shane couldn't overemphasize that enough.

The kitten had sprawled on top of Shane's shoes, eyes drifting closed. If Shane only got to see her in ten-minute spurts, they'd never bond. Eventually, she'd become Damian's on more than just paper. The thought made his heart sink, almost low enough to touch the kitten's head.

"Can we talk more about the name situation?" At Damian's pained face, Shane amended, "Next time?"

Damian blew out a breath. "Sure. Why not."

Shane scrambled to think of something to delay the inevitable, but exhaustion was clouding his brain. "All right, I'll get going. You'll let me know if anything happens?"

"Of course."

Shane reluctantly pried the kitten off his shoes. She'd dug her claws in like she thought she could anchor him there, but he prevailed despite his lurching stomach. He lifted her up to his nose and breathed in. She smelled . . . It was hard to describe. Clean. Like a shaggy rug that had been washed and then laid out to dry in the sun.

She mewed and licked his nose. Shane nuzzled her soft fur, darting a sneaky look at Damian for his reaction. A deep frown dragged Damian's mouth down like an anchor, though Shane couldn't imagine why.

He set the kitten gently on the tile. "I'll be back soon."

Damian made a face he instantly recognized: the same as Dad's the third time Shane had sworn he was moving out for good. It stung worse than the claws had. Apparently, this visit had done little to change Damian's mind about co-adopting. How long would he keep indulging Shane? Long enough for him to prove he was genuine?

He trudged to the front door, hoping his thoughts weren't apparent in the slump of his shoulders. "Good night."

"Good night."

The kitten meowed, and when Shane glanced back, she gave him another slow blink. He blew her a kiss, let himself out, and shut the door behind him. A second later, he heard a *click*; Damian had locked it.

Shane hadn't realized how hot his face had gotten until cool air hit his cheeks. Was every interaction with Damian going to be this charged? And with what exactly? Damian's lack of clothing pointed in one direction while his polite recalcitrance pointed in another.

Shane's phone vibrated against his thigh, and he let out a tepid breath before extracting it. Beatrix had texted.

The Commissioner of Fun let us go for the night. You awake? Want to grab that drink after all?

Tempting, but after the day he'd had, what Shane needed was eight uninterrupted hours of sleep. He might as well wish for a million dollars.

Next time. I'm so tired, I'm seeing spots. I do have a question, though. Shoot.

Shane typed as he walked the short distance to his place. He made it almost the whole way without tripping over a hedge. *Zuko was your first pet, right? How did you learn to be a good cat mom? Are there classes or what?*

The second he unlocked the front door, he was greeted by the smell of fresh basil, courtesy of his window plants. It soothed him, right up until he stubbed a toe on a cardboard box that—in his infinite wisdom—he'd set between the door and the light switch. His phone buzzed again before the meltdown he'd been holding at bay could boil over.

Common sense, mostly. But I did read a book on cat behavior. When I first adopted him, I was convinced my apartment was haunted. Zuko kept staring at empty space like there was something there. Turns out dust motes are a thing, and his eyesight is much better than mine.

Cat books. Of course. Why hadn't Shane thought of that? He listened to audiobooks all the time while jogging or doing chores. Mostly mysteries—nothing like a good who-dun-it—with the occasional comedy and romance sprinkled in. It seemed it was time to switch to nonfiction.

Thanks so much, B. I'll tell you everything tomorrow, promise.

You'd better. My spidey senses have been tingling.

Renewed energy surged through Shane, demoting sleep to an afterthought. As it turned out, what he'd really needed was a plan, and now he had one. He'd learn everything he could about kittens, and then he'd show Damian what a real cat dad looked like.

chapter four

D amian slept like crap. Between the kitten's antics and Shane's visit—every moment of which had been playing on a loop in his head—he'd barely gotten two winks. And they hadn't been consecutive. Even the spring sunlight floating through the windows couldn't lighten his mood.

He rolled out of bed and stretched. His lower back screamed from getting up and down all night. The kitten had needed food, or she'd wanted to play, or she'd tipped over her water dish. On and on it had gone into the wee hours. Her goal must be to make him a creaky old man before he hit thirty.

They'd made it through the first night, though. A promising start.

Damian showered and changed into fresh clothes. Nothing fancy: jeans and one of his many V-neck black shirts. Smothering a yawn, he padded into the living room, the tile cool under his feet. *Someone* had knocked over the one framed photo Damian kept on the coffee table. Said someone was currently lazing on her bed, cleaning a single paw with the deference of an art restorer. He approached, but she failed to acknowledge him.

"Good morning to you too."

She made a small *murrp* in greeting but didn't pause.

Damian righted the photo, stopping to study it. A college-aged Damian had a tasseled graduation cap tucked under one arm while the other was wrapped around a young woman with bleach-blonde hair. And he knew for a fact it was bleached. Up until Hollis had hit those experimental teen years, it'd been darker than Damian's. Last week, she'd been sporting bubblegum pink. By now, it was probably rainbow.

He peeked at the cat. "Remind me to call my sister later, will you?"

She blinked at him, her teensy pink tongue wedged between two of her toes.

"Don't look at me like that. It's not talking to yourself if you have a pet."

She didn't answer, of course. Far too focused on her career as a full-time agent of chaos. Always nice to see more women in high-power positions.

On the subject of work, Damian checked his phone: 8:05 a.m. and he already had fifteen email notifications. At least he'd woken up in time for breakfast, and he'd gotten *some* rest. A small miracle, considering the time that hadn't been eaten by the kitten had been spent thinking about the Jerk Next Door.

Who, Damian had to admit, wasn't actually a jerk. Persistent, yes. A little too optimistic? Maybe. But not a jerk. The kitten had certainly taken to him, and as irritating as that was, Damian had raised enough animals to trust her instincts. Shane also had a talent for catching Damian off-guard, especially late at night when he wasn't thinking straight. Pun fully intended. How had he forgotten to put on a shirt again?

No matter. Shane might have shown his face last night, but he'd give up soon enough. Even perfectly nice people sometimes bit off more than they could chew, and the suggested co-adoption was a veritable cornucopia of problems.

Why was Damian humoring Shane again? It might have something to do with how cute he was when agitated. Or playing with the kitten. Or existing.

Ugh. Someone needed to invent a coffee IV drip. Or fill the sink to the brim so Damian could dunk his head in.

He meandered into the kitchen, and to his delight, the kitten got up and trotted after him. Setting his phone on the counter, he loaded the coffeepot while she busied herself nosing under the cabinets and in each corner. He hadn't let her anywhere near people food, but she seemed to instinctively know to hunt for scraps. Good thing Damian almost never cooked. Well, good for her anyway.

As the coffee brewed, he popped sliced bread into the toaster and hunted in his barren fridge for something to spread on it. He managed to scrounge up a pad of butter and a jar of jam his mom had put in his stocking last Christmas. Or had it been the Christmas before? He unscrewed the lid and sniffed it. It smelled like nothing, which could be either good or very bad.

He held it up for the kitten to see. "You reckon jam goes bad? It's called 'preserves' for a reason, right?"

She responded by flopping over and licking her butthole.

"You have a truly refined palette, madam."

Once he'd scarfed down the toast and had a steaming mug in hand, he walked to the glass backdoor and cracked it open enough for him to squeeze out. The morning breeze was cool and dewy, despite the sun beaming down. Wisps of cloud streaked the deep blue sky. Damian closed his eyes and took a slow breath, filling his lungs with the aroma of freshly tilled earth. He dug his toes into the grass and soaked it in.

It'd make more sense for him to sit at the table on the front patio, but the courtyard had a charming community-garden feel. Leafy trees waved their loaded branches at him, and a working shell-shaped fountain decorated the center. Sometimes, the older residents would sit on its stone lip and chat, their laughter tinkling like the water.

Since he'd started working remotely, this morning ritual was often Damian's only excuse to go outside. Making friends post-college was hard enough, and all his colleagues were older with spouses and kids and mortgages. Not much in common with his thrilling bachelor lifestyle. He'd have to plan a hiking trip soon, or he was going to become one of those cave-dwelling creatures with milky eyes.

He took his first sip of hot coffee and was still reveling in the resultant bliss when a figure appeared at the open gate.

Damian almost dropped his drink in his haste to wave. "Hollis!"

Spotting him, she broke into a jog, her long hair—purple; not rainbow yet—piled into a messy bun. She wore yoga pants and a light tank top like she'd come straight from the gym, and knowing her, she had. "Hey, big bro!"

He pulled her into a hug, and coffee froth spat up from the mouth of his mug. "This is a surprise."

"Yeah, right." She rolled her big brown eyes. "My brother gets a new cat and doesn't tell me? That's grounds for an immediate visit. I texted to let you know I was on the way, but I didn't hear back."

Right, Damian had left his phone in the kitchen. "My bad. I'm still waking up. What a funny coincidence, though. I was just talking about you."

"Really? To who?"

". . . The cat."

Her silence spoke enough volumes to fill a library.

"Don't judge me." Damian glimpsed movement through the glass. The kitten was sharpening her claws on the cat tower Damian had bought after she'd tried to shred his sofa to ribbons. "I have work, but it can wait for a few minutes if you want to meet her. She's *darling*. Most of the time."

"Hell yeah! You think I came all this way to see you?" Hollis winked, then her expression sobered. "I was starting to think you were done with pets for good."

Damian led the way inside, grateful to have an excuse to hide his face. He set the coffee next to his phone, took a breath, and slapped on his best rendition of a smile before turning back to Hollis. "That's fair. For a while, I couldn't see myself getting another one. Not since . . ."

"I know. I'm so sorry." Hollis briefly squeezed his shoulder before plopping onto the couch. "Poor Whiskers. It's so hard when they get old and their bodies don't work as good anymore. She lived a long life, though. Filled with 'nip and ear scritches."

"That's what I tell myself on bad days."

Hollis eyed him. "Had many of those lately?"

"No, it's gotten easier." He'd never said it out loud, but one of the reasons he'd insisted on finding a hyper-specific cat was to buy time. Good thing, too, or in his grief, he might've adopted a whole litter. Fun in theory, not so much in practice.

He stood next to the tower and patted his thigh rhythmically. "Come here, sweetheart."

"Is that what you named her? Sweetheart?"

"I haven't decided yet. I toyed with Tabitha—like Grandma's old cat—but it didn't suit. We also tried Ginger on for size."

Hollis crinkled her nose. "Bit literal, don't you think?"

Damn it. Two against one.

Before long, a furry head nipped out of a hidey-hole. She watched his drumming fingers, eyes widening comically, and then dropped daintily to the floor.

Hollis sat up. "What a cutie! She looks like a fox."

"I know, right?" Damian scooped her up and handed her to Hollis. "She's very well-behaved, but mind your fingers. If she starts licking, biting will follow."

Hollis cuddled the kitten to her chest, scoffing. "You say that as if I don't already know. We've had cats our entire lives."

"Sorry." Damian had been thinking of Shane, as per usual. A sound caught his ear: low buzzing. Had a fly gotten inside when he'd opened the door? He scanned the room but didn't spot anything out of place. "Do you hear that?"

"Hear what?"

"Nothing. Ignore me."

"I've waited years for you to say that." Hollis giggled and scratched the kitten's triangular head. "Is Ginger still in the running? Sorry to be so negative, but I don't think that suits her either."

"Sha— Someone else said the same thing. And to be honest, it was a lazy choice. She deserves a name with a bit more thought put into it."

"What about 'Kit'? Like a baby fox?"

"Isn't Kit a guy's name?"

Hollis narrowed her eyes. "She's a cat. You could call her Dwayne 'The Rock' Johnson, and she wouldn't know the difference."

"Touché. Remember Jennifer, my college friend? The one who blew up my phone over winter break because Barley had ear mites, and she had no clue what to do?"

"Rings a bell. You haven't mentioned her in a while."

They'd fallen out of touch after graduation, same as most of Damian's old friends. He side-stepped the unasked question. "She told me once that her dad threw a hissy fit because she bought Barley a pink collar. Asked if the dog was *gay*, of all things."

"Yikes. As if Barley understands human gender roles. Do animals even see color the same way we do?"

"They sure don't."

QUINN ANDERSON

"People are wild." Hollis heaved a breath, a strand of purple hair escaping captivity to tickle her cheek. The cat swiped at it, but her front legs were too short. "Since we're sort of on the subject, have you talked to Dad recently?"

"If you count texting. Have you?"

"Well . . . no." She nibbled on her lower lip.

Years of experience informed Damian that she was about to say something he wouldn't like. Had Dad started drinking again? Mom had mentioned he'd been tipsy the last time they'd spoken. Hollis opened her mouth, and Damian steeled himself.

Someone *pounded* on the front door so hard it rattled in its frame.

Damian jumped half a foot into the air. "What the fuck?"

Hollis soothed the kitten. She was squirming in her arms like a live wire, probably eager to find a hiding place. "Who could that be this early? And with such a vendetta against doors?"

"Did Mom say anything about stopping by?"

Hollis shook her head.

Damian hurried to answer it before the wood splintered. Shane was standing on the other side with a fist raised. He must've come straight from bed: his clothing was rumpled, and his sandy hair was a mess.

Shane dropped his hand, face flushed. "Where have you been?"

For a second, Damian was too stunned to answer. When he recovered, all he could manage was, "What?"

"I must've called you a dozen times. Are you ignoring me?"

Ah, the buzzing. Damian should've checked his phone.

"Of course not. I stepped outside for a bit, and then my sister showed up. It couldn't have been more than twenty minutes."

He peeked over his shoulder at the sofa. Hollis was leaning forward to peer through the doorway, the kitten still fidgeting in her lap. Her jaw was slack, and when he caught her eye, she mouthed, *Is that your boyfriend?*

Damian's cheeks filled with hot blood. He shook his head before turning back to Shane, praying he wasn't visibly blushing. "Once again, do you know what time it is?"

52

"You weren't asleep last night, and you aren't asleep now." Shane cleared his throat, and when he spoke next, he'd dropped the tone. "May I come in?"

"Or you'll break down my door? You scared the kitten. And me, for that matter."

Shane shifted his weight. "I'm sorry. I got nervous when I didn't hear from you. May I *please* come in?"

The word no was on the tip of Damian's tongue, but his feet had other ideas. He opened the door wider, already scrambling to think of how he was going to explain this to his sister.

Shane stepped inside and gave Hollis a rigid wave. "I hope I'm not interrupting."

"Why *hello* there." She jumped to her feet with dubious enthusiasm. "I'm Hollis, Damian's little sister." To Damian, she mouthed, *He's hot.*

Not for the first time, Damian considered kicking her out.

"Shane. Nice to meet you." Shane jammed both hands into his pockets. "I'm, uh, the next-door neighbor. Or rather, the two-doors-down neighbor. You here to meet the new addition?"

"Yup. And, you know, Damian is a nice bonus." Hollis set the aforementioned kitten on the ground. She scampered right over to Shane and sniffed his shoes.

Damian scowled. He'd thought he'd been imagining it, but the cat seemed more excited to see Shane than Damian. Had to be because Damian was always around, right? Familiarity bred contempt?

Shane looked sidelong at him and grinned. "How'd *Dorothy* sleep?"

"*Ginger* slept fine," Damian shot back. "As did I, thanks for asking."

A total lie, but Shane had started it. Not that Damian was a five-year-old or anything. They stared at each other, and the simmering tension that frequented their meetings engulfed them.

Damian stepped closer and instantly regretted it. Shane's eyes were green as emeralds in the morning light, and Damian's stomach flipped. He shook it off, lowering his voice. "Play it cool, okay? I haven't told her about . . . you know. Us."

"I will if you will."

What was that supposed to mean? Was Damian as transparent as he feared?

The kitten abandoned Shane's feet in favor of food, her paws making an adorable *pit-pat* sound as she bounced across the room. She sat by her dish and yowled at top volume.

"Her majesty is ready for breakfast, it seems," Damian said.

Shane's mouth twitched. "You mean her *meow*-jesty."

Damian must be getting old, because that actually made him chuckle. He opened the pantry by the kitchen and pulled out a can of wet food. The second he popped the lid, he became the kitten's favorite. She dove nose-deep into the bowl like she'd never seen food before in her life. Typical cat. If her dish was half full, it might as well be empty.

Hollis squealed, hands on her knees as she hunched over to watch. "Look at that belly, all red and round. What a sweet little meatball you are."

That innocuous sentence hit Damian with the force of a lightning bolt. He glanced at Shane, not sure why he felt so stricken. Shane gaped back, and an unspoken understanding charged the space between them.

At the same time, they said, "*Meatball.*"

They fell silent, the air almost crackling.

Shane licked his lips. "You sure?"

"Yeah," Damian murmured. "It's perfect." And it was. So much for food names being cliché. He owed Instagram an apology.

"You mean *purr*-fect."

"Get out of my house.

Shane snickered, and Damian joined in dizzily.

"Well," Hollis interjected, bright eyes darting between their faces, "I think we've solved the name debacle. Way to go, team."

Damian wriggled free from whatever odd mood had him in its grasp. "Sis, I hate to say it, but we'll have to catch up another time. I have work soon, and I'm sure Shane came over for a reason." He shot him a pointed look. "Right?"

"Right, um." Shane scratched his chin. "Can I borrow a cup of sugar?"

Damian groaned.

Hollis giggled, but he knew better than to ask what was so amusing. "I'll get out of your hair." She headed for the front door, and Damian dared to hope she'd leave without incident, but as she turned the knob, she peeked over her shoulder and gave him a wink that was visible from space.

He sighed. He was never going to hear the end of this, but he had more pressing matters to deal with. After eating, the kitten—Meatball—had curled up on her bed, disinterested in them both for once. Without her as a distraction, they had nothing to focus on but each other.

Damian rummaged for something to say, but Shane beat him to it.

"You were wrong about ginger girls."

Damian blinked and waited for Shane to elaborate.

"You said they were *extremely* rare," Shane obliged. "I googled it, and while there are more orange males than females, the ratio is eighty to twenty. That's rare, but it's not extreme."

"Ah," Damian deadpanned. "I'll have my retraction written and on your desk before the presses shut down for the night."

"Very funny."

They lapsed into silence once more. Damian retrieved his phone and checked the time for lack of anything better to do. Both Hollis's text and several missed calls from Kitten Thief awaited him, along with three more emails.

"Anything good?" Shane asked.

"Just job stuff."

That seemed to prompt Shane. "Are you going to be late? Should I leave?"

If Damian were a wise man, he'd jump on the chance to evict Shane. Instead, he waved him off. "No, it's okay. I need to check in by nine, but I can technically work whatever hours I like. Assuming all my deadlines are met, of course, and I show up for our weekly meetings."

"Ah." Shane folded his arms behind his head, stiff as plywood. "So, what do you do?"

"I'm a software designer for a tech company."

Shane whistled. "Sounds like a nice gig."

"I love it, when I actually get to do it. I spend most of my time on the phone with clients. They're usually older and need help navigating their computers, and as the youngest employee on staff, that lot falls to me. The amount of code I write varies from week to week."

"Oh, hey." Shane rubbed his chin. "The speakerphone thing makes sense now."

"Huh?"

"Last night you said you'd answered the phone on speaker out of habit. I didn't think much of it, but it makes sense if you spend your days typing and talking at the same time."

Damian shuffled his feet. "I'm surprised you remembered that."

"What can I say? I'm a great listener." Shane waggled his eyebrows.

Damian laughed. A thought popped into the forefront of his mind. Shane wasn't the only one who'd been picking up on context clues. "You wouldn't happen to be a chef, would you?"

Shane beamed. "How'd you guess?"

"I don't know many people who have rants about ginger locked and loaded. Where do you work?"

"You know that French restaurant downtown? La Coccinelle?"

It'd be hard to miss a massive white building with a stone ladybug statue out front. Especially since it was one of the handful of "fancy" joints in town. "I've had a work dinner or two there."

"Then you've probably eaten my food." Shane's chest puffed up like it'd been filled with helium. "I'm their sous chef."

Warmth pooled low in Damian's stomach. He *loved* a man who could cook. Mostly because he couldn't fry an egg without incident. He scrabbled for another question before the inappropriately-horny police threw him in prison. "Do you like it there?"

"Hell no." Damian must have made a face, because Shane added, "It's better now that I've had a chance to establish myself. What you said before about your older coworkers? I totally get that. The culinary industry is pretty accepting, but the guys at my restaurant are . . . set in their ways. Not the friendliest to—" He cut himself off.

Damian quirked an eyebrow. "The friendliest to whom?"

"How did I know you were the sort to say 'whom'?" Shane made a valiant attempt at hiding his face, but Damian caught the blush spreading over his cheeks. "Basically, anyone who isn't an old straight white guy gets a rough shake. Ask my colleague, Beatrix. Or better yet, don't. She'll tell you horror stories that'll keep you up at night."

Damian looked Shane up and down. "You're a white man. And I know for a fact employers are more likely to discriminate against older workers than spry twenty-four-year-olds. So, why—" The dots connected, and Damian could have slapped himself. "Oh. *Oh.*"

Well. That answered a couple of questions Damian had been steadfastly avoiding for the past two days.

Shane's eyes were glued to his shoes. "Problem?"

"No!" Damian bit the inside of his cheek, debating. "Not at all. I'm, uh . . . right there with you."

Was there a merit badge for the most awkward response? Because if so, Damian could join the Scouts right now.

Shane peeked up. "You mean . . .?"

Damian nodded. "Yup, certified gay."

"Guess that makes me an unlicensed gay." Shane's jovial tone was tinged with relief. "What's the certification process like?"

"It involves tequila shots and glitter. I highly recommend it."

Shane chuckled, the sound deep and yet light. The warmth suffusing Damian intensified. Was he reacting this way because Shane was also into men? No, the little crush he'd been refusing to acknowledge had started the moment they'd met. And it was getting harder to ignore.

Before Damian could get his bearings, Shane asked, "So, are you taken?"

Damian's mind blanked. "For a joke? Yeah, all the time."

Shane huffed out a breath that would have been another laugh if it hadn't trembled. "I mean, are you seeing anyone?" When his question elicited no answer, he babbled, "I'm not trying to pry. It's just my dad is always setting me up on these terrible blind dates. He seems to meet gay men everywhere, but if there's a queer scene in this town, I haven't found it."

"There isn't much of one. Trust me, I've done the legwork." Damian had to pry his tongue out from between his teeth before saying, "To answer your question: I'm single."

"Oh, cool. I mean, not *cool.*" Shane's face was redder than Meatball. "I'm not seeing anyone either."

Emergency sirens howled in Damian's skull. Against his better judgment, he asked, "How have I never bumped into you before? I would have remembered you."

Shane smirked. "Oh? And why is that?"

Damn it.

Shane mercifully continued. "I moved in about a week ago. I'm still unpacking and everything."

"That explains it. And the fact that I work from home—a mixed blessing. I'd have to leave my apartment to actually meet people."

"I've had that exact thought about my long hours." Shane's smirk transformed into a kind smile. "Guess we have the same problem."

Damian fell silent, trying his utmost not to think about the obvious solution. At least his luck with neighbors was consistent: attractive men who complicated his life.

"Everything okay?" Shane was fidgeting again. Must be a nervous habit. "I'm not overstaying my welcome, am I? You're awfully quiet."

"You worry too much." Sudden exhaustion swathed Damian's head in fog. He yawned before he could stop himself. Loudly and wide-mouthed, like a lion in a documentary.

"I thought you said you slept fine?" The accusation in Shane's tone was tangible.

Damian wet his lips. "I may have exaggerated."

Shane folded his arms over his chest, and if obvious muscles hadn't bulged, Damian might have stood a chance.

He exhaled. "I got a few winks in. Kittens are a handful, okay? She had to get up a couple of times in the night." More like a hundred, but he kept that to himself. "I wasn't kidding when I said they need a lot of attention."

"You could have—"

A soft meow sounded from the other side of the room, and their heads moved in synch. Meatball had recovered from her food coma and was stretching, her tiny spine arched and her tinier claws extended. She hopped off the bed and trotted over to Shane, where she proceeded to flop on top of his shoes. Within seconds, she was breathing evenly.

Great, now Shane couldn't leave. It was a universal rule for parents of all species: never wake a sleeping baby. Damian wanted to be irritated, but she was so damn *cute*. He bent over and snapped what had to have been his hundredth photo in twelve hours.

Shane went stock-still, probably trying not to disturb her. "Will you text me some pictures of her? I want one for my phone background."

"Sure. Later, if that's okay."

Shane scrubbed a hand down his face. "I already know what you're going to say, but my offer stands. I can take Meatball at night so you can get some rest. It'd be like tag teaming or sharing custody."

Ah, the divorced-parents metaphor was back. Just what Damian needed after Meatball had barely slept with him last night, seeming to prefer her strawberry. And yet here she was, draped over Shane's feet without a care in the world. Comfort obviously wasn't the issue.

The jealousy Damian had been denying rekindled, licking at his bones. Did Meatball love Shane more than him? After three encounters? The thought sent cracks spider-webbing through Damian's calm. He was unflappable in the face of the most aloof cats—they always came around after enough time, affection, and treats—but this burned.

"You can't have her." He winced, surprised sparks hadn't flown out of his mouth. "It's been less than twenty-four hours. She's still settling."

Shane glowered. "Are you going to say that every time?"

"Guess you'll have to wait and see."

At Shane's crestfallen expression, his jealousy warped into guilt.

"I'm sorry," Damian said. "That was harsh. Tell you what, you can visit Meatball again sometime."

"Tonight?"

God, this guy was *relentless*.

"Fine, assuming nothing comes up. Believe it or not, people ask me to do things on occasion." His sister counted, right?

"It might be late, fair warning," Shane said. "I work restaurant hours and all."

"How late?"

"I don't know. Depends on when the executive chef lets us leave. Antoine doesn't own the restaurant, but you'd never guess that from talking to him."

Damian pressed his lips into a thin line. He couldn't blame the bad timing on Shane—he didn't control his hours and obviously didn't like them any more than Damian—but this was already getting untenable. Damian didn't make a habit of staying up half the night. His wild teenage years were firmly behind him, and he had his own job to think of.

He said none of this out loud. Judging by the way Shane's face was falling in increments, he didn't need to. Shane was thinking it too.

The silence stretched thin. When it grew downright emaciated, Damian said, "I guess do your best, and we'll play it by ear."

With a sigh, Shane bent down and picked up Meatball. She mewled a protest at the abrupt awakening but didn't struggle. He brought her to his chest and kissed the top of her head before handing her haltingly to Damian. "I've taken up enough of your time, and I need to get a run in before work anyway. I'll be back for her later."

A promise or a threat?

Damian saw Shane out, Meatball squirming in his arms like she wanted to chase after him. With one last longing look over his shoulder, Shane departed. Damian locked the door and stared at it for a solid minute. Then, without really understanding why, he craned his neck and kissed Meatball on the exact spot Shane had. She purred and rubbed against his cheek. An hour ago, he would have been delighted. Now, he wanted to crawl back into bed.

He gave her one more kiss before setting her down and retrieving his now-cold coffee, determined to get on with his day. He'd set up an office area in the bedroom: a wooden desk by the window piled with notebooks, his work laptop, and headphones. As he settled in for a boring morning of answering emails, his thoughts drifted. Bills. Responsibilities. Meatball.

Shane.

"Goddamn it." Damian rubbed his eyes and forced himself to focus on the laptop screen.

Quiet reigned for five whole minutes before Damian's phone vibrated. A balloon of hope inflated in the back of his mind—mint green with *Shane* printed in bold letters. Damian popped it viciously before tapping the text notification.

Who was that guy??? Tell me everything!

Hollis never could resist meddling.

There's nothing to tell. He lives two doors down.

Technically not a lie, but Damian's heartbeat sped up anyway.

You're getting to know a neighbor? You? Really now.

You'll understand when you're older.

That was sure to send her into the stratosphere. They were only two years apart, but Damian had gotten to do everything first. Drive. Graduate. Leave for college. Tell their dad not to call when he was three whiskeys deep. Normal eldest-child milestones.

You're seriously not dating? I saw the way you two looked at each other.

Have you been reading romance novels again?

He's not straight, is he? Bummer, but I suppose we can't hold that against him.

No, Damian wrote back a little too quickly. *He's gay. Not that it matters.*

Aha! Why not ask him out, then? He's cute, you're cute, and the chemistry is palpable. What's the problem?

At this rate, Damian was going to decompose at this very desk. He worded his next reply with surgical precision to avoid both lying and egging Hollis on.

Dating neighbors is messy. I like this apartment, and you know better than anyone what happened the last time I shat where I ate.

Charming, but there's more to it than that. I can feel it.

Damian huffed. Damn sororal instincts. For a fraction of a second, he debated telling her about the co-adoption, but that'd be like admitting he was considering it. Which he wasn't.

Can we talk later?

Her response was instantaneous.

You're so mean! Why won't you tell me?

Because it's nine in the morning on a Wednesday, and I have things to do today. Aren't you supposed to be working on your thesis?

Spoilsport. You know I won't stop bugging you until you spill.

I'm turning my phone off.

Jerk. Love you!

Damian rolled his eyes but returned the sentiment before setting his phone screen-down on the desk.

For the next few hours, life returned to relative normalcy. He got through a pile of emails and even made himself some lunch. A ham sandwich, but still. He'd bought the fancy nitrate-free kind, which meant he could share morsels with Meatball. She snuggled in his lap and allowed him to feed her like a princess accepting grapes off the vine.

But once afternoon set in, Meatball got a case of the zooms. Damian spent his entire lunch break playing with her, but her energy was boundless. She sprinted the length of the apartment, darting into the bedroom only to skid to a halt. She'd stare at him for a second and zip back out. It wasn't until he heard her gallop a full circuit around the kitchen and then scratch at the front door that a thought struck Damian with a mallet: she was looking for someone.

Hollis. Had to be. Damian had brought an exciting new person into their home, and Meatball had apparently developed object permanence. She wanted to know where the nice lady had gone.

Ugh. His own inner voice couldn't tell a convincing lie.

Damian threw himself into his caseload with savage determination. The hours inched by, but eventually the evening brushed pink and lavender across the sky. After ripping his headphones off and tossing them aside, Damian shut his laptop with audible force.

He trudged out of the bedroom and collapsed on the couch, bone-tired after walking maybe a hundred feet in total. He patted the cushion next to him, and Meatball clawed up an arm. She lay next to him, her hot back plastered to his thigh.

Despite his earlier protests, he stayed up way past his bedtime. Midnight came and went, and he didn't receive so much as a smoke signal from Shane. Who couldn't find the time to send a quick text? Was Shane's job that demanding, or had their earlier talk finally scared him off? Damian could speculate all night if he wanted, which he very much didn't. A mixture of frustration and baffling concern drained the last of his energy.

When he yawned so hard Meatball shot to her feet, he had to pack it in. It seemed he'd been right all along. As soon as Meatball had become inconvenient, Shane had given up. Damian had thought he'd already learned this particular lesson, but a burst of cold disappointment said otherwise.

As he fluffed pillows and pulled back the sheets, he shook his head. What did he have to be upset about, really? Besides the fact that another day had passed and he had nothing to show for it but a few ticked-off items on an endless to-do list.

He sank into bed, already anticipating another fitful night's sleep. Meatball jumped up to lounge next to him, and his delight was radiant enough to guide ships to safety. But before long, she grew restless and resumed sprinting around the empty apartment, searching for someone who wasn't there.

chapter five

C at bed? Check. Food and water? Check. Assorted toys, catnip, and a literal ball of yarn? Check, check, and check.

Shane stood back and surveyed his creation. The kitten corner he'd set up in his living room wasn't as extravagant as Damian's, but he'd situated it under a window that got plenty of light and he'd laid down a cozy blanket. The morning sunshine hit the bed but missed the fish-shaped water dish, exactly as Shane had intended. Meatball was going to love it.

That is, if Shane ever got to have her over. It'd been two days since Damian had last turned him down, and while Shane had intended to try again sooner, he'd been slammed at work. Like, double-shifts slammed. And Chef Antoine had been on him like *beurre blanc* on *poulet*. He must have noticed Shane's not-so-sneaky texting after all. Shane hadn't dared risk it since.

By the time Chef had let him leave, he'd barely been able to stand upright, let alone navigate another mercurial talk with Damian. Sometimes it felt like the only thing keeping him going was sheer stubbornness. That and the thought of one day coming home to find his baby kitty waiting for him. Every day without her punched a hole in his chest. His dad had told him a hundred times that having kids changed everything. It seemed a kitten was a fine substitute in a pinch.

Now that Meatball had a dedicated space, Damian would have to change his tune. On the kitchen table sat two large paper bags filled with a variety of treats. Shane grabbed them and, after some awkward fumbling with the front door, let himself out. Apartment 18A was becoming a familiar sight. Shane elbowed the door in a facsimile of knocking and stood back.

A minute ticked by with the speed of a sloth. Shane was about to knock again when the door opened a sliver.

"Shane?"

"No need to sound so shocked." Shane maneuvered the bags into Damian's line of sight. "I come bearing gifts."

There was a pause, and Shane thought he heard Damian mutter something. Then the door opened, and Damian filled the frame. His hazel eyes were wide, but more noticeably, he was shirtless again.

Shane averted his gaze, blood rushing into his cheeks. "At least this time I know you weren't expecting me."

In his periphery, Damian's mouth opened and closed twice before he shook his head. "No shit. I would've appreciated some warning. As I recall, certain promises were made regarding coming over unannounced."

"Yeah, my mistake. I have news, and the excitement got the better of me."

"How'd you know I'd be home?"

"You're always home." At Damian's sour face, Shane quickly added, "It won't happen again."

Damian sighed and stepped back. "Come in, I guess."

Shane obliged, carrying the bags to the coffee table. Meatball, who'd been lounging supine on the sofa, rolled over and mewed in greeting.

"I'm happy to see you too." He scratched behind her ears, eliciting enthusiastic purrs. He glanced over his shoulder at Damian. "How's she been?"

"Fine." Damian sauntered closer with his arms crossed over his bare chest. He peered into the bags and shot Shane a strained look. "Are you gunning for a World's Best Cat Dad mug or what?"

Shane gasped. "Do they make those?"

"Yes, but please don't buy yourself one. People will talk." Damian paused, chewing on his full bottom lip. "Where have you been?"

He grinned. "Didja miss me?"

Damian stared at him, expressionless.

Shane dug into a bag and pulled out a fish doll stuffed with catnip. Meatball locked eyes on it and crouched into pouncing position. "These are apology toys. Sorry I disappeared for a bit. I've been super busy." He willed Damian to ask with what so he could brag—just a smidgen—about the new kitten setup.

Instead, Damian frowned. "What was so important it made you forget about Meatball?"

Shane's eyebrows shot up. "I didn't forget. I got out of work late, and I mean *late*. Forget the witching hour. It was more like bitching hour." The joke fell flatter than a bad soufflé.

Damian raked a hand through his thick hair so hard, Shane thought he might rip some out. "You said you'd be here. You didn't call. You didn't text. I— We had no idea what happened to you. You could've been dead in a ditch somewhere." He cringed. "Not sure when I became my mother, but the point stands."

What was up with the third degree? Damian normally played it all cool and calm. Shane liked that about him; it balanced out his own anxiety. Shane had been fully prepared to apologize, but it seemed he needed to grovel.

"I'm sorry," Shane said again. "The first night, I was worried I'd wake you. The second, Beatrix had to give me a ride home. I was so worn down, my eyes wouldn't stay open."

Meatball must have run out of patience. She stood on her hind legs to swat at the fish. Shane let it drop, and she jumped on it with the verve of a lioness before kicking the non-life out of it. By far the cuddliest apex predator Shane had ever seen.

Damian was studying the patterned rug under the coffee table like it was the most interesting thing he'd ever seen. "For the record, my phone is always on vibrate. I understand that shit happens, but you should have let me know what was going on."

Shane tried another joke. "You sound like a jealous husband."

"I do not!" He scowled, belying his true thoughts.

Shane's eyes slid down Damian's naked torso, seemingly of their own accord, before landing back on his face. He couldn't pinpoint how he knew, but for everything Damian was saying, there was something he wasn't. "Did you think I was never coming back?"

"Yes."

The bluntness of the answer was almost as shocking as the concept. "What? Why?"

"People leave." Damian shrugged stiffly. "They lose interest. They ghost. It's part of the reason why I think the co-adoption is ridiculous. We haven't even tried it, and we're already having problems."

"I never said it was going to be easy." Shane did his best to project confidence over the blood buzzing in his ears. "But I'm not giving up. I'll never abandon Meatball."

Damian's lips thinned. "I want to believe you. I really do."

A jigsaw puzzle was taking shape in Shane's head—a corner here, a splash of color there—but he was missing too many pieces to see the full picture.

The bags under Damian's eyes, on the other hand, were plainly visible. "Have you gotten any sleep?"

Damian sniffed, and his shoulders relaxed. "Some. Not a lot. After you left, Meatball was running all around. I think . . ."

"What?"

He spit the words out like they tasted bitter. "She was looking for you."

Were he not still in the doghouse—so to speak—Shane would have squealed. Meatball hadn't forgotten him. Hard as he tried not to, he smiled so wide it hurt. His joy must have been obvious, and contagious, because Damian's expression lightened—the sun breaking through cloud cover.

"I'm gonna get dressed." Damian headed for the bedroom but stopped short when his stomach gurgled. Loudly. Meatball's ears twitched and angled toward the sound. "Excuse me. I haven't had breakfast yet."

Shane straightened. "I can make you food."

"No way." Damian waved him off. "I can't ask you to do that."

"You didn't ask. I offered. I'm a chef, and it's quite literally what I do. You may not trust me to watch Meatball yet, but you can trust me to fry an egg."

Was he imagining it, or had Damian flushed when Shane mentioned his job?

Damian eyed him. "You're going to insist, aren't you?"

Shane flashed a sly grin and didn't answer.

"I see. Thank you. That's very . . . kind." Damian hesitated. "My fridge is, uh, pretty empty."

"I'm sure I can scrounge up something."

Damian nodded and disappeared into the bedroom. Shane watched him leave, refusing to acknowledge how much of Damian's ass he could see through his clingy pajama bottoms. Ogling the guy in his own home seemed like a great way to get kicked out, and Damian hadn't needed provocation in the past.

Meatball had grown tired of her fish and was standing on the edge of the cushion, swaying. Huge blue eyes were fixed on the paper bags. Shane might not be a cat expert, but her body language said it all. She wanted more toys, and she knew where they were hiding, but she was too small to make the leap to the coffee table. Christ, she was darling. How did Damian get anything done?

Shane picked up one of the bags and dumped its contents onto the floor. "Go nuts, kiddo."

Meatball took a flying leap, plunging into the toys like they were a pile of autumn leaves. Shane giggled as he plodded into the kitchen, already paging through a mental cookbook. He had three philosophies in life. Always tip twenty percent, never date a man who has to say he's a "nice guy," and food heals all wounds. Once he'd fed Damian, he'd move on to phase two of his plan: begging for a chance to have a sleepover with the cat. Good thing he'd never been the prideful sort.

He opened the fridge and stood staring for so long his front half got cold. It wasn't "pretty empty"; it was a ghost town. No wonder Damian's stomach sounded like a garbage disposal. Shane pushed old takeout containers out of the way until he located a Styrofoam carton. Upon popping the lid, he found two whole eggs. A veritable feast.

The freezer produced somewhat better results. At least Damian had a few kinds of frozen veggies, including broccoli. Between the dusty bottle of oil on the counter and a couple slices of processed cheese, Shane would make do.

He dug around in cabinets and drawers until he located a spatula and a saucepan that looked like it'd never been used, along with plain white plates. He got to work, whisking the eggs and defrosting broccoli tossed with oil over medium heat.

Damian's spice rack was as barren as his fridge, but the basics were present: salt, a pepper grinder, and some dried chives. Shane rehydrated the latter in a dish filled with water, to be added last so the heat wouldn't shrivel them up again. He turned the burner down and poured in the eggs, agitating them gently until small curds formed. It was a dance, a rhythmic one, and Shane knew all the steps. His muscles operated independently of his thoughts.

He was halfway finished when light footsteps announced Damian's impending arrival.

"Hey," Shane called without turning away from the stove, "do you ever cook? Your flatware seems brand new."

"What's flatware?"

"That's an answer in and of itself."

"I'm not completely useless." Damian's voice transitioned to the living room. "Making toast counts as cooking, right?"

"I'm feeling generous, so I'm going to say yes." Shane nodded at the dining table. "Have a seat. It's almost ready."

"Are you going to join me?"

"I'll taste it, don't worry. But I already ate, and there isn't enough for two."

"Why would I worry about you tasting it? Is it poisoned?" Damian's tone was a mixture of amusement and curiosity.

"Oh, right." Shane would have smacked himself with the spatula if it weren't covered in egg goo. "That's a chef thing. You have to check the seasoning as you go, or you might add too much salt. Or worse, not enough."

"Interesting." Damian wandered into Shane's peripheral vision. He was wearing tight jeans and a V-neck. Not black, for once, but spicy green. The color made his eyes look amber in comparison. Almost golden.

Shane stared at him. Had he dressed up? Was it for Shane's benefit? Before that thought train could find a track, the curds finished solidifying. He sprinkled them with salt, a few twists of pepper, and the chives. After plating up, he took a step back to study the final product. Not half bad, considering. He snapped a quick photo—sometimes the simplest meals got the most Instagram attention—then lifted the dish with an exaggerated flourish.

"Breakfast is served." Shane plunked his creation in front of Damian and held out a fork. "Dig in. Mind if I sit with you?"

"Go for it." Damian accepted the fork, scooped up a big bite, and shoveled it into his mouth. Shane waited on tenterhooks while he chewed. After a moment, Damian's face scrunched.

"What? Are they bad?" Shane started to get up. "Shit, I should have asked how salty you like your food. I'll—"

Damian swallowed and held up a hand. "These are the best fucking eggs I've ever had."

Shane's eyebrows rose. Hearing polite, controlled Damian curse out of nowhere was . . . kind of hot, to be honest. "You're not just saying that, are you?"

Damian ignored the question, leaning closer to the plate. "What did you do to make them so good? Whenever I try, they end up dry and rubbery."

"That's common, if it makes you feel better. My dad always says scrambled is the easiest to make poorly and the hardest to make well. He's right. The key is to go extra low and slow. If the burner is set to medium, you're already doing it wrong. Pro tip: take them off the heat when they're a minute shy of being done. They continue to cook so long as they're hot, so mere seconds can be the difference between perfection and rubber."

"Wow. You really know your stuff."

Shane laughed dryly. "I should hope so, or dropping out of college to go to culinary school was a huge mistake."

"Are you sure you don't have a plucky French rat hidden on you somewhere?"

"Nah, though I did love that movie."

Damian ate another mouthful and made a low *mmm* sound that left Shane's skin tingling. "I'd eat like this every day if I could."

"Do you not know how to cook, or do you have no interest in learning?"

"A little of both. It's a shortcoming of mine, admittedly. I tend to abandon things I'm not instantly good at."

Shane nodded. "Relatable. Why don't you think you're good at it?"

"Because I'm not," Damian said with the simple finality of a man who was stating a fact. "My brain is more suited to math, where two plus two always equals four. In a kitchen, you can follow the instructions exactly and still end up with a disaster. It's worse with complicated recipes. I get overwhelmed when there's like fifteen ingredients I've never heard of and have to buy, all for one meal. I know cooking at home is cheaper, but it doesn't always feel like it."

Shane leaned forward in his chair. "I couldn't agree more. Food is supposed to bring people together, but a lot of the big names in my profession are elitist as hell. White truffle this, and Wagyu beef that. Recipe bloggers will unironically say, 'Be sure to use a blowtorch or you might as well throw the whole thing out.' Who owns a blowtorch anyway?"

"I've got one."

Shane could only blink in response.

"Kidding. The look on your face, though. Priceless."

"You're hilarious." Shane gazed into empty space, lost in thought. "Seriously though, simple food made with good technique is the best, and I'll die on this hill. If I had my own restaurant, I'd do things differently. Stick to the classics. And if anyone wanted to make my recipes at home, I'd hand them the card."

"You'd be out of business in a month."

"Maybe, but in my experience, people appreciate a sense of community. They eat out because they want to leave the house, but they still want to feel at home, you know?"

Damian was staring again, head cocked in a way that brought attention to his sharp jawline. Shane tried not to squirm under the intensity of it. His eyes were . . . beautiful. Like October leaves: still green in places but with splashes of brown and gold.

After a moment, Shane wet his lips. "What?"

"You keep surprising me is all."

"In a good way?"

"Are you really going to make me say it?"

Emotions were bubbling up in Shane that he couldn't identify. He used his phone as a distraction. "It's nearly nine. Do you need to get to work?"

"They'll survive without me for a bit longer. It'll be fine."

Shane opened his mouth, not at all certain what he was going to say, but a beeping noise from the living room interrupted. Meatball had climbed free of the toy nest and was playing with some sort of plastic ring. There was a ball inside that rolled around and lit up, chirping whenever Meatball's paws made contact.

Shane squinted. "That's not one of mine. Looks expensive."

"Yeah, I had sticker shock for sure. But she loves it, so worth every penny."

It was petty as hell, but irritation lanced through Shane. "Everything I've bought for her came out of a bargain bin. I hope she doesn't get spoiled."

"No worries there. Cats are born spoiled." Damian's mouth moved as if he'd run his tongue over his teeth. "I don't mean to be invasive, but I'm guessing sous chefs don't make a ton of money."

"Not as much as software developers, apparently." Shane's cheeks were warm again. "One day, when I'm head chef, I'll make real money—the kind you can fold—but for now, I have to suck it up and wait my turn."

"Didn't you move recently? You don't need to buy her toys at all. You've already got 'em."

"Huh?"

Damian swallowed another bite and smiled. "Next time you unpack a box, don't toss it in the recycling. Leave it out for her and see what happens."

"A box, huh?" Shane rubbed his chin. "As someone who has internet access, I'm embarrassed I didn't think of that sooner. I've heard if you put tape on the floor in the shape of one, they'll hop in that too."

"Bingo."

Shane huffed. "I thought the farmer had a *dog*?"

"Your jokes are a real sliding scale."

That got a chuckle out of Shane. "It's hereditary. When you meet my dad, you'll understand. He swears it got worse after I was born."

Now that Shane was thinking about it, Damian had been pretty patient with him as he navigated first-time pet ownership: answering questions and giving genuine advice. Damian might be aloof, but he wasn't unkind. A little pessimistic but not unkind. Blunt, mysterious, and infuriatingly good-looking, but— What had Shane been saying? He'd had a point a second ago.

Distracted as he'd been, he hadn't noticed Damian stiffen.

"Meet your dad?" Damian's eyes were gigantic.

"Oh no. Please don't freak out." Shane waved both hands in placation. "I shouldn't have said 'when.' I meant *if* you met him. Like, randomly someday. You know?" Damn it, he was babbling again.

"I'm not freaked." Damian set his fork down with an audible *thunk*. "But there's something I've been meaning to talk to you about."

"Uh-oh." He chuckled, but it caught in his throat. "That sounds ominous. Should I be worried?"

"It's no big deal, but . . ." Damian took a breath and squared his shoulders. "Listen, we're both adults. I hope we can be honest with each other without things getting awkward. I . . . Well, it hasn't escaped my notice that we're both gay. And single."

Shane swallowed hard. Holy shit, were they going to talk about this? Right now? Shane couldn't pretend he hadn't done some flirting, and on more than one occasion, he'd have sworn Damian was reciprocating. His pulse galloped like it had a shot at the Triple Crown. Oh, he *desperately* wanted to know what Damian was going to say next.

Calm as a still lake, Damian continued, "This goes without saying but just to be clear: we can't date."

Shane almost fell out of his chair. "What?"

"Hopefully I'm not being presumptuous, but I've been getting some vibes." He paused. "Am I imagining things?"

Christ, Shane was going to *combust*. His throat went so dry, it took him three attempts to reply. "No. I've noticed too."

"I appreciate your honesty. The good news is, we can nip this in the bud."

A question rolled off Shane's tongue before he could stop it. "Why, though?"

Damian gave him an odd look. "If we got involved, it'd be a mess. Between living so close to each other and the Meatball debacle, our relationship is already weird enough." He sounded like he was reading out a grocery list. "We might be spending a lot of time together in the future. Let's not complicate things, okay? For Meatball's sake, and honestly, for ours too."

Shane was pretty sure his heart was going to burst out of his chest, *Alien*-style. "Did I do something to make you uncomfortable?" Was it the staring? Damian must have noticed. A heavy wave of feelings crashed over him—hot embarrassment tinged with cold agony.

"Not at all." Damian stretched his long neck to the side until it popped. "Quite the opposite, actually. That's why I thought it'd be best if we cleared the air."

Shane's stomach heaved. And it was silly, really. They hadn't— He hadn't seriously considered *dating*—but now that Damian had taken it off the table . . . Was it weird that Shane was disappointed? Had he liked having the option?

Did it matter if it was never going to happen?

Damian gave him a once-over. "Are you all right? In general, and with everything I said?"

"Yeah, of course." Shane's tongue was a fat slug, lolling in his mouth. "Who said anything about dating?"

"I did," Damian replied in his customary matter-of-fact way.

"That was rhetorical. Obviously we're not going to." Shane forced out a tinny laugh. "You have nothing to worry about. The thought never crossed my mind." All lies were supposed to be equally bad, but that one felt egregious.

"Maybe I shouldn't have said anything." Damian's breath whistled through clenched teeth. "That kinda hurt my feelings. Didn't know I was so repulsive."

Shit. Shane backpedaled like an Olympic cyclist. "I didn't mean it as an insult. I was agreeing, or trying to. I'm focusing on my career right now, and . . . Well, I suppose if I met my soul mate tomorrow, I'd change my tune, but—"

"Forget it. I probably deserved that for springing this on you." Damian picked his fork back up, though the remaining eggs had to be stone-cold by now. "Anyway, you're right. It is obvious we're not compatible."

It was Shane's turn to bristle. "Out of sheer curiosity, what makes you say that?"

"You disappeared for two days without notice, for one thing. I might have let a boyfriend treat me that way five years ago, but I've learned my lesson since."

Shane wanted to be offended, but he was guilty as charged. "Am I ever going to live that down?"

"Oh, and another thing." Damian brandished the fork like a sword. "You're clearly more of a risk-taker than I am. I can't imagine asking a stranger to share their *cat*. There were extenuating circumstances and all, but sometimes I can't believe that happened, and I was there."

Shane fell silent, part pissed off and part acutely aware all of a sudden of how bizarre their arrangement was. He'd been doing his best to pretend it wasn't, but it seemed, not for the first time, that his best wasn't enough.

The cat legally belonged to Damian. He could tell Shane to fuck off whenever he liked, and there'd be nothing Shane could do about it. He'd been treating Damian like an obstacle. A roadblock between him and Meatball. In reality, he'd insinuated himself into a stranger's life without a second thought. And then he'd made demands. He was lucky dating was all Damian had taken off the table.

Apparently, Damian still wasn't finished. "Not to mention what you said about dropping out. College isn't for everyone, but I would've been so stressed wondering if it was a huge mistake. You're a stronger man than me."

A memory clawed its way into the forefront of Shane's mind: his dorm-mates listening open-mouthed as he'd explained he was leaving so he could eventually get a job working back-breaking hours that would neither pay well nor allow him a life outside of it. They'd looked at him like he'd announced he was going to live in the woods, and right now, that sounded like a solid plan B.

He was the world's biggest joke. Meatball deserved a more stable parent. A better parent.

She deserved Damian.

"Hey." Damian nudged Shane's foot under the table.

Shane sniffed, eyes burning. "Hey."

"I'm sorry." Damian seemed to shrink. "I shouldn't have said any of that. I don't know what's the matter with me lately."

"Don't apologize. I asked. It's my fault." All of it was. Defeat hunched Shane's shoulders, and his gaze dropped to the floor. "I should go."

And never come back.

Damian's chair creaked under his weight. "If that's what you want. But, for the record, I'm not kicking you out."

"I know." Shane willed himself to stand, but his knees had weights attached to them.

A soft sound caught his attention. He craned his neck to see behind him. Meatball had sauntered over and was rubbing her body against the back of Shane's chair. She gazed up at him and chirped. Shane heard a small voice in his head say, *Please don't leave me.*

It shook something loose in him, which plunked into his stomach and roiled like water cooling a lump of molten metal.

Shane had taken risks in life. Risks that his loved ones hadn't always understood. But he'd made it past every roadblock, no matter how daunting. He hadn't endured the grueling certification process, or all the times he'd had to suck up his pride and move back home, or Chef Antoine's condescending diatribes just to give up now.

He'd had worse, and Meatball was worth it. Without question.

Shane breathed in, breathed out. "I think I had an epiphany."

Clueless to Shane's inner ramblings, Damian straightened. "You're not leaving, then?"

"I am. For now." Shane pushed his chair back, careful to mind the kitty, and stood up. "You have to get to work, after all."

Damian rose as well. "I don't mind. You made me breakfast."

Shane side-stepped that. "I do want to make one thing clear, though."

"Shane." Damian breathed out. "I really am—"

"Will you be quiet for two seconds?" Shane was moving before he'd registered it. Next thing he knew, he was right in front of Damian, so close he could feel his body heat.

Damian stumbled back, but there was nowhere to go between the table and the wall. "Shane?"

Shane stared him down, not an easy task from two inches below him. "I understand all the reasons why our co-adoption is dicey at best. I understand why you're hesitant, and I even understand why you thought I'd disappeared. What we're doing isn't normal—I get that—but I love this cat. I'm not going anywhere, and if it takes me saying it a hundred times for you to believe me, then that's what I'll do. She's *ours*."

Damian's eyes had gotten big again. "What are you doing?"

"I don't know." Shane breathed hard. "Making my point."

The air between them was electric. Magnetic. Shane had no clue what his next move was, but he wanted to do *something*, so badly it itched. Then he picked the worst possible action: he glanced at Damian's mouth. Damian saw him do it too, if the tremulous breath he took was any indication. He waited for Damian to shove him or tell him to back off, but it never came. Damian just stared, scarlet creeping across his pale face.

Before whatever was about to happen could happen, Damian let out a shriek that rivaled a fire alarm.

Shane jumped. "What?"

"Meatball!" Damian doubled over, and when he reappeared, he had the kitten clutched in his hands. "She climbed up my leg. Fuck, I didn't notice until her claws were nearly at my—" He shut his mouth so hard his jaw clicked.

"Oh, shit." Shane reached for Damian only to drop his arms. "Did she draw blood?"

Damian shot him a flat look. "Want me to take off my pants so you can check?"

Shane's face heated. "That won't be necessary."

Damian set Meatball down, and with her chaos sown, she galloped away. He leaned against the wall, studying Shane. "That was quite the impassioned speech."

"Uh, thanks. Did it work?"

"It left an impression if nothing else." Damian tilted his head to the side. "Pinning me against a wall after agreeing we're not going to date? A bold if confusing choice."

A dangerous reply sprang to the tip of Shane's tongue: There were lots of things they could do that didn't involve dating. If any more blood rushed into his head, Shane might swoon. A long pause followed while Damian searched his face as if hunting for buried treasure. It was all Shane could do not to fidget under the scrutiny.

But then Damian nodded. "I believe you. About Meatball."

Shane scooped his jaw off the tile and snapped it back into place. "Really?"

"Yeah, only a true cat person could rant like that on the fly. We're a histrionic sort." He peeled himself off the wall and winked. "I never meant to discourage you. Well, maybe at first, but I didn't know what else to do. I've never been in a situation like this before, and there's no set protocol."

Shane laughed weakly. "I think we might be the only people who've been in this particular scenario."

"Which means we have to figure it out as we go. Much as I've told myself otherwise, I've known from the moment we met that you genuinely love Meatball. It's obvious every time you look at her."

"I do love her. She stole my heart."

"I still think I saw her first—" Shane started to protest, but Damian held up a hand "—*however*, Meatball deserves all the love she can handle. I'm not agreeing to share her fifty-fifty yet. I still have plenty of issues with that, but if you want to shower Meatball with affection, I won't get in the way."

Shane beamed. "Yet?"

"Don't read too much into it. But I could stand to be more hospitable to the guy who saved me from having to eat another microwave burrito."

"Oh, brutal. What's in them?"

"I don't know, and I don't want to find out."

Shane laughed even though it wasn't that funny, oozing relief. They were settling into something. A truce, or maybe a groove. He wasn't sure exactly, but it was a vast improvement. "How do you stay so fit if you eat all this processed food?"

Damian huffed, but he appeared oddly pleased. "Hey, I had an apple the other day. Local doctors fled in terror."

Shane laughed again, and this time it was sincere.

Damian shocked him yet again by adding, "We can revisit the sleeping-arrangement conversation if you like. Part of the reason why I've been so crabby is because I'm exhausted. And I'm falling behind at work thanks to all the attention Meatball needs. I could use some 'me time,' as my mom calls it."

"I'll think about it." Shane stroked his chin. "Okay, I accept."

"You joke, but sometimes I feel like a single parent. I've always said pets are family, but how the hell do people raise actual children? Multiples of them?"

"Fuck if I know. I asked my dad once what the key to parenthood is, and he said 'Patience. And wine. Lots of the former, and more of the latter.'"

"Sounds healthy." The corners of Damian's lips twitched. "Thanks for not dragging me for admitting I'm being run ragged by a two-pound kitten."

"I would never. Our miniature tiger is a handful." He paused, waiting for Damian to correct him. He didn't, and Shane took it as a sign. "I'm going to tell my parents about Meatball today. They'll want to meet her, Dad in particular. It was his idea that I adopt a pet. Although, he thought it'd be a dog."

"Hm. What's your game plan for explaining our situation?"

"I have no idea. I wasn't certain I should at all. What's yours?"

"I was gonna tell the truth."

Shane regarded him. "The whole truth?"

"And nothing but. Mom will have questions, but it'll be fine."

It seemed Shane had located the source of Damian's chill. "Lucky you. I've been imagining worst-case scenarios all week. My parents are supportive and all, but I've gotten in over my head before. This is one of the weirder stunts I've pulled. I hate making them worry."

Damian tapped his chin. "You get days off, right?"

"Yeah, luckily. Most chefs work all week, but the economy isn't what it used to be. We're closed Sundays, and I get one random weekday. Sometimes two if it's not tourist season. I'm always scheduled Fridays and Saturdays, though. Why?"

"That might work." Damian seemed to be talking more to himself than to Shane. "My mom is coming by Sunday evening to meet her new grandcat, and then we're getting food. That could be a good night for you to have a sleepover. After Mom gets her fill, I can drop Meatball off on our way to dinner."

Shane perked up. "That's perfect. It'll be better if my folks meet her at my place as opposed to some random guy's apartment—no offense. Otherwise, they might think I'm pranking them."

"I feel you. Mom's not going to believe I'm sharing the cat with someone until she sees it with her own eyes."

Shane grinned. "You were one of those kids growing up, huh?"

"Ask Hollis the next time she shows up uninvited. She'll go on an absolute tear about who always got control of the TV remote. It was only seventy percent of the time, I swear."

Shane forced himself to ask the question weighing on his tongue. "So, if I'm understanding all this correctly, I'm going to meet your mom?"

Damian's calm wavered briefly. "I suppose it's inevitable. She's gonna demand an introduction after I explain what's going on, but I figure the damage is done. You've already met Hollis, after all, and she's incapable of keeping her mouth shut. We'll drop Meatball off and leave before your parents arrive."

Shane wet his lips. "I'm meeting your mom in a . . . platonic way."

"If it's too weird for you, we can forget about it. Keep this our little secret."

Tempting, but Shane shook his head. "Nah, secrets only seem to do one thing: get out. Besides, friends meet each other's parents all the time, right?" The word *friends* felt odd in his mouth. Square peg, round hole.

Damian nodded. "I'm glad we talked. I feel better now."

"Me too." Shane checked his phone. "I'm making you late for work. I'll get going. Since it's Friday, I assume you're going to be up late?"

"That's the plan."

"Can I call you later and iron out the details? I'll also let you know if Sunday doesn't jibe for whatever reason."

"Yeah, sounds good."

Meatball reappeared, pawing at Shane's ankle. He picked her up and buried his nose between fuzzy ears, breathing in her sweet, clean smell. "I love you. So much."

Damian opened his mouth only to shut it again, and bizarrely, he blushed. "Okay, wrap it up before I get jealous."

Shane's head shot up. Then realization dawned on him. Jealous because *he* wanted to be the one snuggling Meatball, not Shane. Right, of course. He gave her a gentle squeeze before setting her down. "See you both soon?"

Damian smiled, and he was so handsome when he wasn't frowning that Shane's breath hitched.

"See you soon."

Chapter Six

F or once, Damian's Saturday went according to plan. He got some cleaning done (Meatball declared war on the vacuum) and lazed around (Meatball officially claimed the coffee table as her domain). When a brisk morning warmed into a balmy afternoon, he hiked up a local mountain trail with Hollis in tow.

The fresh air was crisp and invigorating, a welcome reprieve from being trapped indoors all week. The simple beauty of evergreen trees and the crunch of pine needles underfoot never failed to rejuvenate. Thick, purple-bellied clouds promised future rain, but for now, the sun was shining, birds were chirping, and the wind smelled like Christmas.

Hollis was her usual nosy self, asking question after invasive question about Shane. Damian took it in literal stride, beating her up a rocky escarpment as if he could outrace her meddling. No, he wasn't dating Shane. Yes, they were sort of sharing Meatball. No, Damian didn't think it meant anything. It was a random mishap, albeit one that could give karma a run for its money in terms of bitchiness.

Hollis had flashed him a mysterious smile and said, "Funny you should say that. I was thinking it was more like fate."

"You don't seriously believe in fate, do you?"

She hadn't answered, which was almost as alarming as her line of inquiry.

Shane had been slammed at work and hadn't stopped by since their last . . . Damian wasn't sure what to call it. Argument? Chat? Weirdly charged moment? Whatever it was, it had led to an uncomfortable realization: in less than a week, Damian had grown accustomed to seeing Shane on a semi-regular basis. A swarm of questions had been buzzing in his ears ever since, but he was doing his damnedest not to disturb the hive.

When Sunday evening rolled around, it found Damian pacing the length of his apartment while Meatball swiped at his ankles. He'd dressed for a nice dinner and had checked his phone every hour on the hour, as if he could will time to pass faster.

The swap was scheduled for seven, and his talk with Mom the previous night had gone as well as could be expected. He'd told her everything. Mostly. There was no easy way to say, *Assuming this other guy and I keep losing our damn minds, we're raising a cat together.*

Damian had framed it as a funny story. A "you won't *believe* what happened to me the other day" situation. Like he'd gotten a random package in the mail, or he'd found a fifty on the sidewalk. He hadn't mentioned the no-dating talk or the heart-pounding moment in which Shane had seemed a hair's breadth away from kissing him. Mostly because it was his mom, but also because he didn't know what to make of it. He and Shane had agreed romance wasn't an option, and yet . . .

Mom had asked a couple of questions, of course, but for the most part, she'd brushed it off as if it were no big deal. She'd requested more "baby" photos, the story behind Meatball's name, and that was all. It'd been easy. Too easy, in a way that made paranoia tap Damian on the shoulder.

Had Mom been talking to Hollis?

Silly question.

The more he thought about Mom meeting the kitten—and, as a result, Shane—the more urgent the tapping became. He'd thought he'd had a grasp on the reality of the situation, but this? This made it real. For all of Damian's protestations, they weren't considering co-adopting anymore; they were taking it for a test run.

An image exploded into Damian's brain: Shane staring Damian square in the eye from inches away and declaring he wasn't going anywhere. His expression had been equal parts passion and determination.

It'd been a long time since Damian had believed someone when they'd sworn they weren't going to leave.

Jitters swarmed him, worse than the time he'd forgotten to buy groceries and had decided—incorrectly—that he could subsist on coffee alone. What would Shane say if he told that story? Why was Damian constantly wondering what Shane would think or do?

He shook his head, checked his phone again with an unsteady hand, and pored over the plan. Drop off Meatball. Make some innocuous small talk for a minute or two tops. Keep the meeting as succinct as possible, and plead the fifth if necessary. Then get the hell out.

Simple enough, but an errant thought gnawed at the inside of Damian's skull. This was going to be his first time visiting Shane's apartment. He was no cardiologist, but the idea made his heart thump in a way that couldn't be healthy.

Drama queen. It was an apartment like any other, not a window into Shane's soul. He had to be acting this way because Shane was the first attractive gay man Damian had met since . . . Wow, a year or two after graduation. That was depressing. Had it really been so long since he'd had a boyfriend? When had the passing months blended into years?

At least they'd found their compromise. They weren't exactly on the same page—more like Damian was on the recto and Shane the verso—but close enough.

In his agitation, Damian had stopped paying attention to where he was stepping, and his foot made contact with what felt like a garden hose. A loud yowl followed by an orange blur brought him crashing back to the present.

"Oh no, Meatball!"

She streaked away and huddled under the sofa, trembling.

Damian squatted down, his black slacks constricting at the knees. "Sweetheart, I'm so sorry. Are you okay?" He reached out to pet her.

She batted his hand away. Her claws were sheathed, but it didn't look like she was coming out anytime soon. Fuck. At this rate, she'd love Shane more for sure. The jitters transformed into spiders crawling under Damian's skin.

Someone knocked on the door, a welcome interruption to Damian's third existential crisis of the day.

He rose and answered it. Mom stood on the other side as expected, dressed in a sharp navy dress and holding a glass baking dish covered with aluminum foil.

"Hi, Mom." Damian leaned in to kiss her cheek before stepping back.

"Good to see you, honey." Mom strolled inside, brushing short black hair away from her face with a free hand. Steady blue eyes surveyed the apartment before settling on Damian. "Where's the kitten?"

"Hiding under the sofa." Damian massaged his temple. "She's pouting because I stepped on her tail a second ago."

"Poor thing. Bound to happen, though." She handed him the dish. "I made you shepherd's pie and soda bread. It ought to keep you alive for a couple of days. Toast the bread, and then put this in the oven at 375 until the cheese bubbles."

Damian accepted the food. "Thank you. Is it Grandma Aoife's recipe?"

"Of course. If I skipped the godawful raisins, she'd wake up in a cold sweat and book the next flight from Boston."

Damian laughed and stuck the dish in the fridge while Mom strode into the living room. She crouched by the sofa and extended a hand for Meatball to sniff. A small orange head poked out from under the cushions, and Mom plucked her off the ground, holding her like an infant. Meatball snuggled into the crook of her arm like she'd known Mom her whole life.

Seeing them together filled Damian's heart to the brim. But then Mom sighed.

"Something wrong?" he asked.

She shrugged. "It's nothing. I was remembering when you were small enough to fit in my arms."

Damian pulled her into a hug, careful not to disturb Meatball. "Now you're the small one who fits in mine."

She chuckled, but it came out strained.

"Seriously, what's up? I may not have your maternal instincts, but you seem off."

"I was going to wait until dinner to bring it up."

Damian steeled himself. "It's Dad, isn't it? Hollis seemed like she had something to tell me the other day. I thought he might be drinking again."

"It's not that. At least, as far as I know." She set Meatball down and arranged herself on the sofa. "Remember how he and I talked back in February?"

Damian pocketed his hands. "Vividly."

"Well, that wasn't the end of it. He's been calling a lot, actually." She tossed her head like she was shaking off a bad dream. "Years of silence, then he acts like nothing happened."

Damian frowned. "What does he want?"

"He's thinking about moving out west. Says there's nothing keeping him here."

Hot anger burned through Damian. "I guess his children aren't enough of a reason to stick around."

Mom nudged him with a foot. "I didn't come here tonight to speak ill of your father."

"I know." Slamming a mental door shut on the outrage surging through him, Damian added, "It doesn't matter. Dad could live in Australia, and we'd hardly know the difference."

"He says you and Hollis don't make any effort to see him."

"Bullshit." Damian flinched. "Sorry."

Mom waved him off. "I smell it too, kiddo. I told him to his face: 'And whose fault is that?' We invited him to everything for years, but at some point you have to consider the evidence. If he didn't show up the fiftieth time, he's not going to show the fifty-first."

"He claims he wants to see us, but it always has to be on his terms. We have to travel to him and do what he wants to do, which usually involves a seedy bar and enough second-hand smoke to give a shark cancer." Damian took a calming breath. "He might as well leave; it's what he's good at. I wish he would— Why can't he—" There were simply too many wishes in his pounding heart for him to enumerate.

Meatball lounged on the rug between them, and Mom bent down to pet her. With her face hidden, she asked, "Do you think he has any idea how easily we'd forgive him if he'd just say he's sorry?"

Damian's mouth went dry. "He wouldn't even have to mean it. We'd all be flat on the floor in shock."

Mom nodded. "Sad, isn't it? The bar's on the ground, and he still can't stumble over it. I'd love to be angry, but I think I used it all up during the divorce."

"Are you okay?"

"I will be. Thanks for asking. These days, I feel pity for him more than anything else." She exhaled. "Can I give you a nugget of mom wisdom?" Damian nodded, and she continued. "Trust your gut. If something doesn't feel right, get out. Run, don't walk."

Solid advice, but not what Damian wanted to hear as he prepared to share his kitten with a guy he barely knew.

As if sensing his train of thought, Mom eyed him. "On a happier note, tell me about this mysterious new man in your life."

"You're as bad as Hollis. He's not a man in my life."

Mom raised a penciled brow.

"Okay, he's technically both of those things, but you know what I mean. It's really not a big deal." Or so he'd been telling himself for the past week.

"What does he do for a living?"

"He's a chef." At Mom's overjoyed expression, he huffed. "What?"

"Oh, nothing."

He'd expected Mom to have more questions—real ones this time—but she hummed and turned her attention back to Meatball. "Well, I can certainly see how two different people fell in love with this little fox. Such thunderous purring. And it looks like she's going to have a bottlebrush tail."

"Yeah, she's gorgeous. Smart too. She can open every drawer in this apartment and most of the cabinets. It's a real nuisance." He stroked under her chin. "I miss her already."

"Should we get going?" Mom consulted a delicate silver watch on her wrist. "It's time, and I'm curious to meet this Shane fellow."

The nervousness that had simmered in Damian all day boiled over. "Is there any chance I can talk you out of coming with me? I can handle Meatball. There's no real reason for you to tag along."

Mom smiled, eyes twinkling. "Isn't there?"

As expected, there was no sense in arguing. "I'll grab the carrier."

They got Meatball squared away and made the short trip to apartment 20A. Damian had barely finished knocking when the door sprung open.

ARE YOU KITTEN ME

"Hey!" Shane was wearing dark jeans and a blue button-up shirt in addition to a crisp white apron tied at the neck and waist. "You're right on time."

Damian ambled into a bright, cozy apartment, not at all the disaster zone he'd anticipated. Gauzy curtains waved from the windows, and tasteful art decorated the walls—mostly of disembodied hands holding whisks or rolling out dough. It smelled pleasantly earthy, like a garden. Everywhere he looked there were small touches that said someone lived there.

"Did you really move in a week ago?" Damian whistled. "Your place is so neat."

"It'll be two weeks pretty soon." Shane winked but otherwise ignored Damian and the carrier in favor of extending a hand to Mom. "I'm Shane Maguire. It's a pleasure to meet you."

"Linda Murphy. Pleasure's all mine." Mom shook his hand, and her smile took up half her face. "Is that basil I smell?"

A kitchen timer dinged as if on cue, and Shane beamed. "I whipped up some appetizers. No pressure to eat. Damian said you have dinner plans, but I made mushroom ravioli. And bacon-wrapped asparagus. And spinach puff pastry." He rubbed the back of his head. "I wasn't sure if you have dietary restrictions, so I tried for a bit of everything."

"How thoughtful." Mom shot Damian a significant look that he couldn't interpret, let alone translate.

"Please feel free to have a seat, or I can give you a quick tour. Sorry about the mess." Shane indicated three whole cardboard boxes shoved into a corner. "As your son mentioned, I recently moved, and I haven't finished decorating. Although this visit did motivate me to unpack, so thank you for that."

"No apology necessary. Damian told me all about you and your relationship." Having dropped that bombshell, Mom meandered away to admire the artwork.

Shane sidled next to Damian, grinning. "Our *relationship*, huh?"

Damian held up the carrier, positioning it between them. "You want to let Meatball out or what? She's got a lot of exploring to do."

Shane accepted Meatball and set her on the ground, opening the metal latch. She wobbled out, eyes wide as she peered around like a

89

bobblehead. Then she beelined for Shane's kitten corner. It had all the same accoutrements as Damian's but with a blue and red nautical theme, complete with a bed in the shape of a cartoon whale. She jumped on it, clawed it a few times, and curled into a ball. Within seconds, her breathing leveled out.

Shane dug his phone out of a pocket and snapped a dozen photos. "She's so going to take over my Foodstagram. I don't care how many followers I lose."

Damian watched, emotions playing tug-of-war with his stomach: a touch of jealousy but also pure relief. Meatball was okay. Everything was going to be okay. At least for tonight. This didn't sting as much as he'd anticipated, and Mom had said to listen to his instincts.

There were still a couple of things they needed to discuss, however. Damian made eye contact with Shane, glanced at the kitchen, and then returned his gaze to Shane.

"Linda, excuse me for a moment." Shane untied his apron and folded it over an arm. "I've got to grab the hors d'oeuvres." He headed into the kitchen without looking back to see if Damian was following. Which, of course, he was.

Once they were out of earshot, Damian leaned against the counter and lowered his voice for good measure. "You didn't have to do all this, you know."

"Sure I did." Shane tossed the apron aside, grabbed a mitt shaped like a pineapple, and pulled a steaming tray of pastries out of the oven. He set them on the stovetop. "I love playing host. Besides, it's not all for you. My parents are coming over later too, and they expect to be fed by their son, the fancy chef."

Damian hesitated. "Did you tell them about me? I mean, our situation?"

Shane's shoulders stiffened. "I chickened out at the last second. Please feel free to judge me, though I didn't technically lie. I said a neighbor had been helping me with Meatball, since she's my first cat and all. I figure when the time is right, I'll tell them the real truth."

Disappointment punched Damian in the kidneys. Did he want Shane's parents to know about him? Why?

Before he could overthink it, the air infused with the smell of garlic and fresh-baked bread. Damian breathed in deeply before fiddling with his cuff. "This must have taken all day. Can I help?"

Shane made a strangled sound.

It took Damian a second to figure out he was trying and failing not to laugh. "Hey!"

"Sorry. You know what? I could use some help after all." His tone was serious, but his face was red from exertion. "Will you whip me up a quick Mornay sauce please?"

Damian blinked. "Sure. What's a Mornay sauce?"

"It's a béchamel with cheese, usually Gruyère."

"Okay, got it." A grin tugged at Damian's lips. "What's a béchamel?"

Shane clapped a hand over his mouth, but he was too late. A snort escaped. "It's a roux with milk and nutmeg."

Now Damian was struggling not to laugh. His cheeks hurt from the effort. "Ah, I see." He paused. "What's a ro—"

Shane grabbed him by the shoulders. "I say this with love: get out of my kitchen."

Love. That one word knocked all the wind out of Damian's lungs, and the playful mood evaporated.

Damian wet his lips. "You'll have to let go of me first."

"Oh, um." Shane dropped his arms. "My bad."

"No worries." It came out breathless, and Damian winced. He could still feel the warmth and strength of Shane's fingers like they'd been branded into his skin. He cast around for a distraction and spotted a vegetable platter that he could only describe as immaculate. Every slice of carrot was uniform. "How'd you pull this off?"

Shane moved the spinach puffs to a butcher-block cutting board and followed Damian's line of sight, all without once looking at him. "It was no trouble. I have a mandoline with a julienne setting."

Damian didn't speak.

"Not one syllable of that, huh?"

"Afraid not."

Shane cut into a pastry and held up a corner. "Here, try this."

Damian's mouth opened automatically. Shane's thumb grazed his lip, and a hot, buttery morsel hit his tongue. It exploded with flavor: onion, the basil Mom had mentioned, and rosemary? Thyme? Whatever it was, it was delicious. If Damian had been served this in a restaurant, he would have sent compliments to the chef. And possibly a marriage proposal.

"Fuck, that's amazing." Damian was neither exaggerating nor being polite. "You made these from scratch?"

"They're deceptively simple, I swear." Shane fidgeted with an errant spatula. "If you ever want to learn, I could teach you some basics."

"I don't think I'd be a very good student."

Shane peeked up at him, and it occurred to Damian they were still standing an arm's length away. "You never know. You might like it." His lips formed a thoughtful moue. "Huh, that might've been a first too. I turned my own dad down flat."

Bells were tolling in Damian's skull. A warning, or maybe something else. This was so domestic: coming over to Shane's place, eating home-cooked food, chatting and joking around while a beloved pet slept soundly in the corner.

It catapulted Damian back to childhood, before the constant arguing and the dinners consisting of eggshells and broken promises. Back when there had been surprise beach days, movie nights, and lazy Sunday mornings spent building pillow forts. A stable household filled with laughter and affection. Sometimes it seemed more like a dream than a memory.

This—hanging out with Shane—was . . . nice.

And it was getting way too personal.

"Mom," Damian called without taking his eyes off Shane, "do you want anything?"

"Oh, sh—" Shane bit the expletive in half. "Where are my manners? Linda, can I get you a drink?"

"That's very sweet, but I'm fine." She picked up one of the magazines on the coffee table and leafed through it. "Apparently yellow is in. Finally, these designers come to their senses. I'm so sick of everything being beige and 'minimal.' Just say 'boring' and be done with it."

Damian chuckled. His gaze landed on the kitchen table, which bore a faint impression in the shape of a circle. He pointed at it. "Did something used to be there?"

Shane whistled. "Nice work, Sherlock. I had a vase with fresh lilies in it. They were supposed to be for tonight, but then I read somewhere that they're toxic to cats. I tried to give them to Beatrix—my colleague, remember? But I forgot she has a cat too, so they went to the lady next door. She says hi, by the way. Beatrix, that is."

"Does she?" Damian gave him a once-over. "I'm guessing you mentioned me at some point?"

"Oh yeah." Shane smiled. "B knows about you."

The bells rang louder.

Damian cleared his throat. "I'm glad they didn't go to waste, and I gotta admit, I'm impressed. You've really devoted yourself to cat parenthood."

"Not the first time I've engaged in an 'alternative' lifestyle." Shane's smile grew.

Damian was still trying to locate his tongue when someone knocked on the door.

Shane startled and checked his phone. "Uh-oh, my parents must be early."

An absolute cacophony blasted in Damian's head. "Shit. We meant to drop Meatball off and leave. We didn't— I wasn't supposed to—" He had zero idea what he was trying to say.

Shane studied him. "Not ready to meet my folks, huh?"

Damian's tongue absconded to parts unknown, leaving him glued to the spot while Shane answered the door. In walked an attractive middle-aged couple dressed in light, casual clothing.

Shane's father, who sported his same golden-brown hair, wrapped his son in a hug. "Hey, champ. Something smells good."

His mother placed a more conservative hand on Shane's shoulder. "Where's my grandcat?"

Shane opened his mouth, but Mom appeared at his side, gaping. "Bill? Is that you?"

"Linda! What a pleasant surprise."

Shane's dad and Damian's mom embraced like old friends.

Damian rediscovered the English language. "*What*? You two know each other?"

In lieu of an answer, Bill turned to his wife. "Dot, meet Linda, the nice lady from my cooking class."

That sounded familiar. Hadn't Mom said something about the community center?

Shane's face vacillated between surprise and confusion. "Hold up, Dad. This is the woman you told me about? The one with the son around my age?"

"The very same," Bill answered brightly.

Damian could only imagine what sort of expression had crawled over his features. He stared at Shane, and Shane stared back, jaw unhinged.

Dot—Dorothy, Damian recalled from the name debacle—gasped, her brown eyes sparkling. "What a small world! Linda, I've heard such wonderful things about you and your son. Here we were trying to introduce him to Shane, and they've already met. Must be fate."

Fate. Why did that word keep cropping up? Better question: Why did it keep cropping up around Shane? Was the universe trying to tell Damian something? Warn him? Either way, one more freak coincidence, and he'd buy a lottery ticket.

The bells had been replaced by his pulse, pounding with such force he could feel it in his neck. Shane drifted over to him, and the closer he got, the harder Damian's heart thumped.

"I'm guessing you didn't know about this either?" Shane asked, volume on low.

"What gave me away?" Damian replied as he gulped like a fucking goldfish.

Shane laughed, but it came out as a wheeze. "We'd better break them up before the matchmaking starts."

"The what?"

As if cued, Bill turned to Mom. "Are you staying for dinner?"

"Wasn't planning on it, but you can convince me." She breathed in. "Smell those fresh herbs. Damian tells me your son is a chef. He must be very talented."

"The best," Bill declared. "He's funny too. And hard-working. He'll be running that restaurant of his before long."

Shane groaned. "Dad, please don't brag about me while I'm in the room. You're embarrassing me."

"Can't a father be proud of his accomplished and *single* son?" Bill caught Damian's eye and winked.

That jolted Damian into action. "We'd love to stay, but Mom and I are late for a reservation." A complete lie. So much for him being the honest one.

Dorothy pouted. "That's a shame. We'll have to get together another time."

"Name the date," Mom said. "We'll have a family dinner. Bill and I can cook, and after all these classes, it might actually be edible. Maybe next week?"

Fuck, Damian had wandered right into this bear trap. He clapped his hands together, drawing everyone's attention. "So sorry to rush out like this, but we need to get going. And you still need to meet m— *Shane's* cat."

That was harder to say than he'd thought it'd be.

"All right, I'm coming." Mom gave Dorothy a hug and then patted Bill's back. "We'll talk more in class Friday?"

"I'll be there with bells on! Might bring the missus too. Then we can all have a nice, long chat."

If Damian made it through the night without having a conniption, it'd be a miracle. He said his goodbyes, and after pausing to give Meatball some discreet scritches, he ushered Mom out of the apartment. He caught Shane's eye as he crossed the threshold, but his face was unreadable.

As they walked to the car, Mom looked at him sidelong. "Shane seems like a lovely young man."

Damian tensed. "From what I've seen, he is."

"And what a hoot that was, running into Bill and his wife. Had you met them before?"

"No, that wasn't supposed to happen."

"Why not?" Her smile was razor sharp. "If you and Shane are neighbors and nothing more, what's the big deal?"

Damn it. "Mom, have I told you recently that you're very smart?"

Her smile widened. "You could stand to say it more often."

"Have I mentioned how annoying it is?"

She chuckled. "Good, I'm doing my job, then."

He already knew the answer, but he asked anyway: "Are you really going to have dinner with them?"

"Of course. I enjoy Bill's company, and even if I didn't, us parents will do almost anything to make our children happy."

"What's that supposed to mean?"

"Shane's a catch. You realize that, right?"

Damian squinted, wondering if there was an answer to his question in there somewhere. "Why do you say that?"

"His parents adore him, for starters. That's usually a good sign. He's all Bill talks about, besides Dot and the auto shop."

"Shane will be thrilled to hear that. He worries a lot about what they think."

"I can't imagine why. You know, Bill tried to convince me to set you two up. I said no, of course—may blind dates die with my generation—but now that I've met Shane, I could kick myself."

Damian reined in his heartbeat before he had his third cardiac episode of the night. "You're only saying that because I've been single for so long. Worried all your grandchildren will have fur?"

"Joke's on you. I have a backup child." She paused. "I understand your caution, but I hate to think the past is keeping you from your future."

Damian started to protest, but he was struck so powerfully by a thought, it stopped him in his tracks. If Mom had meddled . . . If the Meatball mix-up hadn't happened, and he'd ended up on a blind date with Shane, Damian wouldn't have been disappointed.

He was going to have to deal with that realization eventually, but not tonight. They reached the car, and Damian dug out his keys before opening the passenger door for her. "Where do you want to go for dinner?"

Mom huffed. "I thought you had a reservation?"

"We, um, missed it?"

"Mm-hmm. Well, I don't know about you, but I suddenly find myself in the mood for French."

With La Coccinelle closed on Sundays, they found themselves at a small bistro in the heart of downtown. It didn't smell half as good as Shane's apartment, a fact which Damian did his best not to acknowledge.

Dinner passed without incident, a welcome reprieve. Mom told him all about her new petunias, Hollis's school drama du jour, and the latest gossip from her book club. They'd already discussed her cooking class, and besides Meatball, Damian had nothing to report.

By the time the servers cleared their plates, they'd covered everything but the one question Damian always dreaded: Had he been seeing anyone lately?

He had a canned response ready, but it stuck to the roof of his mouth. He'd been telling Mom—and himself—that work kept him too busy, but that had never really been the case. There were a lot of hours in the day beyond the eight he spent at his desk. If he'd wanted to meet someone, he could have. So, why hadn't he? Was this the dating version of his hunt for a ginger girl?

He'd been coasting for months now, and somewhere along the way, he'd fallen into a routine that had become a rut. Adopting Meatball had been an attempt to switch things up, and it'd worked. But was it enough?

"No dates as of late," he ended up saying. "It's not like I wouldn't love to meet someone, but I guess I don't get out enough."

Mom reached across the white-linen tablecloth and squeezed his hand. "Why don't you try online dating?"

Damian made a face before he could stop himself.

"What? Lots of people meet through their phones these days. Before that, folks used to take out newspaper ads. And before that, I bet there were cave drawings that said 'Hunter 4 Gatherer, must love mastodons.' Humanity doesn't change much, does it? Come to think of it, I can't remember the last time I talked to a couple under thirty who'd met in the wild."

Damian laughed at her phrasing, but his stomach twisted. And it wasn't because the duck confit he'd ordered was rich enough to pay his salary. "I don't have anything against it, but it's tough out there. I already have a smaller dating pool than most, and sometimes I think someone peed in it. You're a single woman. You know what it's like."

She nodded. "Half of them stand you up, and the other half want to hook up."

"Thank you for that mental image. I'll send you my therapy bill."

"Seriously, though. Aren't you lonely? You haven't had a boyfriend since—"

"It's not loneliness," Damian insisted, forcing his face to stay neutral. "I'm *bored*. I'm bored to tears of waking up, going to work, going to sleep, and doing it all again. Adulthood is tedious, and my only consolation is I can go to the store and buy a birthday cake even if it's not my birthday, and no one can stop me."

"I see. Well, you know your life better than I do." Her mouth said one thing while her level gaze said another.

Was Damian lonely? Maybe, but being alone was simple. Uncomplicated. It might also explain why he couldn't stop thinking about Shane. Was he affection starved after spending so much time by himself? Pent-up and fixating on the first cute guy he'd met in ages? Either way, Damian was Tin Man levels of rusty. Things had been better since adopting Meatball, though. Maybe that could be enough after all.

For now.

They wrapped up dinner, and he dropped Mom off at her car. After making her promise to let him know she'd gotten home safely, he trudged to his apartment and let himself in.

"Meatball, I'm ho—" He stopped, his voice echoing around the empty space. How quickly he'd forgotten, and how quickly he'd gotten used to coming home to someone. His phone told him it was still early. He pulled up his contacts, scrolled to Kitten Thief, and hit Call.

Shane answered immediately, as energetic as ever. "Were your ears burning? We were talking about you."

Damian put him on speaker and set the phone on the counter so he could chat and unbutton his cuffs at the same time. "By 'we,' do you mean you and Meatball?"

"Is that weird? Please tell me you talk to the cat too."

"Oh yeah. All the time. And when she meows back, I pretend she's expressing divisive political opinions. She keeps it pretty PC, though. She'd hate to alienate her constituents."

Shane's laughter was deep and gravelly. "Hold on, let me hold the phone up to her. She's making the weirdest noise."

Damian's brain skittered into panic mode. Was it hairballs? Heartworms? Cancer?

High-pitched yowling shot down the line. Alarming, but familiar to most cat owners: the classic get-the-weird-thing-away-from-me screech. She'd probably spotted a shadow she didn't like and wanted to slap the hell out of it, as was the customary feline reaction.

"WHAT ARE YOU SCREAMING ABOUT?" Shane screamed. "Did you forget to pay your taxes? Is the IRS coming for you?"

Damian laughed so hard, he had to grip a chair for support. When he remembered it was mid-April, that set him off again. Shane joined him, and it was a solid minute before either of them collected themselves enough to speak.

"I take it she's adjusted to her new surroundings?" Damian asked between giggle aftershocks.

"Seems like it. I'm sure it helps that our apartments are so similar. Meatball discovered that another orange kitten lives in the bedroom mirror, and she's embroiled in a turf war. Fur will surely fly."

"Aw, the sweet, simple time before they develop self-recognition."

"She's also been— What did you call it? Zooming? Pretty much since my parents left. They love her, by the way. Dad became a cat lady in two seconds flat."

"Call them zoomies if you want to get bullied by teenagers on social media. Remember being a kid and having that kind of energy?"

"I don't think I ever had that much energy. Oh, to be a cozy housecat, with no responsibilities outside of getting eighteen hours of sleep and letting the curtains know they're on thin ice."

Damian laughed again. Had Shane always been this funny? Or had Damian been too busy scaring him off to notice? "Not to change the subject, but I can't believe our parents know each other."

"Right? I thought that sort of coincidence only happened in rom-coms. Did your mom ask a million questions? Dad wanted to know everything but your social security number and blood type, and I'm grateful he stopped there."

"Nah, Mom was pretty chill. She had more opinions than questions."

"Oh?"

"Don't worry about it. Nothing I couldn't manage."

"Lucky. Not that I can blame my dad. I haven't given him a lot of reasons over the years to think I have a handle on this whole adulthood thing."

"Haven't you?" Damian asked. "He seemed to have plenty of confidence when he was talking you up."

"Ugh. He means well. Dad's worked a backbreaking job his whole life, and all he ever wanted was for me to not struggle. He was convinced college was my shot at success, but I didn't know what I wanted to be when I grew up, and I got a bit lost. I still feel lost sometimes." Shane exhaled sharply. "Wow, sorry. Didn't mean to overshare."

Goose bumps popped up all over Damian's body. "Don't apologize." He carried his phone into the bedroom while he changed into sleeping clothes. "You're putting an awful lot of pressure on yourself. You're twenty-four. You're not supposed to have all the answers right now."

"Says the ancient twenty-seven-year-old. Have your many rotations around this Earth granted you the wisdom of the ages?"

"I know where you live."

Shane laughed. "Can I tell you something terrible? About Meatball?"

Damian paused midway through pulling on a shirt. "Sure?"

"Sometimes, she's so adorable, I want to *squeeze* her. Is that awful?"

Damian huffed and finished getting dressed. "No, it's normal. I've read about it. Cuteness can trigger an aggression response in people. Have you ever seen someone play with a baby's fingers by pretending to eat them? It's nothing to worry about. Just don't squeeze too hard, okay?"

"I'll try, but it's a struggle." There was a muffled sound like moving fabric. Damian pictured Shane flopping on his squishy couch and shifting to find a comfortable position. "I think Meatball and I are going to watch a movie tonight."

"Which one?"

"I don't know. I usually pick comedies. I was in the mood for an action flick earlier, but the sirens and explosions might startle the kitty."

"Good thinking."

"What's your genre of choice?"

"Horror," Damian answered without missing a beat. "The campier, the better. None of that torture-porn crap."

"See, I can't do scary. Gives me jitters."

That made sense for Shane. Given . . . Well, everything about him.

Damian, now in his comfiest pajamas, emerged from the bedroom and eyed the sofa. He stifled a yawn with a hand.

"Am I keeping you up?" Shane asked.

"I called you. Seriously, you worry too much." Damian had been pacing around all day. He should be worn out, but despite the yawning, now that he was talking to Shane, he was wide-awake. He must not want to get off the phone. Out of concern for Meatball, of course, and not for any other reason.

"In that case, do you want to come over?"

Damian, who'd been about to cannonball onto the couch, flailed for balance. "To your place? Right now?"

"No, to my super-secret lair. I call it the Citadel of Seclusion. Turns out the Fortress of Solitude was already taken."

Damian chuckled. "Tempting, but that's okay. You've proven yourself to be a capable and suitably neurotic cat owner. I'm sure Meatball will be fine without me for a night."

"Um. I meant in general."

"Huh?"

"I wasn't asking if you wanted to check on the cat. I was asking if you wanted to hang out. With me. And the cat, I suppose."

"Oh."

Damian was quiet for so long, Shane did the nervous-babbling thing. "I've been thinking. I know we agreed not to date—not that either of us wanted to—but we should be friends, right? We have Meatball in common, and now our parents have met." Shane giggled, the high-pitched sound at odds with his speaking voice. "This is awkward as hell. I feel like I'm begging the popular kid to come to my birthday party. Lemme backtrack: We'd love to have you over if you're not exhausted. Or busy. Or whatever."

Was it weird Damian was starting to find Shane's rambling charming? Foreboding rolled over him like cloud banks before a storm. It either heralded rain or lightning, and both possibilities made his lungs spasm.

Damian faked a yawn that turned into a real one halfway through. "Maybe another time. I should get some sleep while I have the chance."

"Right, that makes sense. Meatball's been keeping you up." Shane's disappointment would have been obvious to a toddler.

Guilt smacked Damian across the face. "It's your first real night with her. I don't want to be a distraction while you two are bonding. I'll text you whenever I wake up, probably around eight. We can arrange a swap and maybe talk about the future." Damian grimaced. "Meatball's future."

"Sounds great." An edge of excitement had crept into Shane's tone. "Thanks for letting me watch her. You didn't have to."

Damn Shane's endearing sincerity. It plucked something in Damian's chest. "I should be thanking you. Much as I act like an expert, I'm not used to having to do everything myself."

"Were your previous cats family pets?"

"Mostly. I did have one other, but . . ." Damian's eyes stung. He tried to blink it away, but the pain radiated from inside his ribs.

"Do you want to talk about it?"

A *hell no* balanced on Damian's tongue, but it clung on for dear life. "When I graduated from college and got my first place, I went to the shelter and told them to give me whatever cat had been there the longest. I wanted the oldest, grouchiest bastard they had."

"Why?"

"Because those are the cats that never get out alive. People can be shallow in the strangest ways. Everyone wants a kitten. No one wants the adult with bad legs and a missing eye. It doesn't matter that they love you every bit as much."

Shane sniffed, and when he spoke next, his voice cracked. "What was his name?"

"Her name was Whiskers. She was fourteen years old and a *mess*. A beautiful tortie mess. I used to call her 'pirate kitty.' She had half a tail like a peg leg, and she'd scratched off most of her fur. She was tough, though. Stubborn. I thought she'd live forever. As it turns out, forever is a startlingly short time. I spent several paychecks trying to fix her allergies, her heartworms, and then her liver. It didn't work." Now Damian was sniffling.

"What'd you do?"

"I made her happy and comfortable for as long as I could, but when it became clear how much pain she was in, I had to make a decision. Broke my heart."

Everyone left eventually, whether they wanted to or not.

"That must have been so hard."

"It was, but I had two great years with her and a not so good one. I don't regret it for a second. All the heartache was worth getting the chance to love her, however briefly."

Shane's voice was small. "Meatball's going to live forever, right?"

"Absolutely," Damian lied, and he didn't feel the slightest bit bad about it.

They both quieted. As the seconds dragged on, Damian flopped on the sofa, now properly exhausted.

"Well," Shane said with forced cheer, "that was depressing."

"Sorry. You did ask, though."

"I'm glad I did. That was . . ."

When Shane failed to finish the sentence, Damian prompted, "It was what?"

"Nothing."

Damian yawned. "Come on, man. We're burning daylight here."

Shane sucked in an audible breath and then let it out, his speaker crackling. "I think that's the first thing you've told me about yourself. The first real thing, anyway. It was nice. Sad, but nice."

Damian fell silent, his pulse skipping. Then words tumbled out of his mouth. "What's your last name?"

"What?" Shane asked. But then he seemed to process. "Maguire. Why?"

"That's what I thought you said when you introduced yourself earlier, but I wanted to make sure."

"Yours is Murphy, right?"

"Right." Damian's face was hot again. "I should get to bed."

Shane exhaled again but didn't protest. "Good night, Damian."

"Good night."

They hung up. Damian stared at his phone until the screen darkened. Then he woke it up and edited "Kitten Thief" to "Shane Maguire." After, his arm went limp and landed flat on the cushion next to him, the phone loose in his fingers.

Damian sat there for an endless minute, mind whirring. When his chin drooped down to his chest, he forced himself to climb into bed. Fatigue and churning thoughts warred for dominance. He wasn't sure precisely when he succumbed to sleep, but one thought ricocheted off the walls of his skull long after the others had quieted.

Maybe being friends with Shane wasn't such a good idea after all.

Chapter
Seven

The clock read 8:07 a.m. on a Tuesday, and not only was Shane awake, but he was laughing so hard he couldn't breathe. In an attempt to jump onto the windowsill, Meatball had gotten herself hopelessly tangled in the now-ruined blinds, paws in the air, tail whipping the glass. Like any good father, Shane had scrambled to take a photo instead of helping her.

It'd been a little over two weeks since Damian had first let Shane watch the cat—three since they'd adopted her. In that time, they'd settled into what Shane would dare to call a routine. When he had a free day, he picked up Meatball, kept her overnight, and then returned her to Damian the next morning. So far, so good.

"Poor thing." He rose out of a squatting position. "Want to get down?" He reached for her, but she flapped her paws and managed to flip onto her belly without crashing to the floor. He hovered nearby in case she changed her mind, pulling up Instagram and scrolling through his page.

"My followers are obsessed with you," he said as Meatball rolled like an alligator. Bits of broken blinds went flying. "But don't let your newfound fame go to your head. That's how child stars like you end up bankrupt and starring in bad indie films."

He chuckled to himself as he reviewed the photos. Meatball looked like a Saturday morning cartoon, with her puffy tail and splayed limbs. He selected the most ridiculous shot, slapped a filter on it, and posted.

Within seconds, he had notifications. The internet loved cat content, but damn, people were quick. Most of the comments were benign enough:

Funny!!!

Meatball is a perfect name for a chef's cat!
Want to be a brand ambassador? xo
But then one popped up from Beatrix.
You've posted about her six times today. Someone's pussy whipped.
Followed by a dozen cat emojis.

Shane wrote back, *You know it!* And added an orange heart. Then he untangled Meatball from her plastic jungle gym and collapsed on the sofa. His head lolled, and his eyelids threatened to shutter. Thank God he'd gotten Monday off, or he'd be way too exhausted to deal with kitten antics.

Especially with the way Damian had been acting these past weeks. Ever since their parents had met, their encounters had been brief. They'd chat about work, swap funny Meatball stories, and then part ways until it was time to do it all over again. Totally normal. Except it wasn't.

Something was . . . off. Damian wasn't being *rude*, per se. On the contrary, he was as polite as when they'd first met. And it set Shane's teeth on edge. After all the time they'd spent together, he'd thought they were past the neighborly act. Was this what friendship with Damian looked like? It was what Shane had wanted, so why did he find it so annoying?

It didn't help that Meatball had been sleeping like a baby—in the literal sense. Every couple of hours, she needed water, or she wanted food, or she had to use the litter box. Something in her feline hardware compelled her to announce what she was doing at maximum volume. Lather, rinse, repeat. If Shane didn't get some rest, he was going to be dead on his feet at work later. At least Damian's crabbiness made sense now.

Shane's phone buzzed on the seat next to him. Meatball appeared from thin air and launched herself at it, biting the case like it owed her money. Shane—who might have a career in sleight-of-hand by the time Meatball was grown—snatched it out from under her. She swiped at him but quickly lost interest, sprawling across the cushion and conking out.

Careful not to make any sudden movements, Shane tapped the notification. His mom, who'd joined social media to keep up with "kids these days," had commented on Shane's photo.

My son's beautiful new kitten!

What was it with parents and captioning photos in the comments? Her excitement was infectious, though, and Shane replied, *She loves you! Come see her anytime!*

"Assuming you give me a day's notice," he muttered. "A week would be better. Gotta coordinate with Meatball's other dad."

Having heard her name, Meatball lifted her head, cracked an eye open, and glared.

"Sorry, sweetheart. I'll keep it down."

She made a rumbling sound that would probably become a growl when she got older.

"Please love me. I will pay you to love me. I'll set up a little kitty bank account in your name, and the position of loving me comes with dental."

Meatball slow blinked and sank back into sleep.

Shane had taken to airing his anxieties to her. Everything from irrational fears to whatever latest barb Chef Antoine had lobbed at him. Much as Meatball wore him out sometimes, it helped. Dad was right. The apartment felt fuller. More complete. Or perhaps it was Shane who was fuller.

If only Damian hadn't started acting oddly, he'd almost think his life was coming together. The subtle shift highlighted how much Shane still didn't know about him. He'd received some clues—bits and pieces here and there—but not enough to draw a conclusion. It was a shame, too. The more calm, controlled Damian revealed about himself, the more Shane wanted to see.

Not just metaphorically either.

He shifted in his seat as a warm feeling bubbled in his chest, one that had become as familiar as it was unsettling: Desire. The smoldering kind. He'd made valiant attempts to suppress it—minus that time he'd sort of pounced on Damian—but lately, it'd been banging pots and pans together in his head.

He wanted Damian. Badly. Denying it wasn't an option. Around the second time Damian had answered the door shirtless, the dreams had started. Little flashes at first—pale skin and golden hazel eyes—but before long they'd grown into full-on fantasies. Detailed ones.

Sometimes they were playing with Meatball, and they ended up in a tangle of limbs on the floor. Or Shane cooked a delicious dinner, and Damian thanked him with a kiss that stole his breath. But most of the time, they had wild, furniture-breaking sex—the kind Shane hadn't had since he was a teen.

Damian got this dark look on his face when he was about to say something snarky. It shouldn't be hot, but *Christ* it made Shane want to bite his lip. Hard. The image nestled low in his belly, shooting out tendrils of heat that crackled as they spread. Damn it, his jeans were tight.

He glanced at Meatball. She was snoozing away with one paw twitching in the air. Probably chasing imaginary rabbits.

Shane eased himself off the sofa and tiptoed to the bedroom, shutting the door behind him with a muted *thump*. He had his pants unbuttoned and a hand stuffed into his boxers before he'd hit the bed. The second his fingers wrapped around his cock—hard as stone from two minutes of fantasizing—he hissed.

Pleasure sizzled through him. Shane bit the heel of his palm as he stroked himself with vigor, minimalizing noise as best as he could, but there was no stopping the stream of groans that poured from him. Fuck, he hadn't been this turned on in forever.

He tried—he really did—to picture a generic hot guy in Damian's place, but it was like trying to plug a leak with duct tape. The harder he resisted, the more he pictured Damian's lips on his neck and skimming open-mouthed down his chest, dipping lower to wrap around Shane's di—

Shane came with a moan that would have been thunderous if he hadn't bitten his palm. He milked the aftershocks, biting hard enough to leave marks. When it was over, he lay boneless, panting, and dazed. He'd had actual sex that had been less soul-searing.

After some deep breathing, he managed to grab a tissue off the nightstand with his clean hand and mop himself up. He'd made a mess. The orgasm had shuddered through him, knocking emotions loose as it went. Satisfaction. Confusion. Guilt. Yikes, lots of guilt. How was he going to look Damian in the eye later and pretend he hadn't had an entire catalog of dirty thoughts about him?

Impeccable timing as always, Shane's phone buzzed in his pocket. He ordered himself to ignore it, but as soon as he'd tossed the tissue in the trash, it magically appeared in hand. Fighting off a wave of drowsiness, he directed a bleary eye at the screen.

A text from Damian. Great.

Good morning. How's Meatball? Did you get any sleep?

Polite. Amiable. Straight to the point. Annoyance seared through Shane like he'd been stabbed. It muddled together with lingering arousal until he couldn't tell if he was horny or angry or all of the above. But he couldn't very well get pissy with Damian for texting him good morning.

"Fuck." Shane tossed the phone aside and buried his face in his hands. "So fucked."

Thoughts slogged through knee-deep hormones to reach logical terrain. Their situation had stabilized for the moment, but the future was fragile as glass. One crack could shatter everything, and yet here Shane was, tapping at it with a sledgehammer.

Perhaps it was good that Damian had stopped popping the lid of whatever box he stored his emotions in. Shane had rooted around in it, searching for a person underneath the cool exterior. And he'd found one. One he actually liked. There had been moments when they'd been alone and talking that Shane had dared to think Damian felt it too.

"Stop torturing yourself over something that's not going to happen." He mentally slapped himself. Meatball was the grand prize, and he was too close to the finish line to trip now.

He launched out of bed, as if he could outpace his dirty mind. Buttoning his jeans, he forced himself not to think about how orgasms like that one didn't come every day, no double entendre intended. Remembering Damian's text, he collected his phone and typed a response.

I'm awake, but at what cost?

He hit Send. A minute or so passed before his phone vibrated again.

Meatball's been giving you a run for your money, huh?

Yup. Enjoy your break while it lasts. One of us should be alert at least. What, and I ask this with love, is the deal with her sucking on blankets?

Shane had noticed the behavior last night when he'd tucked her into bed. At first, he'd thought she'd gotten ahold of another scrap of plastic and was eating it. Not that he understood that either.

It's a kitten thing. She'll grow out of it. Hopefully.

Hopefully?

If she's a sucker when she's grown, I'm telling everyone she gets it from you.

That got a snort out of Shane even as cold fingers squeezed his lungs. He really was a sucker.

Before he could reply, Damian double-texted. *When can I have her back?*

And there it was. The joking had almost convinced Shane he was imagining things, but Damian always brought the conversation around to what he really cared about: the cat.

Shane grit his teeth and forced himself to match Damian's polite tone. *My shift doesn't start for a good few hours, so I'm flexible.*

You don't want to keep her for another day?

Shane's heart leaped into his throat, but he squashed it down.

Tuesdays are slow, but I'll still be at the restaurant for around twelve hours. That's too long to leave her by herself. Best-case scenario, she'll get bored and wreck the place.

Shane crept to the door and edged it open, peeking out. Meatball was right where he'd left her. He was sock-sliding into the kitchen when he received Damian's response.

That was an expert cat-dad answer. I'm impressed.

On a scale of one to Meatball-begging-for-people-food, how pathetic was Shane for glowing at the praise?

How about I bring her by on my way to work?

Sounds good. When's your next day off?

Shane would have to check the schedule. He texted Damian as much and promised to update him as soon as he knew.

Damian replied, *Works for me. I'll see you later.*

Shane soaked up as much Meatball time as he could before packing up and transporting her to apartment 18A as planned.

Damian was dressed when he answered, thank fuck, and he smiled crookedly at Shane. "There's my girl. Thanks for bringing her."

Shane was about to snap that she was *their* girl, thank you very much, but Damian stepped forward to take the carrier. Masculine-smelling cologne filled Shane's nostrils and then shot straight between his legs. A hot blush washed over his face as he begged himself not to think about sex.

"You going somewhere?" Shane asked without thinking.

Damian blinked. "No. Why?"

"You're wearing cologne."

"Oh. I, uh, don't remember putting it on. Must be habit."

Shane's heart rattled against his rib cage, and he looked anywhere but at Damian. "Sorry, I've got to run. I'll text you later."

He beat a hasty retreat, picturing Damian staring after him with a frown on his face. Shane didn't stop until he got to his car. The sun radiated with the promise of summer, and a bead of sweat itched its way down his cheek. He took a breath, let it out, and then took another. God*damn*, did Damian have to smell so good? He unlocked the car and drove—carefully, carefully—to La Coccinelle.

Shouting greeted him as he scuttled through the employee entrance. Chef Antoine stood in front of the grill, his face a unique shade of purple. "Either put on a normal apron or get out of my kitchen!"

Beatrix smiled beatifically back at him. "Pink is abnormal? I guess no one thought to tell Elle Woods."

"You know what I mean, Beatrix Kaufman."

"Oh, I love getting full-named. It means I'm doing something right." Beatrix stuck a finger in the air. "The employee handbook specifies that our aprons must be clean and bear the restaurant's logo. It says nothing about color."

"White is our standard, and you know it!"

"Are you in the business of sticking to standards? Is that how you earned your Michelin Star?"

Chef Antoine threw his hands up, bellowed like a belligerent elephant, and stormed off, probably to shout at someone who'd listen.

Shane waited until the coast was clear before he sidled up to Beatrix. "Must be slow if you two are having the apron argument again."

"I had another *Legally Blonde* joke ready to go. Guess I'll save it for next time." Beatrix eyed him. "You look terrible."

"Nice to see you too."

"No really, I'm concerned. Did your new boyfriend keep you up all night?"

"He's not—" Shane shook his head. "It was Meatball. I love my little fox, but she's got a set of lungs on her."

Beatrix tilted her head toward him. "Blaming it on the cat, huh? C'mon, spill."

Shane sighed and relented. "I have a crush on Damian. An honest-to-god high school crush. The kind where you can't think about anything else."

"Yeah, no shit. I figured that out the night we got drinks and you ranted about him for a straight hour. Or a gay one, if you'd prefer."

Shane groaned. "Why didn't you tell me?"

"Sweet summer child. It was so obvious, I thought you knew." Beatrix patted his shoulder. "Crushes pass. You'll get over it in time."

"I'm not so sure." He lowered his voice as a waiter sailed by with a loaded tray. "My emotions are all over the place. I can barely be around Damian. Do you think there's any chance I only feel this way because he's . . . forbidden? For lack of a less dramatic word?"

"Maybe, but that doesn't sound like you. I'd argue that you must really like the guy if you still feel this way after he stole your cat." Shane had almost forgotten that was how he'd told the story at first. How far he and Damian had come. In some ways, at least. "But it's early, right? Give yourself some breathing room. It'll either fizzle out, or it won't."

"And if it doesn't?"

She flashed him the same smile she'd given Chef Antoine. "In that case, you're fucked."

Yeah, that sounded about right. "Let me get washed up and check the schedule. I'll be back to help you with the *mise en place*."

"You'd better. Tonight's soup du jour is onion, and I'm *not* reapplying my mascara."

Shane ducked into the breakroom where a clipboard with the schedule was hanging next to a large basin sink. He scrolled down it with a finger until he got to his name, gasped, and then texted Damian.

I have another day off tomorrow. That almost never happens. Any chance I can have Meatball again?

Leaning over the sink, he rolled up his sleeves and lathered soap to his elbows. By the time he'd dried off, he had a reply. He popped on a set of latex gloves before tapping the notification so he wouldn't have to wash all over again.

I don't see why not. I'll drop her off in the morning.

Shane reread the response, stomach churning like it was eating itself. There had to be some way to get Damian to react. Shane was typing before his brain could evaluate the wisdom of his actions.

Do you have anything going on Wednesday? Besides work?

No. Why?

Maybe we could get coffee. Or have a friendly dinner? I'll cook?

The second he hit Send, Shane underwent a small but not insignificant cardiac event. It was like he was determined to play with fire. Did he have to specify that the dinner was friendly? Christ. If he were smart, he'd limit their contact to picking Meatball up and dropping her off until his libido mellowed out. But it seemed he wasn't interested in doing the smart thing.

Damian's reply was a long minute coming.

We could have dinner, I guess.

Shane huffed. *Try not to sound too enthused.*

Sorry, I was thinking.

Before Shane could ask about what, the chat log indicated that Damian was typing. Then he stopped. He started again. Stopped. Whatever was on Damian's mind, he didn't seem to understand it either. Shane was debating how long he could safely linger in the breakroom when Damian finally found his tongue.

Wednesday works. The only thing I have to do the next day is attend a quarterly meeting at the office, and it doesn't start until noon.

So, theoretically, we could watch a movie too? I'm willing to give horror another shot if you have any recs.

He sounded desperate, because he was. Several deep breaths were all that kept him from having a meltdown as he waited.

I'll see how I'm feeling. We're on for dinner regardless. It'll be nice to see Meatball on one of your days. I miss her when she's not around, much as I love sleep.

Shane experienced the full spectrum of human emotion all at once. Everything from joy to terror, revolving like a carousel. Did Damian just want more time with Meatball?

I know what you mean.

It's my turn to feed you, though. Okay?

That was a nice gesture, tempted as Shane was to ask if the dinner would be fit for human consumption. *Sounds great. My place? Around seven? You can bring Meatball then so you don't have to make a double trip.*

We'll be there.

Shane tucked his phone away, pulse pounding, and asked the empty room, "What the hell am I doing?"

The fluorescent lights buzzing overhead seemed to answer, *No clue, but you'd better figure it out fast.*

By Wednesday, Shane had worked himself into a proper froth.

Without Meatball to distract him, errant thoughts were free to swarm his brain. His few interim conversations with Damian had been stilted. It was Shane's fault, too. It was like he'd forgotten how to interact with humans. Had he always been this awkward when crushing on a guy? It'd been so long that his memory was fuzzy.

He'd called Mom that morning—as he usually did on his days off—and asked if she remembered how he'd been with his handful of ex-boyfriends. She'd given a typical maternal response: "You were charming, sweetie! Maybe a bit excitable, and you had a tendency to ramble. But it was cute."

So, in other words, awkward.

"This is going to be a disaster," he muttered to himself as he unloaded groceries out of a paper bag: a few staples, gourmet cheese, a frozen lasagna in case Damian's food genuinely wasn't edible, and a bottle of wine. Instinct had informed him Damian was a red man. They could toast to their new . . . friendship? Did Hallmark make a card for what they had going on?

After squaring everything away, Shane changed into a crisp shirt—black, for no particular reason—and whatever jeans smelled the least like onion. He dived dramatically onto the couch and reviewed his Instagram (Meatball, Meatball, some actual meatballs, and more Meatball), until the proverbial clock struck seven.

There was a knock at the door, and Shane's pulse went into overdrive. He hopped to his feet and answered it, scrabbling for a joke to open with. "You know, people could set their watches to you."

Yikes, not his best work.

But Damian smiled. "People our age don't wear watches." His hair had been combed back, and he'd thrown a red bomber jacket over his usual dark clothes. It hugged his chest and emphasized his lean build.

Shane must have stared too long because Damian cleared his throat. Shane startled and said the first thing that popped into his head. "My parents wear them."

"Case in point." Damian hefted the carrier. "Did you miss us?" Meatball mewed from inside.

Shane studied him. Damian seemed casual enough. Maybe a little too casual. An honest answer pushed against Shane's lips, but he swallowed it. "It's great having Meatball again so soon. Thanks for bringing her over." He spotted a loaded plastic bag in Damian's other hand. "Is that dinner?"

"It is."

"Here, let me take that." Shane carried it over to the kitchen table and tugged it open. Reaching in, he pulled out a clear plastic container filled with sauced pasta. "Did you make this?"

"God no." Damian shut the front door and set Meatball down on the tile, fiddling with the carrier latch. "Not trying to poison anyone. It's takeout. I hope Italian is okay."

Shane beamed. "It's perfect. One of my favorites."

"I assume French is at the top of the list."

"You'd be surprised. The richness wears on me after a while, and the next thing I know, I'm wolfing down cheap street tacos. You said you have an Italian grandmother, right? You must know where to find the authentic stuff."

"Funnily enough, most of my relatives are Irish. A good chunk of them have that rare black-hair, blue-eyes thing going on. I must've been late the day they handed out those genes."

"Your eyes are beautiful, though." Shane bit his tongue, literally. "I mean. Um."

Damian breezed on like he hadn't heard. "Anyway, the Irish aren't exactly renowned for their food, so I went with a safer branch of the family tree."

"Good call, though I do enjoy colcannon."

Now free, Meatball raced into the living room, skidded to a halt with her claws extended, and strutted to the back door. She sat with her nose pressed to the glass, eyes huge as she peered into the courtyard.

A frown threatened to crawl over Shane's face. Was there somewhere Meatball would rather be than here with him?

"She's hit that phase where she's curious about the outside world," Damian said, reading his mind. "She'll sit in the window and watch bugs and birds for hours. God forbid someone walks by with their dog."

"I probably would too if I was stuck in an apartment all day, every day."

"Hey, I resent that remark. Besides, she's got two apartments now. Can you believe it's almost been a month since we adopted her?"

Shane feigned surprise as if he hadn't been thinking about it all week. "Oh hey, it has. Seems like yesterday." He finished unpacking what amounted to a small feast. "You certainly covered all the bases."

Damian ran a hand through his combed hair, ruffling it into perfect disarray. "I wasn't sure what you'd like."

"I like everything but cilantro, so no worries there." Shane wound the bag into a knot and set it aside for later. He had a feeling Damian was going to take the leftovers home so he could live off them for the next week.

Damian folded his arms. While not as muscular as Shane, the jacket fabric tightened to straining. "Why not cilantro?"

"To some people, including me, it tastes like soap. It's a shame too. I've been told it's delicious, and it's an important acid component in a lot of international cuisine."

"I'm going to pretend I understood that." Damian shifted his weight from foot to foot. "You want to eat now, or what?"

Shane eyed him. "I'm not usually hungry this early. You?"

"Nah."

"Grab a seat then and relax. Neither of us has to work until late tomorrow." Shane had meant it to be comforting, but Damian's shoulders tensed. He quickly asked, "Do you drink?"

"Alcohol? Not often. But on special occasions, sure."

Shane grinned. "Does our first dinner together qualify as a special occasion?" He retrieved the wine, plunking it down on the table. Judging by the container of *bistec* he'd spotted, red had been the right call. He fetched two stemmed glasses and a corkscrew, the latter of which he extended to Damian. "Would you like to do the honors? Unless you don't know how to open wine. I could teach you."

Damian stared at the corkscrew like Shane had offered him a live rattlesnake.

Shane glanced between it and him. "What?"

"You— I—" Damian wiped his mouth with the back of a hand. "Come with me." He marched over to the sink.

Heart hammering, Shane followed. "Is everything okay? Worried Meatball will overhear?" He laughed, but Damian didn't join in.

Damian was gazing out the window, but after a beat, he turned to Shane. "Is this a date?"

Shane's mouth actually popped open. He scrambled for something to say—a denial—but his mind blanked.

A glossy strand of hair fell across Damian's brow, and he swiped it away. "Listen, I don't want to make things weird, but your shirt, and the wine—"

"*My* shirt?" Shane squawked.

Damian continued as if he hadn't been interrupted. "I'm probably overreacting, and that's on me, but we had an agreement. You said we should be friends for Meatball's sake, which makes sense, but then you invite me to dinner and a movie—kind of a classic combination, you know?—and you look so nice, and— I— Okay, I have no idea what I'm saying, but do you get me?"

Shane's mind whirred as it processed the word deluge, but he managed a weak smile. "I must be a bad influence on you."

Damian squinted at him.

"You're rambling."

A snort burst from Damian, and he clapped a hand over his mouth.

Shane seized the opportunity to clarify. "The wine is a hostess gift. When someone cooks for you, or brings you food in this case, you're supposed to contribute a bottle. Or dessert. Flowers. Whatever."

Damian's tongue made a fleeting appearance as it swept across his bottom lip. "Host*ess*?"

"You know what I mean, you uncultured swine. Didn't your mother ever teach you these things? It's called having manners." He'd meant to say it in a joking way, but it came out forced. Damian's tongue had drawn Shane's attention to his mouth, and he begged himself yet again to *stop thinking about sex.*

Thankfully, Damian relaxed. "Now that you mention it, I remember my grandma—the Italian one—proselytizing about never showing up to someone's house empty-handed."

"There you have it. This is not a date." Shane's mouth got drier with every word. Then he blurted out, "You think I look nice?"

"What?" Damian turned burgundy. "No."

He was lying. It wasn't written on his face so much as tattooed. An ache Shane couldn't identify lanced through him. He glanced away for a second to gather himself only to peek back and find Damian staring at him.

Shane gazed into his eyes, unable to move, and as seconds ticked by, their hazel color darkened with intensity. This time, there was no denying the heat that sprang up between them, practically sparking. Not tension. Not friendly camaraderie. *Heat.*

Damian took a step forward, expression bewildered. If Shane could string a thought together, he'd guess Damian had no idea he was moving. Damian peered down at him from inches away, pupils huge. Shane's breath caught, and then he did the worst thing possible.

He shivered. Visibly.

Damian's lips parted. Whether it was to speak, or—oh fuck—do something else, Shane would never know.

Something sharp dug into his ankle, and he shrieked like a bird of prey. Meatball had grown bored of staring out the window and had found a new plaything: Shane's leg. Damian doubled over laughing as

Shane detached her from his ankle—yelping as each individual claw popped off his skin—and deposited her several feet away.

He glared at Damian. "It's not funny!"

"The clawing, no." Damian gasped for air between giggles. "But the noise you made? Very much so. Scientists can stop guessing what dinosaurs must have sounded like."

The mood evaporated. Kitten-blocked. Typical, and if Shane was being honest, welcome. What would have happened if Meatball hadn't interrupted? When Damian recovered, his eyes dropped to his shoes. His face was still flushed, and the pink tinge was lovely against his fair skin. Was he thinking it too?

"Everything all right?" Shane asked through gritted teeth.

Damian's reply was almost inaudible. "Maybe I shouldn't have come."

"What? But, Damian, we—"

A soft *pat pat pat* sound interrupted, which was perfect, because Shane had no idea what he'd been about to say. He glanced down. Meatball was scratching her ear. Nothing new there. Shane looked back at Damian, swishing words around in his mouth. Before he could formulate anything resembling a coherent sentence, Meatball scratched again, her back leg blurring.

"Uh-oh," Damian said.

"What's 'uh-oh'?"

The blush vanished. "She hasn't been outside, has she?"

"Of course not." Shane scratched his own cheek.

"Are you itchy too?"

"No. What's going on?"

"Don't freak out, but I think it might be fleas."

"*Fleas*?" Shane cried. "She doesn't have fleas! I didn't give them to her!"

"I said don't freak out." Damian side-eyed him, but it wasn't unkind. "And I never suggested you did. She got out of a shelter filled with animals three weeks ago, remember? She probably picked them up there. They can lie dormant if need be. Man, I could kick myself for not giving her some preventative meds. Do you know how to check for them?"

"I think so." Shane sighed. "Can you show me?"

In lieu of answering, Damian picked up Meatball. "Come here, you little bastard."

Shane gasped and would have clutched his pearls if he'd been wearing any. "Don't name-call the kitten!"

Damian fingered around her belly and throat, sticking to the white parts. "What? It's true. Cats don't have a concept of marriage."

Despite his protests, Shane had to admit, that was kind of hilarious. "If anything, she's a *love child*."

Any mirth he might have felt fizzled out, however, when Damian pinched his thumb and forefinger around a dark shape, visible against Meatball's throat. He pulled his fingers away with whatever it was trapped between them. "Yup, we've got a flea. Only the one so far, but where there's a flea, there are eggs."

"Oh my God." Shane pressed his hands to his temples. "This must be my fault. The restaurant lets people bring their dogs onto the patio. I bet I picked up a flea at work and brought it home."

"There's no point in speculating. We'll never know for certain where she got them."

"Well, we know it wasn't you. You never leave your apartment." Shane was doing an impressive impersonation of a toddler.

"Hey, not never." Damian's mouth was pursed, but the corners kept twitching up. "I know you're a first-timer, and it's scary when something inevitably goes wrong, but will you please stop shouting?"

"But I infested the baby!"

". . . The *baby*?"

"Don't tease me. This isn't the time."

"Okay, okay." With his fingers still pinched together, Damian handed Meatball to Shane. "I'm going to drown this sucker, pun intended, in soapy water. You keep Meatball calm, which will require calming down yourself. Think you can handle that?"

"I'll try." Shane accepted her and cradled her against his chest. "I'm so sorry, love."

Damian filled a cup in Shane's sink and then plunged his fingers in before yanking them back out. "Okay, the evil flea has been vanquished. You can also trap them using tape in a pinch. Do you have shampoo?"

"For me or the cat?" Shane shook his head. "Duh. No, I don't."

Damian dug out his keys. "I'll grab mine and the pills I picked up. Don't blame yourself. This was bound to happen eventually, even with an indoor cat."

"Thank you. You're so prepared." For all the books Shane had read, they were entrenched in their first real crisis, and he was useless.

"Years of experience. Back in a bit." Damian let himself out and closed the door. His footsteps made a decrescendo in the direction of his apartment.

For lack of anything better to do, Shane deposited Meatball on the sofa and then opened the wine, dumping an ill-advised amount into a glass and gulping down half of it. He made a mental note to call his dad and thank him for never letting him adopt anything bigger than a bread box growing up. Parenthood was hard.

Within minutes, there was a brief knock on the door, and Damian let himself in. He carried a large mixing bowl containing plastic bottles and a box with a picture of a kitten on it. "Meatball, sweetheart, you're not going to like this."

Shane scrutinized the supplies. "What are you going to do?"

"*We* are going to give Meatball a bath, dry her off, and then dose her with a topical insecticide. Trust me, it's a two-person job."

It was Shane's turn to not know what any of that meant, but if it helped Meatball, that was all that mattered. "Tell me what to do, and I'll do it."

"Good attitude." Damian removed the bottles, dumped a good bit of one into the mixing bowl, and filled it with sudsy water. "Feeling better?"

Shane hovered next to the sink. "Not really."

"Can I let you in on a secret? I was pretty freaked out for a minute there myself."

"I'd never have guessed. You're so . . . together, if that makes sense."

"There's a trick I can teach you if you're interested. It might not work for you, but it's worth a shot."

Shane perked up. "Please."

"For the record, it's important to feel your feelings, but when they get overwhelming, I ask myself a simple question: Can I do anything about this?" Damian shut the water off and faced Shane. "If the answer is yes, focus on doing it. If not, then there's no sense in dwelling. Especially at night. If the sun's gone down and you find yourself reliving past mistakes, stop it. Say it out loud if you must. 'No more thinking about this until morning.'"

"Solid advice." Shane paused. "Easier said than done, though."

"Oh, you bet, but with enough practice, it'll come naturally. Hold Meatball, will you? She's going to use every weapon in her kitty arsenal to get away."

The bath was a messy affair, complete with non-stop yowling from Meatball and most of the water sloshing onto the floor. Damian remained serene throughout the process, whereas Shane's hair was sticking up almost as much as the cat's by the end.

When she'd been thoroughly washed, they wrapped Meatball up in a dry towel and situated her on the sofa to sulk. And sulk she did, shooting them regular baleful glares.

Damian assessed her as he wiped off his hands. "I wish I could explain that this is for her own good."

Shane assessed him in turn. "You really have had cats all your life, huh? I don't know what I would have done if you hadn't been here."

"You did great. But yeah, I have. Turns out being gay doesn't exclude you from loving pussy."

Shane stared unblinkingly at him.

Damian snorted. "Fair enough. You would have been fine, okay? You might not have realized she had fleas until they started biting you, but you'd have gotten there."

"How reassuring." Shane's shirt was damp and clinging to his chest. "Guess I should change."

Damian glanced at him only to quickly turn away. "If you want."

"Out of curiosity, do you like all animals, or just cats?"

"Everything but birds. I find them unnerving. Whenever I look into their eyes, I get this weird feeling that they remember when they were dinosaurs, and that knowledge gives them power."

Shane laughed. "That might be the best description of birds I've ever heard." Movement caught his eye. Over on the couch, Meatball was shaking. "Is that normal?"

"What?" Damian followed his line of sight. "She seems fine to me."

"She must be freezing!" Panic sent Shane rocketing into outer space. "Is she sick? Should we take her to the vet?"

Damian brushed him off. "She's damp. Will you stop being a helicopter parent? Give it ten minutes, and she'll warm up."

"But she's shivering!"

"So?" Damian's cheeks were twin red apples. "People shiver. It happens."

What? *Oh*. Shane had to pant for breath before he could speak. "Right, yeah. Of course. I'll, um, try to relax."

Hesitating, Damian reached over and rubbed Shane's shoulder before snatching his hand back like it'd burned him. "Listen, you can salt my opinion to taste, but I've bathed plenty of irate cats in my day. The baby is perfectly safe."

Shane stole the phrase and added it to his lexicon before grinning. "What did you call her?"

Damian sighed. "Fine, I admit it. We're single fathers, and this is our daughter."

"We could have our own sitcom."

"No one would watch it."

Meatball meowed as if to say, *I'd watch it.*

Shane cooed. "She's so expressive."

"Right? Almost seems like she understands sometimes. But everyone thinks that about their pets."

Ten minutes passed—long enough for Shane's body heat to dry his shirt—and exactly as Damian had said, Meatball stopped quaking and fell asleep still snuggled in the towel.

"Okay, I may have overreacted," Shane admitted.

"Just a smidge." Damian's voice was strained, like he was fighting back another bout of giggles. "We'll keep an eye on her, and if anything changes, we can go to the emergency vet."

"All right. Are you hungry?"

"Starving."

"Thank God, because I'm starting to think you didn't bring enough food."

Shane pulled out plates, and they sat down to eat in relative peace. Shane let Damian take the steak in favor of a container of fresh gnocchi in a butter-sage sauce. He'd wolfed down a quarter of it before he remembered he needed air to live.

"Good?" Damian took a sip of wine. As it turned out, he did like reds.

Shane swallowed his bite. "Very."

"No critiques from the expert chef?"

"I might have added a twist of lemon to balance out the richness, but otherwise, it's *superbe*."

"*Tu parles français?*"

"*Un peu*, because of my job. But not much, and not well."

"Good." Damian chuckled. "That's the only thing I know how to say."

Shane finished his plate and sat back with a satisfied groan. Meatball started squirming, unable to free herself from the swaddling, and Damian handled it before Shane could rise from his seat.

"Thank you," he said when Damian returned. "Being a dad sure is tough, huh?"

He'd meant it as a joke, but Damian didn't laugh. "Sometimes. It's been easier since you've been around, though."

"Same to you."

Damian swirled wine around in the glass, face pinched. Shane was about to ask if something was wrong when Damian exhaled. "Well, I suppose we can't avoid talking about this forever."

Shane had to reboot his brain before he could ask, "About what?"

Damian, having taken a bite, waved a fork between them, and Shane thought he might hyperventilate. But then Damian said, "The co-adoption. I've been acting like it's still theoretical, but we're well past that. We should discuss the future."

Shane should've been elated. He'd been working toward this exact conversation all month. But disappointment weighed on his chest, heavy as an anchor. "All right. Let's talk."

chapter eight

Damian quickly discovered that when it came to Meatball, there wasn't much to discuss. The problem—for lack of a better term—was that they agreed on everything.

Meatball would be a strictly indoor cat. Neither of them was willing to risk another flea infestation. Or her getting hit by a car. Or a neighbor mistaking her for a cuddly stray and falling in love. She had two dads already; that was plenty.

As soon as she was big enough, they'd take care of a few things Damian referred to as "routine cat maintenance": a collar and ID tag, vaccinations, getting her spayed, and so on.

"I'm happy to cover the majority of her bills." Damian monitored Shane's face for his reaction. "Since you're still working your way up the ranks."

"No way." Shane waved a dismissive hand. "We'll divvy them up. Paying for her care is the one way I get to be her dad on paper. Plus, fair is fair."

Damian considered arguing the point, but his whoever-makes-more-pays-more philosophy only applied to romantic relationships. "If you insist."

The strangest thing they agreed on was that their arrangement had been working so far. And smoothly too. Meatball was thriving and didn't seem at all bothered by being shuttled back and forth. Good thing Damian wasn't a betting man; he would've lost a lot of money.

Shane sipped his second glass of wine. "I want to have Meatball on more than just my days off."

Damian pursed his lips. "Hmm. That's not unreasonable, but I don't love the idea of her being home alone for long stretches."

"I could give you a key to my place." Shane's tone was awfully insouciant for someone who'd dropped a bombshell. "You can check on her whenever you like. Or hell, I don't mind if you hang out here while I'm at work."

Before he could stop it, Damian's imagination grabbed hold of the idea and sprinted for the horizon. He pictured himself lounging around with Meatball, waiting for Shane to come home, like a fifties housewife. Sitting on his couch. Using his shower. Lying on his bed. Phew, that last image made his jeans tight.

Damian's face burned. "I'm not super comfortable being in people's space when they're not home."

"I knew it." Shane nodded. "You're an underwear thief."

"*Shane.*"

"All right, fine. How about when she's older? Everyone's always saying they grow up so fast. I'm actually looking forward to her getting bigger. She won't seem so fragile."

"You'll get your wish soon enough. But believe me, bigger cats mean bigger problems."

"I have another idea that's more immediate. I've been thinking about asking my boss if I can work the breakfast shift."

"Oh?" Damian's eyes darted between the bottle and his own empty glass before he sighed and topped himself off. "What would that mean?"

"No more getting home at two in the morning. No more accidental overtime when something goes wrong during dinner service, as it always does. And Antoine almost never comes in before noon, so I wouldn't be as stressed out."

"That all sounds great."

"If he says yes, it will be. Or if he's in a bad mood, he might fire me on the spot for impudence or whatever."

Damian frowned. "It's not that extreme, is it?"

"I'm exaggerating a little, but my field is really competitive. And backbreaking. Chef is always telling us how replaceable we are. Helps keep our morale at a healthy rock-bottom low. Sometimes I don't know why I—" Shane scraped a fork around his plate, though he'd inhaled all his food. "But if it does work out, my schedule will be closer to yours."

Shane didn't state the implication, and he didn't need to. Damian read him loud and clear. "There'd be no reason why we couldn't share Meatball fifty-fifty."

"That's the goal." Shane smiled. "Scheduling, shared custody, and late-night conversations over wine. Is this what being divorced is like?"

"Yes," Damian answered. Shane gestured for him to elaborate, but he ignored it. "To be perfectly clear, you're changing your schedule because *you* want to, right?"

"Yeah. But also for Meatball. And for you, in a way. I don't like bothering you in the middle of the night."

Precisely what Damian didn't want to hear. "You're a grown man, so I'm not going to lecture you. But—"

"Knew there was a 'but' coming."

"*But* you shouldn't build your life around other people. They're unreliable, and schedules change. We don't know what our lives are going to look like in a year. Or hell, a month. You should do what's best for you and forget everyone else."

Shane's lips formed a thin pink line.

"What?"

"I'm sensing a pattern is all."

Damian gulped some wine and steeled himself. "Care to share with the class?"

"You've brought up the fact that you can't count on people more than once. Specifically, that people leave. You thought I was going to pull a disappearing act until I showed you otherwise."

Damian winced. "You think I'm cynical?" Wouldn't be the first time he'd heard that particular accusation.

"Not *cynical*. I doubt a cynic could love animals as much as you do. From your point of view, I'm sure you're being practical. And protecting yourself."

"You have a theory as to why that is?"

"Nothing solid, but a picture is starting to form. There's got to be a story behind it, and I'd like to hear it."

Damian considered him. He hadn't expected Shane to pick up on the context clues he now realized he'd been broadcasting. But he should have. Whenever Damian pushed Shane away, he came back in force. When Damian did open up, Shane met him where he was. And most alarmingly, Shane hadn't run screaming.

Yet.

Damian still didn't know what he would have done earlier in the kitchen if it hadn't been for Meatball. But he'd been ready to do something. Or someone.

No. Bad Damian. That was the wine talking.

"I'd rather not get into it, if that's okay. At least, not tonight." Damian stared into empty space. "It's a big bummer, and I don't want to spoil our evening."

"It won't spoil anything, promise. I want to understand you, and I can't do that without context. Did an ex-boyfriend screw you over or something?"

Damian let out a tight breath. If only it were that simple, but his issues went way back. Delving in would take more time and wherewithal than he currently possessed, but Shane had that look on his face—the one that said Damian couldn't wriggle out of this. He had to give him something, and ex-boyfriends hit much less close to home. Literally. "I only have two real exes, and I wouldn't say either of them screwed me."

Shane batted his eyelashes.

"Get your mind out of the gutter, please," Damian said as his brain went to the same filthy place. "They were . . . fine."

"'Fine'?" Shane cocked his head to the side. "That's it?"

"If they'd been more than fine, I wouldn't still be single. I dated one through most of college, and it ended when we graduated. He was from out of state—like, other-side-of-the-country out of state—so we understood our relationship had an expiration date."

"But you dated him anyway? Knowing it was going to end? That doesn't sound like you."

"Yeah, because I learned my lesson. I would never do that today. I saw it coming—like a check-engine light—and yet I was heartbroken all the same when he decided to go home."

"Was there a part of you that thought he might stay?"

"A small one. I was young and naïve. Of course I hoped it would magically work out, like in a cheesy movie. It was nearly three years of my life. But he told me from the start what was going to happen, and I didn't listen. That's on me."

Shane nodded, eyes somber, but didn't speak.

Damian took that as permission to continue. "My second serious relationship was with this guy named Ed. He was cute, funny, nice, and so on. Ticked all the right boxes. We dated for a little over a year before we called it quits."

"It was a mutual decision?"

Damian hesitated for a fraction of a second too long.

Shane whistled. "He dumped you like hot garbage, huh?"

"Thank you so much for your tact."

"What happened? You don't have to answer if you don't want, but I can tell there's more to the story."

Damian rubbed his forehead, certain he could feel a wrinkle forming. "You might not have picked up on this—and sorry if it sounds arrogant—but I'm pretty good at remaining calm in stressful situations. Maybe too good at times."

Shane burst out laughing. At Damian's raised eyebrow, he said, "Yeah, I've noticed. What about it?"

"Well, I'm like that with boyfriends too. Relaxed, laissez-faire, passive. Whatever you want to call it, I'm the 'it'll be fine' guy. I don't need a lot of maintenance, and I operate under the assumption that most day-to-day troubles will turn out okay in the end."

Shane blinked. "And Ed *didn't* like that?"

"He hated it. He said I wasn't putting in any effort. Relationships are work, sure, but I didn't think ours needed to be worked on every day. He wanted drama and passion, and I just wanted someone I could peacefully coexist with. I've always thought that's the key to a successful partnership."

"Most married people would agree with you, in my opinion."

"I appreciate that. Anyway, for our one-year anniversary, we had this big party with all our friends and family. Everything seemed fantastic. I thought . . . I thought we might be headed for marriage, you know? Then a week later, we got into a fight. I don't remember what about, but I do remember him shouting that even arguing with me had gotten boring." Damian's pride stung at the memory. "He left me then and there."

Shane slumped in his seat, scowling at the ceiling. "The fucking nerve."

Of all the responses Damian had expected, that wasn't one of them. "Huh?"

"I can't fathom finding stability *boring*. I've been searching for it my whole life. It would have done me so much good to have someone like you around, telling me it'll all be fine."

Damian swallowed around the lump that had appeared in his throat. "Different strokes, I guess. There's something about Ed you need to know, and then I— Some of my decisions should make more sense."

Shane straightened. "What?"

"I had another apartment before I moved here, and Ed was my next-door neighbor. That's how we met."

Shane's mouth formed a perfect "O" of surprise. "The lack of personal stuff in your place. You said you moved in a hurry. Damn, I can't believe I didn't put two and two together. I'm guessing the breakup wasn't civil if you had to get the hell out of dodge."

"To put it mildly. Despite dumping me, Ed apparently considered himself the injured party. Whenever we ran into each other—which happened every other day—I was a picture of politeness. But that seemed to piss him off. I knew he had a vindictive streak, but if I'd known how far he'd go . . . Eggs were thrown at my windows, and my packages mysteriously disappeared. He'd have aggressive sex—real or faked, I have no idea—and I'd hear everything through the thin walls. I mean *everything*."

Shane cringed. "Ouch. Awkward."

"Not the worst of it, unfortunately. My car was keyed too, and that was when I decided to break a lease for the first and hopefully last time in my life. I can't prove any of it was him, but as far as I know he was the only person who hated my guts. I'm not too proud to admit the way his revenge escalated kinda scared me." Damian inhaled slowly, trying to calm his spasming heart. "I never want to go through that again."

"That's *horrible*," Shane said. "Ed sucks. If you want my take, it sounds like he was trying to get a rise out of you. And he picked a truly sick way to go about it."

Damian fell silent for a moment as he mulled that over. "Get a rise out of me?"

Shane's mouth puckered. "Again, I don't understand Ed and I never will. What he did was completely out of line. But having been on the receiving end of your polite detachment, I can confirm it's a little annoying. That's probably part of what set him off, along with his obvious mountain of issues."

His stomach churned. "Was I really that bad when we first met?"

"First met?" Shane huffed. "You were that bad yesterday, dude. Ever since our dating talk—which makes way more sense now, you were right—you've been different. I wasn't going to mention it, but since you're opening up ... Might as well rip the bandage off."

Shit. Shane *had* noticed the distance Damian had tried to put between them. He struggled to keep his face neutral. "I thought I was being friendly, like you wanted."

"Is that what you were doing? Pro tip: No one likes it when someone they've gotten close to acts like nothing happened. There's civility and then there's denial."

Side-stepping that with all the grace of newborn giraffe, Damian said, "I have to admit I made mistakes as well. Before I knew what Ed was really like, I let him walk right out the door. Didn't try to win him over or make any flowery declarations. Same with my college boyfriend. Both times, I told myself that one day, when I truly loved someone, I'd fight for them. I'm starting to wonder if that day will ever come."

"Ed wasn't worth the effort. You made the right call, and you don't have to admit anything after what he did. It's honestly generous of you to say he was 'fine.' I would have called him a different four-letter word."

"I don't want to be the guy who talks shit about his exes. It's not like he hit me."

"Doesn't have to be physical to be abuse." Shane's eyes were glassy. "I have the opposite problem. I obsess over every small issue until they become big, and I self-sabotage. Most of my relationships only lasted a couple months. Apparently, being an anxious mess is a turn-off."

Damian grinned. "Ed would have loved that. Maybe I should give him your number."

"Ed can go fuck himself, because I'm sure not going to."

It was so unexpected, Damian almost choked on his laughter. "Jesus, did he dump you too?"

"I'm heated about this, bro." Shane gesticulated as he spoke, reminding Damian of the Italian side of his family. "He didn't need to chase you out of your own home. You didn't do shit except want different things than him."

"But see, it was the lack of shit that bothered him."

"If someone thinks a dearth of problems is a problem, then they need a hobby. Arguing isn't passionate; it's exhausting. I'm busy enough without someone demanding I entertain them every second of the day."

"It wasn't that bad, but I see your point. I haven't given up hope that I'll find my fellow boring homebody eventually. I'd like to do the cliché American Dream thing. Buy a house, build a picket fence, and start a family." Damian glared at his drink. He hadn't meant to say that last part.

"You mean kids? The non-furry variety?"

Too late now. "Yeah, and if that's going to happen, I need to get moving. I'm pushing thirty and all."

"Will you shut up?" Shane snorted. "Do you know how many people would love to be as 'old' as us? When you're forty, you're going to see photos from now and wonder how you ever thought you were a dinosaur."

"Look who's doling out sage advice all of a sudden." Damian's smile widened. "While you're at it, got any dating tips for me?"

"Hell no. Asking me for relationship advice is like asking Meatball what escrow is." He glanced at the kitten, still dozing on the couch, before turning back. "It's nice knowing I'm not the only one who's a bit lost. Especially you."

"Why me?"

Shane did the thing with his mouth where he looked like he was tasting words for seasoning. "I envied you when we first started talking. I still do now and then. You seem so *steady*. But since spending time with you, you've gotten, I dunno, real? Less perfect. More human." He shrugged. "I'm rambling again. Ignore me."

There were a number of things Damian wanted to say in response, but what came out was, "I haven't been able to do that from the start."

He couldn't speak to what Shane was thinking, but his head was screaming at him. They had so much more in common than he'd ever expected. Close-knit families. Relationship struggles. Jobs they loved despite unique challenges—Shane's stress and Damian's isolation.

All of which had led to their fateful meeting. Something had been missing from both their lives, and they'd tried to fill the void with Meatball. There was a pun in there somewhere, but Damian didn't care to dig for it.

"We've gotten off topic," Damian finally said. "Let's talk about our cat."

Shane smiled with teeth. "We've talked about her all night, but sure. Change the subject right as things have gotten interesting."

Damian pinched the bridge of his nose. "I know you think it's fun to call me on my bullshit, but I have a genuine question."

"Okay, shoot."

"Do you worry that Meatball loves me more than you?"

Shane's eyes widened cartoonishly. "How did you know?"

"Call it a hunch. To be honest, I've been torturing myself about it too."

"Oh, thank fuck. I thought it was just me." One corner of Shane's mouth lifted. "Is that the real reason you spoil her with toys and towers and treats, oh my?"

"I do *not* sp—" Damian exhaled. "The point is, she loves us both, and we should accept that for the sake of our collective sanity."

"I'm down if you are. I could use one less thing."

"Same. Although, you've seemed less anxious lately."

"Yeah, Meatball has helped, flea-panics notwithstanding. It's nice having someone around. Someone to talk to, whether she understands or not."

"I know what you mean."

In true Beetlejuice fashion, Meatball had been summoned by her name. Shaking herself loose from the towel, she meandered over and jumped up on the table, snuffling at their plates. Shane made a shooing motion, but Damian plucked her off the surface and dropped her to the ground from thigh-height.

Shane *screeched*. "You threw the baby! Is she hurt?"

Damian couldn't help but laugh at his shocked face. "I didn't throw her, and she's fine. Cats aren't like dogs. They're basically tube socks filled with springs. You can chuck 'em across the room and they'll stick the landing. I don't recommend it, though. It can be hard on their joints, and in a fight, she'd kick our clawless, fangless asses."

Shane worried his bottom lip. "All right. If you swear she's fine, I trust you."

Did he have to say it like that? All open and vulnerable?

Damian cleared his throat, choosing now to reinforce a subject he'd been avoiding. "On that note, there's something else I want to discuss. What happens when one of us has *plans*?" He emphasized the last word, hoping Shane would pick up on his meaning.

But alas, Shane cocked his pretty head to the side. "Plans?"

"Yeah, while we're semi on the subject of romance." He drew a fortifying breath. "We've navigated our schedules and our families, but what about personal time? One of us is bound to go on vacation, or throw a party, or—gasp—get a boyfriend. Are we going to cover for each other or what?"

Shane sat up straight. "Are you dating right now? It didn't occur to me that your situation might have changed since the last time we talked about this." Was Damian imagining it, or did Shane seem disheartened? And why did it make Damian feel like he'd been sucker punched?

"No." He crossed his arms over his chest. "But I've been considering getting back out there sometime in the near-distant future. My mom's been pushing me, and she has a point. It's been long enough."

Shane tutted. "Between your mom and my dad, we'll be married within a year."

Damian's heart skipped several beats. "What?" A second later, he got Shane's meaning. "Right, the blind dates." They'd be married to *other people*.

Shane breezed on like he had no idea what he was doing to Damian's medical history. "If you have any success, let me know. I've only ever gotten stood up. Or propositioned."

Boy, did Damian not want to think about Shane having casual sex. Not for prudish reasons—he'd had plenty of it himself. But with Shane's classic good looks and sculpted body, it was all too easy to picture him at a gay club, drawing every eye in the room. He would have drawn Damian's.

Damn, the wine must be hitting harder than he'd thought. It'd been a hot minute since he'd had alcohol of any sort. He checked the bottle to see if it was carbonated; his whole body felt light and bubbly.

It wasn't. The bubbles were all in his head, and they were heading for lower ground.

"I wanted to thank you again."

Damian startled. "For what?"

"For giving me a chance, and then a second chance." Shane waved around them. "For tonight too. This has been fun."

Damian recognized a cue when he heard one. Dinner was over, and it was time for him to leave. He drained the rest of his wine in two gulps. Hopefully, he wouldn't stumble on the way back to his place.

He pushed back his chair and stood up. "I had fun too. Can I help with the dishes?"

"Nah, I like washing up after a good meal. It's relaxing."

"You're welcome to take a crack at my sink anytime."

"You'd have to cook first." Shane snickered and joined him in standing. Damian was about to say goodbye to Meatball when Shane gestured to the couch. "Make yourself comfortable. I'll only be a minute."

Damian's heart somersaulted. What did Shane want to do on the sofa?

All sorts of X-rated possibilities flashed through his mind faster than he could swat them away. Eloquent as a politician, he mumbled, "Huh?"

"Right. You never said if you wanted to watch a movie too. Care to join me, or do you need to get going?"

Oh. That seemed innocent enough after their talk, and it meant more time with Meatball. And Shane.

"I can stay for a while." Damian detached the roots his feet had sunk into the floor and headed for the living room. "What movie were you thinking?"

Shane paused in clearing the dishes to smile brightly. "*Cats.*"

Damian narrowed his eyes.

"Kidding! So serious. I was going to put on a popcorn flick. Anything too thought-provoking before bed, and I can't sleep."

"Same."

Shane indicated the bottle on the table. "There's a swig or two left, if you want."

Against every instinct he had, Damian refilled his glass. He was fairly buzzed, but if the movie was two hours long, that'd be enough time for him to sober up before bed. It wasn't like he was driving, and after being so tightly wound, it was nice to feel loose.

He sat on the far end of the couch. Not pressed against the arm or anything—that would be suspicious—but over enough to give him space to breathe. To his utter joy, Meatball hopped onto the seat next to him and circled around twice before forming a fuzzy orange ball. He gave her some gentle ear scratches, and she purred like an engine.

After soaking the dishes, Shane padded over, his socked feet making soft noises. His shirt had long since dried, but it still hugged his body, highlighting his musculature. Damian had been trying and failing not to stare at his broad shoulders whenever Shane turned around. The closer Shane got, the harder it became, and it wasn't the only thing getting hard.

Damian ripped his gaze away and sucked in a breath. Was it too late to fake an emergency?

Shane eased himself down next to Meatball, closer than Damian would have liked, and when he reached over to pet her, their fingers touched.

Honest-to-God sparks flew. They sizzled up Damian's arm, and judging by the way Shane snatched his hand back, he'd felt them too. Shane was quiet as he fumbled for the remote, eyes glued to the TV on its wooden stand.

Damian watched him, either too tipsy or too horny to care if he noticed. Shane's fingers were thick and calloused as they worked the buttons. He must spend his days hauling crates of produce around, working up a sweat, hard arms corded and glistening. Before Damian could stop himself, he imagined large hands raking through his hair, tugging hard, and—

What *was* this? His brain was on rails, headed straight for raunchy terrain. It kept poking him with needling thoughts, like how Shane was perfect kissing height. And the fact that Damian hadn't told his own mother some of the things he'd shared with Shane.

As the TV flashed on, Damian forced himself to focus. Nothing was supposed to happen tonight. Or ever. But impaired as he was, Damian struggled to remember why it shouldn't. There were reasons—he knew there were—but they fluttered out of reach, gossamer as butterflies.

Shane selected a screwball comedy, and Damian watched it so closely, he could have aced a quiz. A tense eon later, his glass was empty, and the credits were rolling. He stared at the screen, afraid to look at Shane. If Damian glanced over and Shane was watching him too, he wasn't sure he'd be able to stop himself from leaning in.

Panic squirmed in his gut like a trapped animal. Then a thought occurred: he hadn't heard so much as a throat-clearing from Shane in the past half hour. Bracing himself, Damian peeked over.

Shane was out cold, having apparently handled the wine as well as Damian. He'd curled his long legs under himself, and his head had lolled onto the back of the sofa. He bore a striking resemblance to Meatball. When he shifted in his sleep, the aforementioned muscles flexed distinctly under his shirt.

Christ, Shane was hot.

What?

Damian rubbed his eyes, suddenly engulfed in bone-deep weariness. He set his glass on the coffee table and leaned over, intent on shaking Shane awake. But Meatball reached out in her sleep and wrapped socked paws around his wrist, holding it to her chest.

Damian, powerless to resist her, relaxed into the cushions. A couple more minutes couldn't hurt. His elbow—bent to accommodate Meatball—touched Shane's thigh, warm and firm. They fit well, despite the awkward position. A thought trundled through his hazy brain, something about puzzle pieces, but it dissolved before he could pin it down. The angle was straining his neck, and he let his head fall against Shane's shoulder. Just for a second.

If asked, Damian would swear up and down that he never closed his eyes, but when they opened again, sunlight had flooded the apartment. He squinted against the brightness, temporarily blind. He was stretched out on his side, and he wasn't alone. Something hot and solid was pressed to his chest. If given three guesses, he'd only need one.

Shane's long limbs intertwined with Damian's. His face was peaceful, chest moving in rhythm with deep breaths. Ash-blond eyelashes fluttered against his cheeks, and he smelled like fresh laundry. Clean and sweet. At some point, Damian had taken off his jacket and thrown it over both of them. His cologne mingled with Shane's scent in an alarmingly enticing way.

Damian's left arm was numb, his mouth tasted like old socks, and he had enough kinks in his neck to host a fetish event. So why was he harder than he'd ever been in his life? Fuck. Dread surged through him, almost powerful enough to blot out the searing arousal. But not quite. This was exactly what he'd been trying to avoid, and here he'd let it happen. Hell, drunk him had encouraged it.

In his panic, his thoughts skittered. This was the first time he'd slept through the night while Meatball was present since they'd adopted her. She lay at their feet, though a feathery toy clutched to her chest had replaced Damian's wrist. The little minx had gotten up at some point without waking either of them. And yet she'd happily trumpeted her every move before.

"Bastards," Damian murmured. "The whole lot of them."

As he absorbed the picture the three of them presented, dozing together in a pile, a thought rang in his head like a bell: this was what it'd be like if they were a family.

He scrubbed his brow with a free hand, harder than was necessary. Logically, this was an accident, and not that big of a deal, assuming he could get his dick to behave before Shane woke. Yet panic was tying sailor's knots in his intestines. Damian was the calm one. He was the one who kept cool under fire. And he was in serious danger of throwing up. Why couldn't he control himself when it came to Shane? Especially after Ed?

When an answer he wasn't ready for roared in his ears, he slammed a mental door shut and shoved a fact blockade in front of it: They hadn't even known each other for a month. This changed nothing. It meant nothing. He'd been single and lonely for too long. That was all.

Shane's words from the previous night reverberated in his head: *"There's civility and then there's denial."*

He whipped out his phone, wincing as it informed him the battery was at twenty percent, and checked the time. His lungs unclenched, and the breath he'd been holding whooshed out. If he'd slept through his meeting, it would've been the perfect cherry to top an already belligerent day.

Extricating himself involved muscles he hadn't known he had, but he managed it. Once free, he bent down and shook Shane awake.

Shane shot into an upright position, blinking owlishly at the apartment. His movements jostled Meatball, and she growled without lifting her head.

"Where . . ." Shane rubbed his eyes, and when they settled on Damian, they widened. "Oh. Oh, shit."

"Morning to you too." Damian brushed some of the wrinkles out of his shirt. "You'll never guess what happened."

"Damn, I underestimated how tired I was." Shane shook himself like a dog drying off, and his gaze landed on Meatball. He smiled at her, and Damian would have sworn the sun must have moved from behind a cloud; the entire room brightened.

Another wave of panic sent him reeling. He grabbed his jacket and yanked it on. "I have to go."

Shane's head whipped up. "What? Why?"

"I gotta get out of here." He pocketed his phone and stumbled toward the door. "You can keep Meatball for a while longer." Maybe if he threw Shane a bone—a loaded phrase—he'd let Damian escape without talking about this.

Shane climbed to his feet and wobbled for balance, one eye refusing to stay open. "Wait, what's going on? Why are you in such a rush?"

So much for that.

"I'm not," Damian said as he practically sprinted to the exit and fumbled with the knob. Damn it. Shane had locked it, like a reasonable adult. He flipped the dead bolt with shaking fingers.

"Damian."

With a sigh, he turned around. Shane was standing with his feet apart and arms crossed over his chest, scowling and looking . . . fucking *hot*, with his hair in disarray and his eyes vivid green in the light.

This time, Damian couldn't blame the errant thought on alcohol. Shane was sexy. He could protest all he liked, but his body wasn't going to let him pretend otherwise.

"Something's up with you," Shane said. "I can feel it. Is this because we slept together?"

They flinched at his word choice simultaneously, and the energy between them electrified.

Damian's breath caught in his throat. "I have a meeting."

"Yeah, at noon."

Shit. If only he hadn't given Shane details.

"What's really wrong?" Shane asked. "Tell me."

"Nothing's *wrong*." Damian wasn't sure if he was being truthful.

Shane hesitated and then blushed. "If this is about the moment in the kitchen . . ."

"It's not." Damian swallowed. "I mean, it is, but it's more than that. It's everything. There's something else I haven't— We can't— I don't— We've been over this. Our situation is already complicated enough."

Shane's expression was so soft, so filled with longing. "It doesn't have to be."

Damian was no longer certain if he wanted to escape or throw himself into Shane's arms, but either decision was going to have consequences. "I need to think things over."

"Think *what* over?" Shane waved between them. "What do you think this is?"

What was that old phrase? The million-dollar question.

He gathered his nerve, but it disintegrated like a spiderweb. "I'm not going to bullshit you. We both know what's happening here, or almost happening, and that's part of why I need time. I'm not like you, Shane. Not after Ed. I test the depth of water with one foot, not two."

Shane mercifully didn't bother denying it. "For how long? I swear to God, if you get all polite and distant again, we're going to have a problem. Your ex fucked you over, and I get that, but I'm not him."

Damian inhaled, exhaled, and tried to exude calm. "Listen, level with me here. I'm very confused. My head is saying one thing, and my body is laughing at it with both middle fingers in the air. I've never been the sort of person who sees signs, but now they're everywhere in bright neon lights, and I don't understand what that means. I swear I'm not trying to be a dick."

"You must be a natural, then." Shane's face turned an apoplectic red. "This is rich coming from you. You realize that, right?"

Damian's hackles rose, but he smoothed them down. Shane had a point. "Yes, I'm being a hypocrite. When you left for two days, I threw a hissy fit, but now I'm pulling my own disappearing act. You have every right to be pissed. I'm not— I'm not fucking perfect, okay? I don't know what I'm doing. I have to *think*. Please try to understand. Please?"

Shane muttered something under his breath.

Against his better judgment, Damian asked, "What was that?"

"I said I don't understand you at all."

Words burst out of Damian as fast as he could regret them. "Then let me go."

Shane opened and closed his mouth several times. After a beat, he scooped Meatball off the sofa and held her between them like a shield. "Fine. Goodbye."

It sounded so final.

Damian paused, stomach spasming, before reaching for the knob once more. Slowly, like part of him was waiting for Shane to stop him.

Shane stroked a finger under Meatball's chin. "You were right after all."

Relief inundated Damian, and he glanced over his shoulder. "I was?"

"Yeah. People really do leave." With that, Shane turned his back. On the conversation, and on Damian.

Eyes stinging, Damian stood frozen on the edge of a precipice. He scrambled to think of something he could say to salvage this. When no brilliant reply was forthcoming, he let himself out.

He was halfway to his apartment before the breath he'd been holding burst out of him as a sob. Ordering himself to keep it together, he stabbed his key into the lock. His fingers shook, but he managed to turn it and stagger into his apartment. Out of habit, he opened his mouth to announce he was home, only to shut it with a sharp *click*.

He was the world's biggest asshole. Shane's voice reverberated in his head. *"Your ex fucked you over . . . but I'm not him."* Damian believed him—truly—but he'd made a promise to himself: never again. He couldn't break that on a whim, no matter how handsome said whim was. And kind. And funny. And a great listener. And— And—

Panic wrapped around him like an octopus, cold and slimy. He shouldn't have bailed. Thinking be damned; he should have stayed and talked this out. But what would he have said? Would Shane have listened after that pathetic display? What in God's name was Damian going to do?

He had no idea, but he knew who to ask.

As calmly as he could manage, he set down his keys, took off his shoes, and breathed until his hands steadied. Then he called his mother.

She answered on the first ring. "Hi, kiddo. How are you?"

"I fucked up, Mom. Big time." Damian paced around his living room, caged-tiger style.

"Are you okay?" Keys jingled. "You sound upset. I can be there in fifteen minutes."

"Don't worry, I'm fine. Well, no, I'm a sentient trash can, but everyone's alive, and I still have ten fingers and toes."

"What happened?"

Phew. Where to begin?

"It's about Shane. The guy you met a couple weeks ago, remember?"

"Meatball's other dad?" And there was the entire crisis in a nutshell. "Yeah, I remember. What a darling young man."

Damian bit back several inappropriate responses. "We had a fight. It was my fault, and I have no idea how to fix things. If they *can* be fixed."

His phone buzzed against the side of his face. His heart performed several cartwheels before he realized the text wasn't from Shane.

Just have sex with him already.

"Hollis?" Damian gaped at the screen before putting it back to his ear. "Mom, is Hollis there with you?"

His sister's muffled voice shouted, "Yes, and she's sick of you dancing around your boyfriend!"

"He is *not* my—" Damian sighed. "Mom, I'm scared."

He hadn't said those words since he was ten. He'd had a nightmare about the last time they'd gone to the zoo, and he'd asked Dad to buy him one of the elephant-shaped balloons. Only Dad had bought too many and had floated away into the sky. How prophetic.

"What are you scared about, sweetie?"

"Shane and I have been getting to know each other. For Meatball's sake, you know? Things have been . . . weird between us."

"What kind of weird?"

The heart-pounding kind. The butterflies-in-the-stomach kind. The I-have-to-throw-you-down-and-kiss-you-right-now-or-I'll-stop-breathing kind. Oh God, did he really want to talk about this with his *mother*?

"I think he likes me." He hadn't officially confirmed it, but Shane at least wanted to have sex as much as Damian did. He hadn't imagined sparks flying like a wildfire. He said absolutely none of that to her.

Mom gasped. "That's wonderful!"

"It's a disaster!" Damian huffed and dialed back the volume. "Ever since we met, my life's been changing. I'm doing all sorts of things I never would have considered before. It's like I can't stop myself."

Mom was quiet for a long time.

"Mom?" Damian prompted.

"Are you in love with him?"

"*What*? No!"

"Are you sure? I suppose it hasn't been very long, but that sounds like love to me. Or infatuation, at least. Sometimes when two people are right for each other, a month is all it takes."

"It's not love. It can't be. It's too fast, way too fast."

Fuck, what if it was? Damian's pulse rocketed to the Moon. He could *not* be in love with Shane.

Mom must have let out a breath; her speaker sputtered. "Why don't you go on a date with him and see what happens?"

The catalog of reasons Damian had compiled came pouring out. "What if it doesn't work out? What if he ends up hating me like Ed did? What's going to happen to Meatball if we break up?" If Shane thought passing her back and forth felt like being divorced now, he'd learn how wrong he was.

Mom affected the long-suffering tone Damian had heard many times throughout his moody teen years. "What if it *does* work out? What if you get everything you've been searching for?"

And that was petrifying enough to melt even Damian's cool.

He wiped sweaty palms on his jeans, trading the phone back and forth. "How likely is that, though? That Shane is the man I'm supposed to be with? You said yourself hardly anyone meets their future husband in the wild anymore."

"All right, let's say you break up. Will he try to take the cat?"

Damian started to point out that Shane couldn't, but the words were foul on his tongue. He replied with a deeper truth. "No. He would never do that."

"Then what are you worried about? I don't know exactly what Ed put you through—and please spare me the details, or I'll go full Mama Bear—but you seem certain Shane isn't a bad person. Do you think he won't want to see Meatball anymore if it means seeing you? Maybe the real reason you don't want to date is because you'd rather have him in your life at all than risk losing him."

A semitruck stocked with self-awareness plowed through Damian's apartment and flattened him. "Please don't let that be right. I'll ship myself to a monastery tomorrow if that's right." Icy fingers played his rib cage like a xylophone, matching his staccato pulse.

"I'm afraid it might be, sweetie. You're forgetting I've met this young man. Did you think I was that interested in his wall art? I was watching you two the entire night. You were both polite enough, but I might as well have not been in the room. The way you gravitated to each other . . . It was obvious, and my eyes aren't what they used to be."

Damian plopped onto the couch, heavy as stone. "I didn't ask for this."

"Life doesn't wait for permission. It happens whether you're ready or not."

"We argued though. For all I know, I've already ruined everything before it could begin. Shane likes me because he thinks I have my shit together, but lately I've been a mess." Although, Shane had also said he enjoyed seeing Damian's imperfections. Was that still the case? "What should I do?"

"Oh, my sweet boy. I may not know how to make a marriage work, but I know about love. It's seldom a bad thing, even when it ends. If you never take any risks, you're going to miss out on all the blessings life has in store for you. You've put up walls over the years. Thick ones. I was starting to worry no one could knock them down. But it seems a chef with anxiety and a rambunctious kitten were the right combination for the job. How long can you keep standing still?"

It was excellent advice. Top-notch parental wisdom, straight off the vine. The question was: Could Damian follow it? He'd thought he'd been comfortable with his life how it was, but as the days had blurred by, he'd been screaming for a change. When one had fallen in his lap, it'd sent him spiraling.

Why had he left Meatball with Shane? Not that it mattered. They were going to have to see each other eventually, and the thought alone made him hyperventilate.

When his lungs functioned as intended again, he said, "Thanks for listening, Mom. You've given me a lot to think about."

"What's your plan?"

"Hell if I know. Right now, it's to get to work. It's meeting day."

Mom tutted. "I wouldn't wait too long if I were you. In my experience, absence makes the heart forget. Can I give you one last insight?"

He braced for impact. "Of course."

"A lot of people have walked out of your life, and I've seen the toll it's taken on you. Especially your father. You've been hurt, and that's real, but it's not a reason to close yourself off. Maybe Shane is your person; maybe he's not. There's only one way to find out. Regardless of what happens, you're not alone. Your sister and I will always be here for you. Always."

Mist covered Damian's eyes, and he blinked it away. "I love you."

"I love you very much, my son."

Hollis shouted, "I love you too, sentient trash can!"

The call disconnected. Mom had probably hung up to scold Hollis, as if that had ever dissuaded her.

Damian sat on the sofa for a long minute, staring at his phone until the screen dimmed. Several email notifications taunted him—reading material for the meeting—but he ignored them in favor of replaying scenes from earlier.

The thing that struck Damian the most was how unsurprised Shane had been. Confused, yes. Angry? Absolutely. But not surprised. Come to think of it, he'd done a solid impersonation of a younger Damian as he'd watched him walk out the door.

Damian hadn't fought for any of his lovers. Why should Shane fight for him?

Cold trickled down his spine, like something wet had touched the back of his neck. He hesitated, mind whirring, and then tapped his phone's home button until it lit up. A text was written and sent to Shane before he could lose his nerve.

Thanks for having dinner with me. I'm sorry about this morning.

He reread it a dozen times and concluded it was the worst apology ever penned.

A reply appeared, and Damian's lungs iced over.

I thought you needed space? Sounded like bullshit before, but now I think it's the best idea you've had in the past month.

Technically, he'd asked for time, but same continuum ballpark. Shane's underlying meaning was clear: *I'm pissed and don't want to talk to you.* And Damian deserved nothing less. This was what he'd demanded, damn it.

He attempted to go about his day, but hours dragged into years. If Damian said a single coherent sentence during the meeting, it was news to him. He barely remembered going to the office at all, outside of the hair-raising detour he'd taken past Shane's place. The windows had been dark.

Several centuries later, when night had fallen and Damian hadn't heard a single peep out of Shane, he broke down and texted again. The kitten was still neutral territory, right?

When can I pick up Meatball? Or do you mind bringing her here?

Damian's phone became a watched pot that never boiled. He consulted it every few minutes as he microwaved dinner and opened a book only to close it again. Shane must be working, but that hadn't kept him from responding before, back when Damian had been holding all the cards.

The unease simmering in him was starting to scorch. In a fit of pique, he sent Shane a third text, and this one was heated.

Are you ignoring me?

Less than a minute passed before Shane's response appeared and kicked Damian in the teeth.

I'm doing what you asked. You don't want to discuss things, and I don't see how we can cat-swap without talking.

Hm. Good point.

I can ask Hollis to get her?

I guess that'd work, but I'd rather wait until we can be adults about this. Enjoy your thinking time.

Yup, Shane was pissed all right. There wasn't much room to read between the lines. If Damian wanted to see Meatball anytime soon, he was going to have to talk to Shane.

About everything.

Chapter nine

S hane had Meatball to himself for three days. Three fantastic, lazy days filled with cuddles, romps, and treats. She even behaved herself while he was at work, only knocking everything off the coffee table twice. It would have been a perfect weekend if it weren't for the giant elephant perched in the corner of the apartment.

Damian hadn't reached out since their last exchange. Shane had certainly checked enough times. Whenever he stress-reread the texts, he ended up feeling sick all over again. Most of his pique was directed at Damian—where it belonged—but some of it was aimed at himself. Why'd he have to fall asleep? Why had Damian, for that matter, if he was so opposed to the idea?

But their catnap hadn't caused this, easy as it was to point a finger. Damian had been cagey for weeks, and something had set him off. Wasn't hard to guess what either. Damian had more or less stated it before making his grand exodus.

They were attracted to each other, and that freaked Damian out. Funny, considering Shane was the one who had something to lose. When Damian had opened up, it'd explained some of his skittish behavior, but not all. A piece of the puzzle was missing, and until Damian decided to share, there was nothing Shane could do but kill time. Damian would come for Meatball eventually, and then Shane would—

He had no clue, but if someone offered to end this waiting game in exchange for one of Shane's fingers, he might sacrifice a pinky.

It was Sunday again. Shane's day off, and Damian's too. There was nothing to stop them from hashing this out—no bosses, no plans, and no obligations. So why hadn't Damian contacted him?

Meatball lounged by her bowl, having gorged herself on a whole can of wet food, probably in preparation for a growth spurt. As Shane finished washing the dishes from lunch, he glanced at her. "Think I should bite the bullet and text him?"

She flopped over, stuck a socked leg in the air, and cleaned each of her pink toe beans individually.

"Yeah, I know. We should let him come to us. But who knows how long that will take?" He maintained a light tone to avoid stressing the kitten, but his jaw kept clenching.

His phone dinged, and it appeared in hand as if it'd been there all along. Ugh, Chef Antoine. What could he want on a Sunday?

We need to talk when you get in tomorrow, Maguire.

Ah, he wanted to scare the living shit out of Shane, as per usual.

About anything in particular, Chef?

Your sloppy work and your future at the restaurant. Or lack thereof.

Perfect. Exactly what Shane needed right now, though not unexpected. He'd been scattered since the day he'd met Damian, and as always, anything short of perfection wasn't good enough. Was it sad he was grateful he'd been called *sloppy* and not something more abusive? That couldn't be normal, right?

Groaning, he pocketed his phone and drew several breaths that were meant to be steadying but left him seeing spots. He should be a shaky mess at the thought of being fired, but it seemed he'd hit his emotional capacity.

Meatball meowed, and when she rolled onto her belly, her striped face was illuminated by a stray sunbeam shining through a window. Shane gasped and hurried over for a closer look. When he reached down and cradled her cheeks, she tensed but didn't resist.

"Your eyes! When did they change?"

There were thick green rings around her pupils that hadn't been there a week ago. Shane had hundreds of pictures to prove it. A memory flashed into his head. One of the first things Damian had ever said to him had been about Meatball's baby-blue eyes. Seemed like years ago.

Shane waited until she struck a cute pose—which took two seconds; every pose was cute—and snapped a close-up. He paused, thoughts battering his skull like a stormy sea, before texting it to Damian. No caption. He'd either get it or he wouldn't.

As Shane had hoped, Damian wrote right back. *Green! Oh my God, since when?*

Damian sounded amiable enough. Shane's fingers blurred in his haste to keep the conversation flowing. *Right? Could have happened overnight at the rate she's growing.*

Maybe they'll be amber by the time she's an adult, and we'll have a Halloween kitty. Or you and her will match.

Before, Shane would have cracked a joke about a family resemblance. Damian would have groaned and pretended it was terrible, but that would have egged Shane on. Now, exasperation clawed up his esophagus. *We'll* have a Halloween kitty? Was Damian in full-blown denial or trying to be nice? Either way, it was lost on Shane.

You could see them in person, you know. Or are you going to leave Meatball with me forever? I have half a mind to let you.

A minute ticked by. No response. The urge to find a pier and fling his phone into the ocean was growing stronger by the hour.

As Shane was writing an ill-advised and scathing addition, a new message appeared. A brief one.

I'm sorry.

A start, but not enough. Shane deleted what he'd written and composed anew. *For anything in particular, or are you repeating your earlier apology?*

For everything.

Shane stared at the screen, suspicion and curiosity battling for supremacy. On impulse, he hit the Call button next to Damian's name.

It went straight to voice mail.

Shane growled and typed, *Answer your fucking phone, Damian.*

Come over.

What?

What? Shane replied.

We need to talk, and I've been avoiding it long enough. Bring Meatball with you. Please?

Shane composed a refusal out of sheer spite before shaking his head and erasing it. He packed Meatball up and made the short trek to apartment 18A. Before he could knock, the door flew open.

He sucked in a breath. "What the hell happened to you?"

Damian's hair, normally tousled to perfection, was sticking up at random angles. His shirt was hanging off him, and bags had been piled under eyes so wild they would have better suited a spooked horse.

"Hi." Damian opened the door wider and stood back, barefoot and ashen. "Come in."

Shane fought the instinct to march into Damian's kitchen and force a sandwich down his throat. If this was some sort of tactic, it was *not* going to work.

He gritted his teeth and sidled past. For a moment, they stood chest to chest, and Damian stared at Shane from inches away. Shane's breath caught, cracking his resolve, but then Damian's shoulders slumped. He moved aside, putting physical and metaphorical distance between them.

"Here's Meatball." Shane placed the carrier on the kitchen table and opened it. "Safe and sound."

Meatball exited, hopped to the ground, and trotted to her food dish. She was definitely going to do some growing soon. If only her other dad would follow her example. Shane shoved the thought aside.

"Thanks for bringing her on such short notice." Damian shut the door and stood in front of it like he wanted to be near an exit. "Have you seen any more fleas?"

"No, and I checked several times. I think we caught them early." He surveyed Damian, irritated for a stunning variety of reasons. "You look awful."

"Thanks." Damian's tone was wry. "I haven't been sleeping well."

"Or eating, if I had to guess."

Damian shrugged. "Don't worry about it."

"I won't," he lied. He waited for him to continue, but Damian seemed content to stand there interminably. "Is that all you have to say to me?"

Damian breathed out, and a few errant strands of hair danced around his face. "I'm working up to it. I'm sorry for how long this took. My mom said this thing that sent me into a tailspin. Didn't mean for it to last three days." He hesitated. "Do you want coffee or—"

"You're stalling. I didn't come here to chitchat."

Damian exhaled again and took a step forward, his expression pinched. "I'm sorry."

"You've said that. Maybe try being more specific."

"Do you want me to explain, or do you want to give me a hard time?"

Shane folded his arms over his chest. "Oh, my bad. Am I not making this easy for you?"

"Sarcasm. My old friend."

"I think I've earned the right at this point. Every time we start to get close, you push me away. Why?"

"I gotta open a window." Damian tugged at his collar and trudged into the kitchen. "Need some air." He undid the latch above the sink and pushed up the glass. A pleasant spring breeze swirled in that did nothing to cool Shane's ire.

He eyed the countertop. "Meatball can't get up there?"

Damian waved him off. "I've done it plenty of times, and we're both here to watch her. It'll be fine."

"I've heard that before."

Damian sighed and came back, leaving a solid six feet of distance between them. "I'm sorry I pushed you away, okay?"

"Which time?" To his horror, Shane's irritation was waning the more he looked at the absolute train wreck standing in front of him. "Is it me? Did I do something wrong?"

"No, please don't blame yourself. This is my fault. It was a combination of things. It had been such a long time since . . . I got overwhelmed. Does that make sense?"

It did, but fortunately the anger came roaring back. "What was so overwhelming? Us getting to know one another? Falling asleep together and nothing happening? Jesus, dude, it's not like I proposed."

Damian's eyes widened. "I didn't— It wasn't—"

"You said you wouldn't bullshit me." Not anger, Shane realized absently. Something much hotter and more mercurial was smoldering in his veins. "We both know what's going on here, and I'm not going to dance around it. Tell me: Why are you so afraid of us being attracted to each other? Unless I've completely misread this." He wanted, needed to hear Damian say it. "Do you feel the same?"

Damian's cheeks pinkened, but he didn't object. Good thing too, or Shane might have screamed. Damian drew a breath that audibly caught in his throat. "I . . . Fuck, why is this so hard?"

When the silence dragged on, Shane prompted, "You can be honest with me, Damian. I'm a big boy, and evasiveness hasn't exactly benefited you in the past."

A long pause followed. Then Damian murmured, "I feel it too."

Shane stepped into the kitchen. "And you still don't want to do anything about it. Is that it? You've been blaming this on Ed and the neighbors thing, but I'm starting to wonder. I can take a hint if you're just not interested. I work all the time, and I don't make as much money as you, and—"

"God, please stop acting like you're the disappointment here. It makes my chest hurt. You're not a failure now, and you weren't one when you dropped out, no matter what the mean voices in your head say." There must have been something interesting on the ground, because that was the only place Damian would look. "It's not that I don't *want*. But I got it into my head that if anything changed, it would ruin everything."

Shane's skin tingled at the emphasis. That last part should have deterred him, but for the first time in days, hope kindled in his chest. "You want me?"

Every line on Damian's face had misery stamped into it. "I do."

Shane's insides lurched. "Is wanting me so horrible you have to run away?"

Damian shook his head. "Shane, you need to be smart about this. Meatball is legally mine. If something happened, and our relationship soured . . ."

Shane's pulse was nearing critical mass. "You wouldn't let me see her anymore?"

"I like to think I would never do that to you, but things could get ugly. I've been through it before, more than once. That's why I said upfront we shouldn't complicate things."

Shane rubbed his eyes. "Haven't I proven I'm not like your ex?"

"I didn't think my ex was like my ex, or I never would have dated him. People can change, trust me. You have to be careful." He said it so quietly, he must have been talking to himself.

"So, what? All of this is to protect me? I'm a grown man; I can make my own choices."

Damian toed a crack in the tile underfoot. "And what, you're choosing me? The dick who keeps jerking you around?"

"You're not a dick, even if you insist on pretending otherwise. I'm choosing to try because I can't ignore what's right in front of us anymore. Meatball is yours, and I'm playing with fire. I've known that from day one. But I've been taking risks my entire adult life, and I'm not afraid."

For the first time, Damian looked small to him. "I am. I'm fucking terrified."

"Why though? You got a deep, dark secret or something?"

"No, it's pretty mundane to be honest. Ed and my college boyfriend aren't the only ones who—" He tugged at his shirt again, and a sliver of flat stomach peeked out from under the hem. "I don't want to get into it right now. I feel like I'm falling apart."

"Too bad. I'm not dropping this until you tell me the truth."

"Can we have lunch first or something?"

That gave Shane pause, but he moved closer, within arm's reach. "I don't know if I can wait much longer. I'm about ready to walk."

Damian's head whipped up so fast, his neck cracked. "You said you'd never abandon Meatball."

"Yeah, *her*. You, on the other hand."

Shane had meant it as a snarky joke, but the second the words left his mouth, he knew he'd said the worst possible thing.

Damian's face went bone white. "You should go."

"Damian."

"No, you've got a point. Why should you stick around? I'm obviously not as perfect as you thought."

"*Damian*. Come on. That was mean, and I shouldn't have said it."

"I'm so tired, I can't think about this anymore. Or anything ever again." Damian's head lolled on his neck like a marionette with cut strings. "Go ahead and leave. I won't stop you. Hell, I won't blame you."

Shane stood rooted to the spot, heart hammering. Part of him wanted to do exactly as Damian had suggested. But a bigger part saw what was really happening here. Underneath the logic and calm, Damian was shattering in front of his eyes.

His arms reached out on autopilot and held Damian by the shoulders. Damian pushed him away, but it was half-hearted. His fingers ran hot trails down Shane's chest.

Shane drew a breath that trembled. "You said you'd fight."

Damian squirmed in his grip. "What?"

Shane felt Damian's muscles working through his shirt. If he wanted to get away, he could. Damian was choosing to stay, and as they stared at each other from inches away, energy crackled.

"You said that one day, when someone was really important to you, you'd fight for them. You want me, but do you care about me? Enough to fight?"

Damian's color was returning, mostly pink. "I— Shane, I don't want to make a mistake."

"Fine." Shane released him and stepped back, lungs collapsing like popped balloons. "That's all I needed to hear."

"Are you leaving?" Damian's voice cracked.

"Look at me."

Damian did, and his eyes *burned*.

"If you don't want me to waltz out that door, take a risk. Test the water with both feet. I don't ca—"

In a move Shane never would have predicted in a hundred years, Damian grabbed Shane's face and kissed him.

Hard.

Shane stumbled from the force of it, and Damian followed. He kissed like he was as hungry as he looked: desperate, open-mouthed, and with teeth. For a second, Shane was too shocked to react, but then he kissed back with enthusiasm. Christ, it felt good to finally touch Damian. Like something that had splintered was knitting together inside him.

The small of his back hit the kitchen counter, and Damian pressed him roughly against it. He made a sound low in his throat like he'd taken a bite of the world's most luxurious dessert. Damian's body was hot—feverishly so—and firm as he pinned Shane in place. One of the hands holding Shane's jaw slid into his hair and grabbed a handful. A bolt of pure pleasure shot straight down Shane's spine, and he moaned against Damian's mouth.

Damian tightened his grip, fingers digging into Shane's scalp, and slipped his tongue past Shane's lips. Shane melted into it, nerve endings firing. He hadn't been kissed like this in . . . ever. So eagerly, and with such deliberate intent. Why hadn't they done this sooner? Through the blanket of arousal wrapping around him, he couldn't remember. All he knew was he wanted more. Now.

He fisted Damian's shirt and hauled him closer. When their hips met, two things became clear: Shane was hard and Damian was too. Damian pulled back enough to look Shane in the eye. His irises were gone, eclipsed by deep black, and the intensity of it turned Shane's bones to jelly.

"You wondered if I wanted you?"

Shane had to pant for breath before he could reply. "Yeah."

"Does this answer your question?"

Words failing him, Shane nodded. Damian tugged on Shane's head, exposing his neck, and mouthed it, his breath as hot as the rest of him. Shane's knees actually quaked as a hand found its way under his shirt and raked blunt nails across his stomach. He should do something. Touch Damian back. Kiss every inch of him that he could reach. But his brain had short-circuited, and Damian's hand was dipping lower. Christ, was he going to . . .?

"I'd have given this up," Damian murmured against his throat, tongue darting out to lick Shane's pulse point. "Want you so much. Would have never admitted it if it meant still having you."

Before Shane could begin to process that, something poked him from inside his own skull. Much as it pained him to do it, he dragged his mouth away and gasped for breath. "Hold on a sec."

Damian's face was buried in the crook of his neck. "Don't wanna."

Why did this have to feel so *good*? Shane couldn't remember why he was stopping it. "Damian. Fuck, *Damian*."

"Please do." Damian had found his way to Shane's earlobe and was doing something with his tongue Shane couldn't describe, but it shot straight to his dick. Shane was about to flip him around and shove him against the nearest flat surface when the same something from before jabbed him again.

He pulled back. "No, seriously. We can't."

"Why not?" Damian dropped his hands and stepped back. The few inches between them felt like miles after finally, finally being so close.

Shane had to reboot his brain before he could answer. "This won't solve anything."

"Do we need a solution right now?" Damian's pout said he already knew the answer. "Can't we just . . . you know?"

"Much as I would love to fuck our problems away, they'll still be here when we resurface." Another poke. He frowned. "Something's wrong."

"What?"

Shane had to blink at the room around them to clear his mind. When it did, arousal was swept away and replaced by undiluted terror. "Where's Meatball? This is around the time she usually interrupts us." One of several reasons they'd never gotten this far.

Like a rubber band had snapped, Damian was out of the kitchen in an instant. "Meatball? Sweetheart?"

No soft pattering of paws met his call.

Shane pushed off the counter and rounded it into the living room so fast he stumbled. "Meatball? Meatball!"

"I'll check the bedroom." Damian was already sprinting in that direction. "Look under the sofa."

They trashed the place, including turning the cat tower upside down in case she'd somehow wedged herself into a corner. By the end of it, they were standing in the kitchen again, heaving for oxygen. Every cupboard and pantry door was open, but Meatball was nowhere to be found.

As they stood there gasping, they turned in perfect unison and stared at the open window above the sink.

Damian looked like he'd been hit with a brick. "She can't have."

Shane's strength abandoned him, and he hunched over, hands on his knees. "It's the only explanation."

"She *can't* have." Damian yanked at his hair. "How did we not notice?"

He tried to shrug, but his shoulders refused. "We were distracted." He'd gone from wanting that kiss more than anything to cursing it so fast he had whiplash.

"Why the fuck would she leave the apartment?"

"You've seen the way she stares out the glass, remember? She's curious about the outside world."

Damian shook from head to toe. "Shit. We've got to find her. I should have put a collar and tag on her the first chance I got. I'll never forgive myself if something happens to her. She could be *dead*." He'd said it at a normal volume, but the word might as well have been a gunshot.

Shane had been plunged into an ice bath. He drew in a slow breath and released it as gradually, but it didn't help. "What should we do?"

"Gather up whatever she sleeps on and plays with the most. If she's nearby, she'll be able to smell herself on them." Despite the plan, Damian didn't move. He clutched his chest. "I think I'm going to be sick."

"Hey." Shane rose to his full height and squeezed Damian's arm. "Remember your motto? 'It'll be fine.' We'll find her. She can't have gotten far."

Damian exhaled, shuddering. "All right, let's go. We're wasting time."

They grabbed what they needed, including shoes for Damian, and headed into the courtyard. Shane arranged Meatball's bed, plus a feathery toy, on the welcome mat. "There. This is home."

To think, the idea of Damian's apartment being her home had haunted Shane. Now it was their best chance.

Damian nodded, arms wrapped around himself, but his eyes were scanning the bushes. "I see something red!" He flung himself into the brush. A second later, a cardinal exploded out of the leaves, squawking with indignation. It flew away, and he shivered despite the afternoon sun.

"Damian." Shane tugged his sleeve. "You've got to stay calm."

"How can I?" Damian whirled around. "How can *you*?"

"Because you taught me how." He started down a paved path, gesturing for Damian to follow. "Remember the flea scare? You said to ask myself a question: Can I do anything about this right now? I can, so that's what I'm doing." He might burst into tears at any moment, but having a task to focus on helped—and a Damian to placate.

Damian wobbled after him, his face vacillating between white and blotchy red. "I'm surprised you remember that."

"Of course I do. It's good advice. And it got easier with practice, like you said." The calm Shane was exuding was mostly bravado—he hadn't had *that* much practice—but he didn't tell Damian that. He paused at the fountain and surveyed the landscape. "We should split up. We'll cover more ground that way. And let's be sure to check my apartment, too. She might head there."

Silence.

He glanced back at Damian. "What?"

"You're right, but"—Damian brushed the back of Shane's hand with his own—"can we stick together? If I'm left alone, I'll explode."

After years of relying on the support of others, there was something deeply moving about being the one to provide it. It was Shane's turn to be stable, to be needed. He considered reaching for Damian's hand, but their earlier fight was still fresh. And unresolved.

"Let's take your mind off things while we search."

Damian headed for the gate. "What could possibly distract me right now?"

Trailing after him, Shane kept his tone light. "We could talk about the kiss. Or, uh, the other thing that almost happened."

Damian shot him a look so withering, it could have desiccated a Redwood.

"What? It was unexpected, is all. It's either that or your deep, dark secret. Your choice. You're not out of the doghouse—or cat tower, I suppose."

"You and your dad jokes," Damian muttered.

"If you still need convincing, Meatball might hear our voices and come running."

That jostled Damian into action. He cupped his hands around his mouth. "Meatball! *Meatball!*"

"Or shout her name until you're hoarse. That works too."

Grumbling, Damian rolled a shoulder in an imitation of a shrug. "Fine. Deep, dark secret it is. Speaking of dad jokes, remember when I met your folks?"

"Vividly." That was the night Shane had realized his attraction to Damian went deeper than surface level.

"Did you happen to notice I only had the one parent?"

"Yeah, but I figured your dad couldn't make it or something." Shane gasped. "Is he . . .?"

"He's alive. Last I heard, anyway."

"Oh." He rubbed the back of his head. "Then why?"

"Fuck if I know." Damian paused to peer under a raised flowerbed. "He might as well be dead for all the effort he's put in over the years. He missed my last ten birthdays and both of my graduations. What did it for me, though, was when we threw a party for Hollis after she got into grad school. She was so proud of herself, and so certain he'd be there. She cried for days."

Puzzle pieces were once again falling into place. "Does he live far away or something?"

"Nope, he's got a bachelor pad right outside of town. I bumped into him at the grocery store once. If it were possible to die from awkwardness, I'd be cold in the ground." They reached the gate. "We'll head left and check the perimeter?"

In lieu of an answer, Shane started walking, inspecting the hedges with an attention he'd never once shown them. "I'm guessing you don't talk much."

"If you count texting every few months as talking." Damian breathed sharply. "I know how this sounds, for the record. Like I'm a big baby with daddy issues. It's why I didn't bring it up sooner. But my father was the first man to ever walk out on me, and I can't pretend it didn't have an impact."

"Of course it did. And I don't think you sound like a baby at all." Shane tried to imagine his life without Dad and winced. "What happened? I hate to ask, but as someone with a close family, I'm struggling to wrap my head around this."

Damian shrugged, scanning any trees with branches low enough for an industrious kitten to reach. "Tale as old as time. Mom filed for divorce, and Dad decided that meant he didn't have to be a parent anymore."

"Like, at all?"

"He kept up pretenses when we were little. He'd have us on weekends, and we'd do stuff around town. I'd dare say it was fun. But as we got older, it was like he didn't know what to do with us. Or he didn't want to deal with our complaints about his drinking and smelly apartment. He stopped showing up for everything except major holidays, and after a while, that stopped too. The grocery store run-in was the first time I'd seen him in years."

"Jesus," Shane said for lack of a more eloquent comment.

"Like clockwork, every few years he reaches out and says he wants to see us. We cave and arrange a meeting. Then he'll cancel because he can't smoke in the restaurant, or the zoo doesn't serve beer. Who the fuck gets drunk at the *zoo*?" Damian scoffed. "Eventually, we wised up. He only wants us when it's convenient."

"I could maybe understand not wanting to see Linda after the divorce, but why not keep in touch with his own children? It sounds like I've fought harder for Meatball than he has for you, and she's a cat."

"Yup, you have. And I've asked myself that same question a million times. I've never come up with an answer that didn't make me want to punch a wall. When I was a kid, I blamed myself. If only I'd been smarter, nicer, better at sports, maybe he would have stayed. When I got older, I blamed the alcohol. Now, I blame him. He was a deadbeat who abandoned us, plain and simple. Happens to lots of people."

"That doesn't make it any easier."

"Doesn't it? Some kids have no parents at all. It could be worse, and I hate to complain. Ruins my image as the 'it'll be fine' guy."

He was probably trying to be funny, but Shane's heart ached. "Aren't you the same man who told me it's important to feel your feelings? You're allowed to grieve." He chewed his bottom lip. "Can I ask a sensitive question?"

"Might as well. This is a sensitive conversation."

"Do you hate him?"

Damian stopped short, face blank. His brow furrowed for a solid minute before he started walking again. "No. Maybe for a while in my rebellious teen years, but not anymore. It doesn't serve me to hold on to negativity. That's probably a selfish way of looking at it."

"I think it's wise."

"Thanks. It wouldn't make any difference, but sometimes I wish I knew why. Why weren't we enough? Why wasn't he happy being married and a father? That's all I've ever wanted, and he tossed it away. I've been asking myself these questions for a decade, and it's frustrating knowing I'll never get answers."

They reached a corner and rounded it in unison without exchanging a word. Loud techno music emanated from the next building over, grating on Shane's nerves. Damian was finally opening up for real, and anything might cause those doors to slam shut again.

Shane hunted through a mental catalog of questions. There were dozens of them, too many to cover in one conversation. He'd have to prioritize. "That all sounds very . . . final. Is there any chance you might reconcile someday?"

"Nah," Damian said flatly. "Like I said, we wised up."

"Good."

Damian's head jerked toward him. "Huh?"

"*Good*. You didn't ask for my input, but I'm giving it anyway. You should cut him out of your life like the tumor he is."

"I'm surprised to hear you say that. You and your dad are obviously close. I thought you'd want me to give him one last chance."

"Hell no. Sorry, but your dad's a raging asshole. He's been playing relationship chicken, neither in your lives nor out. My guess is he's getting on in years and realizes he might need you and Hollis, so he's not willing to shut the door completely. For the record, I don't believe in 'daddy issues.' What he did reflects on him, not you, and he's not making any effort to rectify the past. You have every right to tell him to never contact you again."

Damian fell quiet before wetting his lips. "Funny you should say that. He's been threatening to move ever since his 'ungrateful' children stopped returning his calls."

"Let him. Good riddance."

They made it past the pulsating music. Shane couldn't tell if it was the ensuing calm, Damian's story, or the fact that they hadn't spotted Meatball, but he'd never been more tense. "If you don't want to talk about this anymore, I understand."

"It's okay." Damian stretched his neck side to side. "Kinda feels good to get it all out. And to have someone objective say it's not my fault."

Shane's resolve broke, and he reached for Damian's hand. "I wouldn't say I'm objective."

Damian's mouth twitched up. He squeezed Shane's fingers before releasing them. "The fucked-up thing is, sometimes I worry I'm just like him. He was always kind of a loner, and when his marriage hit the skids, he didn't fight for it. He gave up immediately and blamed everyone but himself." He stared at the grass, arms dangling at his sides.

"You're *nothing* like your father." Shane blinked at his own forceful tone.

"Aren't I?" Damian peeked up. "I let people walk out of my life. And it's hilarious, really, because all I've ever wanted was for someone to *stay*."

"But you're here now. Fighting. Having this conversation with me even though it's hard."

Damian laughed, but it came out choked. "Well, yeah. I need you."

"You do?" Shane searched his face.

It was a long time before Damian spoke. "I do."

The sincerity with which he said it knocked the air from Shane's lungs. He smiled and nudged Damian with an elbow. "That means a lot to me."

Damian kicked the grass. "I still can't believe I almost . . ."

"What?"

"Nothing. We need to keep looking."

"That was an obvious dodge, but all right. How are you feeling?"

"I'm kinda annoyed, actually."

Shane startled. "What? Why?"

"You were right. Talking got my mind off things for a while." Damian laughed, but it came out rough. "Now you know everything, so that bandage has been ripped off. Ready to run for the hills?"

"Nah, I think I'll stick around." On the contrary, the impulse to hold Damian was overpowering. But the image of Shane cradling him in his arms like an overgrown cat threatened to dissolve him into hysterical giggles. "You make so much more sense now. I don't blame you for not trusting me at first."

"That's okay. I blame myself enough for the both of us."

"No, really. You've got a math brain. Two plus two equals four, right? You recognized a pattern of behavior that caused you pain, and you avoided it. It's a very human thing to do."

"If by 'human,' you mean 'self-sabotaging,' then yeah, it was human all right."

They checked the entire perimeter, scoured the courtyard again, and Shane went so far as to lift Damian onto his shoulders so they could search the roof.

Meatball was nowhere to be found.

In a last-ditch effort, they returned to the altar they'd built outside of Damian's apartment. Her bed and toy were undisturbed. As easily as the panic had subsided, it came surging back.

Shane wiped his dry mouth with a hand. "What now?"

Damian tapped his chin. "Don't worry, I've got a plan. The cat expert has returned now that I can breathe again."

"Glad to have you. What can I do?"

"We'll make a flyer on my laptop. We both have a million pictures of Meatball, but pick one that clearly shows her markings and any other distinguishing features."

Shane snapped his fingers. "Her eyes. We need a recent one."

"Smart. We'll take the flyer to a copy store and get a million printed up. Once we've put them all over town, we'll go door to door. Maybe someone's seen her."

"Do you really think she could be d—" Shane cut himself off.

Damian looked at him sidelong. "Don't say it. Don't so much as think it. It'll be fine."

"Yup, you're back all right. It seems only one of us is allowed to be a disaster at a time."

"Not a bad system, if you ask me."

The plan took all day, but they followed it to the letter. They stapled flyers onto telephone poles and knocked on door after door. Damian switched to talking about coding as they walked, which was about as interesting to Shane as drying paint, but he didn't complain.

It kept them distracted and from bursting into tears every time someone told them they hadn't seen the kitten on the poster.

No one had. Not in their building. Not in all of Windy Groves. Not for miles around, way farther than an average cat's territory would extend. By the time they admitted defeat, the sun was setting, and Shane's feet felt like they'd been ground down to stubs.

They slogged back to Damian's place, backs bent and heads lowered. Damian let them in, and the apartment seemed so empty, Shane ached. Long shadows spilled like ink across the floor, and Meatball's missing bed stood out in sharp relief despite the dim light.

"I don't understand." Shane collapsed on the sofa and ripped his shoes off, massaging an ankle. "Where could she be?"

Damian flopped next to him and went boneless. "She's so tiny. She must be holed up somewhere. What I don't get is why she didn't come out. We were talking the whole time. She must have heard us."

"Maybe she didn't." Shane flinched. "That's a bad sign, isn't it?"

"It might mean she's really far away." Damian's throat moved as he swallowed. "I don't want to think about the implications."

"Please let her be alive." Shane spoke to the beams of gray light stretching across the ceiling, or perhaps beyond them. "I don't care if she's missing an eye, or a leg, or if she needs round-the-clock care. I'll take it, so long as she's still with us." He glanced at Damian. "How are you holding up?"

"I'm scared to *death*. I've never had a cat disappear for more than a few hours before, long enough to get hungry and wander back."

"Speaking of which, you never ate lunch. Or dinner. Are you starving?"

"I should be, but food is the furthest thing from my mind." Damian scrubbed his face with a hand. "I can't stand this waiting around. I both can and will weep like an infant."

"Remember the other bit of advice you gave me? The sun's down. Give yourself permission to stop stewing for a few hours."

"You were right. Easier said than done."

Shane hesitated before rubbing Damian's shoulder. It was hot from being in the sun all day. "Let's talk strategy, then. We'll rest up and start fresh in the morning."

"Tomorrow's Monday. We have work."

"We'll call out. Family emergency."

Damian nodded. "I was hoping you'd say that. But if you need to go in, I understand. From what you've told me about your boss, he's not going to accept a missing pet as an emergency. I'd hate for you to get reprimanded. Or worse."

Shane huffed. "With all the commotion, I almost forgot. Chef Antoine wants to have a 'talk' with me tomorrow. I might as well bail; I'm fired either way. Sometimes I forget why I went the fine-dining route. It's so unforgiving."

"Why did you, out of curiosity? You obviously love food, but it's never sounded like you love your job."

Shane shrugged. "Everyone said I had to or I'd end up 'flipping burgers.' According to the culinary world, that's the worst thing that can happen to a trained chef. More elitist bullshit. But landing this job made me feel like I'd finally proven myself, and that kept me going through many a mental health crisis. If I loved cooking one iota less, I would've burned out months ago."

"You ever think about doing something else?"

Shane chuckled dryly. "Oh, all the time. But what? Food is my life. Not to be the cheesiest, but it's how I show people I care. And, as you know, I don't have a degree to fall back on. I'm trapped."

Damian studied him. "If you say so. Try not to add any more stress to your overloaded plate. You're not going to get fired."

"When you say it, I almost believe it." Shane's fingers lingered on Damian's shoulder. "We make a good team."

Damian leaned into the touch. "Do you want to spend the night?"

Despite bone-deep weariness, Shane shot into an upright position. "Uh, Damian?"

"Not like that." Damian flicked a wrist. "I'm too tired for that, and it doesn't seem like the right time." His head drooped in Shane's direction. "Does it?"

"No," he agreed as certain parts of his body insisted he wasn't exhausted after all.

"I meant stay over in case Meatball comes back in the night. We can take shifts watching and calling for her."

Shane fell back against the cushions. "Works for me. I'm guessing I'll take the couch?"

"Can't." Damian yawned. "Already taken. By me."

Shane's heart gave one extra hard beat. "You want me to sleep in your bed?" He imagined burying his face in lush pillows that smelled like Damian's cologne. It plucked a string that had grown taut in his belly.

"No." Damian's eyes were sliding shut. "Stay with me. Please?"

Such a vulnerable, tender request, but frustration clawed at Shane. It took him a second to locate its source. "The last time we fell asleep together, you had a meltdown."

At his bitter tone, Damian roused. "And I'm sorry about that. I'll say it as many times as it takes. Do you at least understand why now?"

"I do, and I don't need another apology." Shane let out a slow breath that convinced his teeth to stop grinding. "I don't know what I need."

"You mean one honest adult conversation didn't magically solve our problems?" Damian laughed, but it was weak. Then he raised a hand only to drop it into his lap. "Did I ruin everything?"

"No." Shane meant it. "Talking helped, but I guess I'm the one who's skittish now. Part of me is worried I'll wake up tomorrow, and we'll be back to square one. You've pulled a hot-and-cold act on me before."

"Shane, I stuck my tongue down your throat earlier. I think we're safely in 'hot' territory."

"There's more to relationships than sex." Though they'd certainly taken to it like fish to water. "I need to know where we stand before anything else happens. Are we doing this thing or not?"

"By 'this thing,' do you mean are we boyfriends?"

Shane kept his face neutral. "What do you want it to mean?"

Damian's mouth scrunched to the side. "We might consider going on an actual date before we make it official."

"If you think about it, we've sort of been on one. Does dinner and a movie ring any bells? And you've met my parents."

Damian nodded. "We were kinda in denial when we swore that wasn't a date, huh? I'd like to take things step by step if that's okay. There's a lot left to learn about each other, and that takes time. But I can promise you something right now: I'm done pushing you away. It won't happen again."

Shane's stomach acid churned. "I want to trust you."

"But you don't?"

Shane fell silent. Then a recent memory popped into his head. "You said something earlier that I didn't know what to make of in the moment."

"When? And what?"

Shane eyed him. "When we were kissing. Something about not doing this so you could have me?"

There was enough light left for Shane to see Damian's face turn neon red. "Damn, I was hoping you didn't hear that."

"What did you mean?"

"My mom was the one who suggested it. She thought I might be avoiding the obvious attraction between us because I wanted you in my life so badly, I wasn't willing to risk an ugly breakup. She was right."

Shane's pulse picked up pace. "You mean that?"

"Yeah." Damian scrutinized his face. "Piss-poor logic, huh?"

"No, it makes sense. And in a weird way, I'm flattered."

"You've done so much for me today." Damian's voice was breathy. "You said we make a good team, but the truth is, we're a great one. I would have completely broken down if you hadn't been here."

"It was your own advice I was repeating."

"It was more than that. I thought I was the crisis-handler, but I fell apart, and you picked up the pieces without anyone asking you to."

"You helped me too. This sounds like an after-school special, but I've learned a lot about myself from this. I'm not as much of a catastrophe as I'd thought."

"Can I ask you for one more thing, Shane?"

Shane scratched his chin. "Depends. If you need an organ donor, I have to ask my mom first."

Chuckling, Damian patted the cushion next to him. "It's been a long day. Will you hold me for a while?"

Exactly what Shane had been wanting to do for hours. Instead of answering, he heaved himself up and crawled next to Damian, who moved to make room. They lay on their sides, facing each other. Damian's warm breath tickled his cheek. The residual light from the now-set sun was fading by the second, but neither of them moved.

Damian's eyes darted around Shane's face as if he were memorizing it. "You want to sleep?"

A minute ago, Shane would have already been snoring. But inappropriate as it was, having Damian's lean body pressed up against his was awakening more than his mind. He slung an arm around Damian's waist. "I'm getting a second wind."

"Me too." The intensity of Damian's gaze, studying him from inches way, was scorching. It was too dark to see their color, but Shane could picture the glint of gold around Damian's irises.

It was like Shane had been hypnotized. He leaned in before he could think it through. Damian met him halfway, lips as warm and firm as the rest of him. Shane kissed him slowly, deeply, like he was savoring a fine wine's bouquet. Damian's hand found its way to his chest, and fingers dug in. It burned, and Shane gripped Damian's waist with equal possessiveness.

The kiss went from a slow exploration to downright filthy in seconds. Tongues became involved, followed by teeth. And fuck, Shane wanted more.

He broke away with a gasp. "I'm sorry."

Damian shuddered, breath coming in pants. "I'm not."

"I said I'd just hold you."

"I'm really not complaining. I'm so fucking tense, something's got to give." Damian nosed Shane's jaw. "You smell good. Gives me this odd urge to bite you."

Now *that* got Shane's attention. His body and brain were officially awake, but he forced himself to ask, "I thought we were too tired?"

"For actual sex, yes. But maybe we can—" Damian angled his torso so their hips aligned. Damian's cock nudged against Shane's, the heat and hardness of it obvious through the denim.

Shane hissed. "Fuck, that feels good. Why does it feel so *good*?"

"Because we're finally here." Another shudder wracked Damian, and as close as they were, it ricocheted through Shane too.

"*Finally*," Shane agreed. They'd barely touched, and he was already dizzy.

"I'm not always great at telling people what I'm feeling, but I'm fantastic at showing them." There was a dark promise in Damian's tone. "Let me show you."

Words failing him, Shane nodded.

"Take this off." Damian yanked at Shane's shirt hem. "This is going to get messy."

Oh *hell* yes.

Shane whipped it off and threw it across the room like it'd caught fire. Not missing a beat, Damian fumbled with Shane's fly, and merely having his hands in that general area was enough to make Shane's nerve endings sing. Damian got Shane's jeans open and his boxers pushed down in record time. When Damian curled strong, confident fingers around his cock, Shane moaned. Loudly.

"Fuck, Damian."

"Next time." Damian bit down on the junction between Shane's neck and shoulder, and that felt almost good enough to make Shane come on the spot.

Through Herculean effort, he got his fingers to work Damian's pants down his thighs, and then they were groin-to-groin. It was awkward, lying on their sides like this and still mostly clothed, but when Shane rocked their hips together, Damian made a noise so deep and visceral it was more sensation than sound.

Between Shane's artless thrusting and Damian's—extremely talented—fingers, Shane was right on the edge.

Echoing his thoughts, Damian grunted. "I swear I normally last longer than this."

"I won't judge if you d— Oh *fuck*, do that again." Damian had given Shane's dick a squeeze on the upstroke, and Shane had actually seen stars.

"Like this?" Damian repeated the motion, and right as his fist reached the head of Shane's cock, Damian locked their lips together. He dipped his tongue into Shane's mouth in a way Shane instantly recognized: it mimicked sex, and the intent—the promise for the future—was so powerful, Shane unraveled.

He came with a shout. It was all he could do to keep his hips moving until he both heard and felt Damian follow after. His bones were liquid, and there wasn't enough air in the room. His gulped breaths tasted like Damian: salt and soap and cologne. It filled Shane even as he emptied and went limp, utterly spent.

It wasn't until after, when he was coming down, that Shane realized how dark the room had gotten. His eyes adjusted, and he made out Damian next to him, his jaw slack.

Shane kissed the corner of his mouth. "Better?"

Damian nodded and rested his sweaty brow on Shane's bare chest. "Much."

"We should turn on a light."

"Are you volunteering to get up? Because I'm not."

Now that Shane wasn't so horny, the weariness from before swept over him. He summoned the last of his strength, tucked himself away, and climbed to his feet. He fumbled with a lamp in the corner; it flooded the room with pleasant yellow light.

When he turned back to the sofa, he was treated to the sight of a disheveled and thoroughly debauched Damian, more naked than not and covered in sweat. Among other fluids, which were threatening to become incriminating stains.

"Wait right there."

Damian's answering grunt said it all: he wasn't planning on moving anytime soon.

Shane considered snagging his discarded shirt off the ground before dismissing the idea. He headed into the kitchen, grabbed a clean dish towel, and mopped the mess off his own stomach before taking care of Damian.

Ridiculous as it was, he wanted to blush as he wiped Damian down and got him back into his underwear. He hadn't seen everything. Yet. What would it be like in the future, when they had all the time in the world to touch and taste and discover? The thought alone almost got Shane going again, but he was tired with a capital T this time.

Damian muttered, "Too good to me." He hauled himself part of the way up only to flop back down. "Ugh."

"Need some help?"

"Please and thank you." Damian accepted Shane's arm and used it to get upright. Once there, he blinked at the room, looking like a kitten who'd gotten their nose booped. It took all of Shane's willpower not to do it.

Having collected himself, Damian leaned past Shane and peered out the back door. The light from the lamp illuminated Meatball's strawberry bed: empty.

Shane rubbed Damian's back, cool from drying sweat. "We'll keep searching."

"She must be so scared."

"Or she's having the time of her life. Chasing bugs and scaring birds and rolling around in the grass." Shane tried to inject some joviality into his tone, but it came out pleading. "I blame myself."

Damian squinted at him. "For Meatball running away? How is that your fault? I'm the one who opened the window."

"I let you."

"I didn't notice Meatball escape."

"Neither did I." He sighed. "We sound like an old married couple. She'll turn up. It'll be fine."

"Hey." Damian frowned, but his lips kept twitching up. "That's my line."

Shane dignified that with a kiss, a chaste one. His stomach gurgled. "I think I have enough dregs of energy left to butter toast. Any chance you're hungry now?"

"Starving." Damian kissed him again with such pure longing, Shane couldn't breathe. Against his lips, Damian whispered, "Less so since we met."

Chapter ten

🐾

"**W**ake up, Damian. It's morning."

Shane's voice reached Damian through layers of fog. He grunted but didn't move, splayed out on his stomach with his face planted in a pillow.

Strong fingers massaged Damian's shoulder. "Hey, Sleeping Beauty. Want some breakfast?"

Damian stirred, cracking an eye open only to slam it shut again. The room—his bedroom, he recalled—was saturated with bright mid-morning sunlight. The gauzy curtains did nothing to block it out. He'd only meant to sleep for a few hours, but it seemed his body had taken the reins.

He rolled onto his back, the gray top sheet soft and warm against his bare chest. Shane was perched on the mattress next to him, still wearing Damian's pajamas. The faint scent of fresh coffee emanated all the way from the kitchen.

Waking up to a hot breakfast and a hotter man? Damian could get used to this.

"I'm awake, I'm awake." The pillow next to him smelled like Shane: herbs and piney shampoo. He stared at the ceiling for a second, letting delicious memories from the night before wash over him, but then a cold remembrance brought him crashing back to reality. He rocketed up in place. "Did she . . . ?"

Shane flinched and looked away. "No sign of Meatball. I called for her until my throat was raw. I'm surprised I didn't wake you."

Damian cursed viciously and wiped his face. "I must've been out. Sorry."

"Don't be. You didn't miss anything, and one of us should get some rest." Shane's breath whistled through his teeth. "This isn't how I wanted to start the day. I was going to bring you breakfast in bed and pretend nothing's wrong for a couple minutes."

"I appreciate the thought, but I was gonna ask about her as soon as I was conscious." He reached for his phone on the nightstand, and when the screen lit up he cursed again, invoking a couple minor religious figures for good measure. "I forgot to email my supervisor last night and tell her there's a family emergency. Good thing she's understanding."

"Speaking of work, I've been thinking I might go in later after all."

"Really? Why?"

"I don't want to say it, but I guess I have to." Shane's back bent like someone had hung weights from his neck. "I'm starting to lose hope. What will we do if she never comes back?"

"Hey." Damian scooted closer. "Don't talk like that."

"I'm serious, Damian. If she doesn't show up today, she'll have been missing for twenty-four hours. How long before we have to assume she's either gone for good or dead?"

A lump blocked Damian's throat, and swallowing did nothing to dislodge it. "There's a lot more we can do. We'll check the shelters— all of them—and the pound. We'll go door to door again. Hollis and our parents will help, no question. I bet Beatrix will too from what you've told me. And there are local groups on social media specifically for missing pets."

Shane sniffled. "And if none of that works?"

"Then . . ." Damian had no idea.

Shane shook his head. "This is so unfair."

"It is. And right when everything was— I'm so sorry. I hate this."

Shane's eyes were bright, but not with their usual cheer. "Without her, what happens to us?"

Damian's lungs were doing cartwheels. "What do you mean?"

"She brought us together. She *kept* us together, long after we might've given up. We've made a lot of jokes about being parents, and I know that's all they are, but have you heard what can happen to a couple when they lose a child?"

A couple. Was it possible to be overjoyed and completely miserable at the same time?

"Shane." Damian had to clear the rasp from his throat. The urge to cry, to wrap his arms around Shane and squeeze him, was overwhelming, but that wasn't what Shane needed right now. "I'm going to say something that you won't want to hear, but you have to listen. Okay?"

Shane sniffled and nodded.

"I love Meatball so much, and this has been absolute hell. But cats don't live as long as humans. We knew when we adopted her that someday we'd have to say goodbye." At Shane's crestfallen look, Damian cracked and pulled him close. "I don't think for a second that day is today."

Shane rested his head on Damian's shoulder. "What if it is, though? Will we survive it?"

Shane was asking about their relationship, but with the way Damian's heart was splintering into shards, the question could have been literal. If Meatball really was gone, it would rip them both to shreds. Grief had a way of either bringing people closer or dividing them. Which would it be in their case?

"We will. If, and I do mean if, something happens to Meatball, we'll get through it together. We can't guarantee she'll come home in one piece, or that she'll have perfect health, or that she'll live to a ripe old age. But *when* we get her back, we can make sure she spends every day she has left happy and loved."

Shaking his head, Shane released a long breath. "I can't believe she's gone."

"She's not. She'll never be gone. When you love someone, they live in your heart forever. It's cliché, but the truth often is."

Nerves clawed at Damian even as he injected as much confidence into the words as he could. Shane had a point. They'd already been through the proverbial relationship wringer. But Damian had almost lost Shane once, and this time, he was ready to fight.

Shane lifted his head, and his eyes bored into Damian's. "Promise me."

Damian read him loud and clear. "I promise. It'll be fine."

"Okay." Shane's mouth twitched. "Well, on that note, I'm leaving."

"What?" Damian swung his legs around to sit next to Shane, but they got tangled in the sheets. He flopped, fishlike and surely attractive, until he was free. "Why?"

"You have no food in this house, my guy. I'm pretty sure the eggs in your fridge are close to hatching."

"Thanks for the miniature heart attack." It occurred to Damian that they were sitting on a bed. Grinning, he leaned over and kissed Shane's jawline. "Is food all that's on your mind right now?"

Shane gasped when Damian nibbled his throat, but he pulled away. "Tempting, but I don't think even you can get me in the mood right now."

"I get it."

Shane shimmied like he was shaking off rain. "This is going to sound so selfish—I should be worrying about Meatball, and I am— but I keep wondering about my parents."

"What about them?"

"What am I going to say if she doesn't come back? That I lost my first-ever pet within weeks of adopting her? They're going to think I fucked up, as per usual."

"Shane, you're putting too much pressure on yourself again." Damian elbowed him gently. "Your parents love you, and pets run away sometimes. If they judge you, I'll show up at their house, politely inform them that I was the one who opened the window, and flee into the night, never to be seen again."

That got a laugh. "All right, good point. I'll get provisions, and then I'm afraid I'll have to leave again. I want to get my final boss battle with Chef Antoine over with. Swear you'll call me if you so much as see a red blur?"

"Of course." He tilted Shane's chin up and pecked him on the mouth. "I'll miss you."

Shane's lips tickled Damian's as he spoke, "Since when are you such a romantic?"

"Says the guy who wanted to bring me breakfast in bed." Shane was right, though. Their current crisis notwithstanding, Damian felt . . . light. Before, he'd thought something was missing, but it was more like a weight had been removed. How had he not realized how stagnant he'd been? It'd taken Shane and all of his annoying, endearing persistence to make him see it.

After Shane returned with enough groceries to feed Damian for a month, they ate a quick meal and chugged coffee like their lives depended on it—which they did, in Damian's undercaffeinated opinion.

He walked Shane to the door, not bothering to put a shirt on. Shane's lingering look over his shoulder as he strode away—full of heat and intention—could sustain Damian through a harsh winter.

Back inside, he rushed to the glass door and peered out. Still no Meatball. He unlocked it and reached down to pat her bed. As he'd suspected, it was damp with dew. Not exactly a cat magnet. He left the toy where it was and added some others for good measure before tossing the bed in the dryer.

He let his boss know what was going on and received a professionally sympathetic email in response, along with a list of clients who needed follow-ups. The world didn't stop turning for a missing pet, no matter how much he wanted it to.

He managed to wash one whole plate before he found himself staring out the door again. Then he scrubbed a spatula only to go onto the patio and call for Meatball with it still soapy in his hand.

Today was going to be the longest day of his life.

He invented chores to complete and threw himself into them. By noon, the kitchen was sparkling, his bed had been made for the first time since college, and he was considering waxing the floors. He was saved from buying an extremely overpriced buffer he'd never use by an electronic ding.

Digging Meatball's bed gingerly out of the dryer, he prayed enough of her smell had lingered. He picked up her toys before setting it back outside and placing them on top. His heart throbbed as he stood there uselessly, flexing his fingers at his sides.

"Meatball, sweetie, where are you?"

The courtyard was mercifully empty. If he'd had to make small talk with a well-meaning neighbor, he might explode. He left the door open, not the slightest bit concerned about bugs or his electric bill. It was amazing what grief could do to a man's priorities.

He plopped onto the threshold, sinking like an anchor. He'd been afraid of this. As soon as Shane had left, a breakdown had crept over him, thirsty vines that were already constricting.

Grandma's cat, Tabitha. "Pirate kitty" Whiskers. Now Meatball.

Rationally, there was nothing he could have done for the first two, but if Meatball died, it was his fault. No arguing with it. After a year of searching for his precious ginger girl, he'd let her slip through his fingers. There was an analogy in there somewhere, but if Damian connected the dots, he really would cry.

Eye sockets aching, he reached behind him and pinched the lip of her food dish before carefully transferring it outside. They'd debated leaving it out the night before, but it could attract raccoons who would absolutely attack a kitten.

"Please be okay," Damian said to Meatball, himself, or maybe God. "Please."

His gaze drifted to the fountain in the center of the courtyard. As he listened to water gurgle from sculpted spouts, a sense of numb calm enveloped him . . . for three seconds, until he spotted something orange sticking out of the water. It was on the opposite side, partially obscured by a stone fixture and thirty feet away, but Damian recognized it instantly.

A tail. A striped ginger tail.

Oh *fuck*. Had she drowned?

Damian's heart slammed against his ribs. He was on his feet so fast, he saw spots. He spared one thought for the fact that he was both shoeless and shirtless before he sprinted to the center of the courtyard, the ground hot under his feet even as his body iced over. In his head, he chanted *please, please, please*.

"Meatball!"

The most beautiful green eyes Damian had ever seen blinked up at him from the lip of the fountain. She wasn't *in* the water. She was leaning down for a drink, her tail sticking up for balance.

She was alive.

Damian abandoned dignity and got down on his knees, holding out trembling fingers for her to sniff. "It's me, sweetheart. Come here." If he startled her and she ran off again, he'd fling himself into the sun.

Meatball ignored his hand and stared at him. Then she chirped her head off and bounded right over, pawing at the stone. Damian's heart was going to *burst*.

"Baby!" Damian grabbed her and cradled her to his chest. "Thank fucking God. Your dad and I were scared to death. No more strolls around the neighborhood, okay?"

She was damp and shivering, but she was *alive*. Beyond looking a bit scrawny, she didn't have any obvious signs of injury. Nothing a warm bed and a few good meals couldn't fix.

Damian's arms trembled as he carried her back to the apartment, sunlight and honey coursing through his veins. She didn't struggle, and when they got close to the door, she started meowing her head off like she recognized it. At least she hadn't been without fresh water for a whole day.

He got her inside, shut the door, and locked it tight before remembering her food dish was on the doormat. Not taking his eyes off her for a second, he retrieved her belongings and put them back in their rightful places. Meatball dived nose-deep into her bowl the second he set it down and started gulping. The sound she made was akin to a snake inhaling a mouse. Damian had never heard anything more wonderful.

Much as her every movement was suddenly fascinating, he had to tell Shane. The call rang five times before going to voice mail. Shane must still be talking to his boss. Damian snapped a photo of the returned Meatball and was texting it to everyone in his contacts list— including Shane and several numbers he didn't even recognize—when a call popped up. Shane.

"Hey," Shane said breathlessly. "Good news or bad?"

"She's back! We found her!" Damian was one decibel shy of thunderous.

Shane shouted wordlessly, right into Damian's eardrums. "Thank fuck! I'll come straight home."

Home.

Damian was still recovering when he heard a specific jingly bang— something metal had dropped onto the floor: a pot?—followed by Shane yelling, "I don't care, I have to go!" Another bang, and this one Damian definitely recognized: a heavy door slamming shut.

"What was that all about?" he asked.

"Doesn't matter. I'll be there as fast as traffic will allow. Don't let her out of your sight."

"Way ahead of you."

"Damian, I— You're so . . . Do you know how much I—" Shane must have stilled, judging by the sudden quiet.

"I know." And to Damian's surprise, he did. "Come home."

They hung up, and Damian sat loose-limbed on the sofa, pulse skipping like it was playing hopscotch. The bottoms of his feet were filthy from dashing across the courtyard. He willed himself up, double-checked all the doors and windows, and went into the bathroom to scrub them clean.

By the time he'd finished and assured himself with several ear scratches that Meatball wasn't a figment of his imagination, someone rattled the front doorknob.

"Open up!" Shane called, banging on the wood.

Damian did, only for Shane to scoot around him, teetering for balance. "Where is she?"

Damian's body filled with helium. "Living room, safe and sound."

Shane dashed in that direction, skidded to a stop, and turned back to peck Damian on the mouth. "Hi."

"Hi." Damian smiled.

Then he was off. "Meatball! Are you okay?"

She yowled and ran over to sniff Shane's shoes. The sight was so familiar, so perfect, Damian stood back and hugged himself, drinking it in. Shane squatted down and pet as much of Meatball as he could reach while she purred and rubbed against his legs.

"I almost can't believe it," Shane murmured, ostensibly to himself. "Is she real? I know she's real, but is she?"

"She is," Damian said. "And I felt the same when I saw her. Our little escape artist seems perfectly fine. She's not limping, and I didn't spot any blood or injuries. We can take her to the vet to be sure."

"No, let her enjoy being home for a while. We'll keep an eye on her, maybe give her another flea treatment when she's settled."

"Good call, Cat Dad."

Shane rubbed under her white chin. "I hope you enjoyed your travels, gorgeous, because that's never happening again."

Damian resisted a sudden impulse to giggle. "Never."

"Where did you find her?"

"The fountain in the courtyard. In hindsight, we should have watched it like hawks. She'd need water before food after all."

Shane frowned. "She wasn't there yesterday, though. We searched the entire complex."

"I know, right? Where was she? I suppose it doesn't matter."

"I have a theory, and you're going to think it's ridiculous."

He grinned. "Now you have to tell me."

Shane stuck a finger in the air like a professor giving a lecture. "I've been thinking about it. She disappeared right as things between us were, uh . . . Let's say coming to a head, right?"

"So?"

"I bet she was strolling ten paces behind us the whole time, waiting for us to talk it out before she reappeared."

Damian snorted. "Do I need to remind you that Meatball isn't a person?"

"No, but she's definitely a matchmaker. Think about it: When we met and were dancing around each other, she'd sit on my shoes so I couldn't leave. The flea debacle forced us to bond, and she didn't wake us up the first night we slept together."

"She also interrupted several charged moments in which we might have 'bonded' sooner. And she disappeared during our first kiss."

"I think she knew it wasn't the right time. We were acting on physical attraction instead of getting to know each other. She made us slow down and focus on what's important. I'm telling you, the kitten is a puppet master." He rubbed behind Meatball's ears. "Isn't that right, you little bastard?"

Damian laughed. "I thought she was a *love child*."

"All right, I admit it. Cats are bastards. But this *petite boulette de viande* is *our* bastard."

"What's that mean?"

"Meatball, but she's more like a cupid. My dad could learn a thing or two from her."

"Does he need to?" Damian teased. "Planning on going on another blind date?"

Shane turned the most delicious shade of pink. Damian took a mental snapshot for later. If Shane wasn't that hue the next time they kissed, Damian would have to step up his game. And there was definitely going to be a next time. The knowledge was as fizzy and light as champagne bubbles.

Damian meandered over to the sofa and sat down. Shane followed suit, but he switched from squatting to sitting with his legs crossed on the floor. Meatball crawled into his lap and attacked his untucked shirt. He cooed over her, neck bent.

Damian watched them play for a bit, blissful and content before their phone conversation blared into his thoughts. "Hey, what happened at your job? I heard you shouting at someone."

Shane's head popped up like a bud that had burst into flower. "Not my job anymore!"

Damian sucked in a breath. "What?"

"I quit. Isn't it great?"

"*What*? When? Why?"

"Throw in a *where* and a *how*, and you're halfway to a journalism degree." Shane winked before sobering. "It started out civilly enough. I went in and asked Chef— Huh, I guess I don't have to call him that anymore. I asked *Antoine* what he wanted to talk about. He yelled, I stood there and took it, yadda yadda. Nothing unusual so far."

Damian blinked. "Yeah, getting screamed at by a fellow grown adult. Totally normal part of the work week. Was that the straw that broke the camel or whatever?"

"I'm getting there. When Antoine ran out of breath, I told him I was unhappy too, which set him off again. Privilege this, and it's-an-honor-to-cook-under-me that. Normally, I'd back off, but I swear I had some kind of epiphany. Only instead of discovering gravity, I rediscovered my backbone. And my priorities. With Meatball in danger and you distressed, I couldn't bring myself to care what he thought."

"Your backbone was never missing," Damian assured. "I still think about the time you told me in no uncertain terms that you weren't going anywhere. It was weirdly comforting for obvious reasons. And kinda hot. I should have known then and there."

Shane eyed him. "Known what?"

"Later. I want to hear what happened next."

"Well, Antoine didn't find it hot." He frowned. "There's a sentence I never thought I'd say. Anyway, then you called, and I knew the second my phone rang that it was about Meatball. I said I had to answer, and Antoine threatened to fire me on the spot."

Damian whistled but didn't interrupt.

"It should have sent me into a full-blown panic, but instead, I felt this wave of relief. I told him to do it and stormed out." Shane smirked. "You should have seen his face. Plenty of people have quit on him, but they usually disappear quietly. I think Beatrix was the most shocked. She's already texted to ask if I've been replaced by a pod person. Had to be done, though. Nothing was going to stop me from getting to Meatball. And you."

Damian's body warmed, but he still had questions. "Will you have to move back with your parents?"

"Not for a while. I have savings and all, responsible adult that I am. But if I do, it was worth it. I was so determined to hit some imaginary adulthood benchmark, I couldn't see how miserable I was. All because a bunch of jerks tried to convince me I have nothing to offer."

"It did sound like a pretty toxic environment."

"Yeah, I was starting to believe them. As soon as I asked myself why I gave a fuck, I realized I didn't. I could hear your voice in my head. That soothing tone you use when you're talking someone off a ledge? It told me it was okay to give up, that I wasn't a failure if I admitted I was wasting my time."

"So, that's it? You're never cooking again?"

"Oh, no. I'm not quitting entirely. But there's something better out there for me, and I finally worked up the courage to find it."

"For the record, as someone who's seen you when you get off work, I think you made the right call. But are you sure this is what you want? There's no going back."z

"Absolutely." Shane beamed. "La Coccinelle isn't the only restaurant in town. With my experience, I'll get hired somewhere else. Somewhere more my style. I'm sure of it. Or, hell, flipping burgers might be beneath Antoine, but I'll do whatever I have to." Shane stopped petting Meatball and gazed blearily at the room around him. "Man, I thought I was going to freak out once reality set in, but this feels *amazing*. I'm free."

His enthusiasm was both tangible and infectious. "It's wonderful seeing you so confident."

"You deserve a share of the credit." Shane rose to his feet with Meatball draped in his arms. He eased himself onto the couch, careful not to jostle her. "You were the one who got me thinking about all the expectations I'd placed on myself. And you reminded me that doing something else is always an option. So long as I'm breathing, it's not too late to try again."

Damian brushed a thumb across Shane's jawline. "Seems we're a good influence on each other."

"I agree." Shane pressed his cheek into Damian's palm. "Of course, if I'm still unemployed in a couple of months, I might sing a different tune. If I can't pay my rent, we won't be neighbors anymore."

"That won't happen. You're one of the best chefs I've ever met, and the most dedicated. I've picked up some tips just from listening to you. Besides, you can always crash with me."

Shane stilled, eyes wide.

It took Damian an embarrassing amount of time to realize what he'd implied. "I'm not asking you to move in! I meant you could couch surf. Temporarily."

"Oh, so I'd be sleeping on the sofa?" Shane pressed his lips into a thin white line, but a snort burst out anyway.

"I mean, you don't have to. Unless you *want* to. I didn't— That is to say—"

Damian's protests were silenced by a sudden, firm kiss from Shane. Damian melted into it, gripping Shane's shirt so he could tug him closer.

Shane dipped his tongue into Damian's mouth, tasting him, before pulling back enough to speak. "I've got to stop doing that."

"Kissing me?" Damian dug his fingers in. "Because I could do this all day. In fact, I might."

"No, teasing you. You're so sexy when you're flustered, I can't help myself."

"We're alone and have nowhere to be." Damian's voice was raspy. A combination of lust and impatience made him squirm in his seat. "Isn't there something you'd rather be doing?"

Shane shuddered. "Before, we said it wasn't the right time. But now?"

Anticipation zinged down Damian's spine. "Now."

Shane grabbed Damian's chin and kissed him with heart-stopping enthusiasm. Damian groaned and pressed against him, reveling in the heat of his body. God, every part of Shane was incredible, from his broad shoulders to the hint of stubble on his jaw. He scraped it down Damian's neck, and goose bumps popped up all over his skin.

When eager fingers dragged their way from his chest to his stomach and then lower, it was all Damian could do to keep breathing. His cock perked up, begging for attention.

And it was about to get it.

Meatball chose that moment to fling herself into Damian's lap and come dangerously close to clawing something she *should not claw*. He broke the kiss with an impressive and very masculine shriek, shooing her away with one hand while he shielded his poor genitals with the other. Oblivious, she took that as an invitation to play, swiping at his fingers.

"Meatball, no!"

Shane made a faint wheezing sound, somewhere between a laugh and a groan. "Meatball, yes. Did she . . .?"

Damian glared at him. "She sure tried, and it's not funny."

"Gotta disagree with you there. What do we do? Punish her?"

"We can't," Damian grumbled. "She doesn't understand what she did wrong."

"Is there some way to communicate that to her?"

"Nope. Welcome to cat ownership. They spend your money, claw your furniture, and have no concept of personal space. Little fuckers."

Shane gasped and pretended to cover Meatball's ears. "Don't say 'fuck' in front of the b-a-b-y!"

Okay, Damian had to admit that was funny. "Still think she's a matchmaker?"

"Of course." Shane smiled, taking Damian's hand and entwining their fingers. "You're here, aren't you?"

Damian thought his heart might sprout feathers and soar heavenward. At which point, Meatball would attack it. Fucking cats.

Shane's expression darkened. "If you're still in the mood, there's somewhere else I'd like you to be." He tugged on Damian's hand, eyes darting between him and the bedroom.

Damian swallowed. "Meatball, we love you, but we have to lock you out now."

They stumbled to their feet, stymied by their refusal to stop touching each other for a single second. Damian fisted a hand in Shane's shirt and used it to drag him into the bedroom, closing the door firmly behind them. Meatball stuck her paws through the crack at the bottom, but before her antics could distract him, Shane was on him.

He shoved Damian back against the wood so hard, the frame rattled. When Shane kissed him this time, it was urgent, hungry. Damian dissolved under the onslaught, boneless and weak-kneed. Shane slid a thigh between Damian's legs, and pleasure sizzled through him.

Shane broke away long enough to look at him, mouth bruise-red. "You sure you want to do this?"

"Feel for yourself." Damian arched his hips and rubbed their lower bodies together, his erection lining up with a matching bulge.

Shane hissed and pressed them harder together. "God, you're making me lightheaded." His breath tickled Damian's ear. "Can't *believe* I'm saying this, but maybe we should go on a date first, or—"

"Shane, I could be naked by now."

That got Shane's undivided attention. He gripped Damian by the shoulders, flipped him around, and guided him toward the bed. The backs of Damian's knees hit the mattress, and he fell onto it. Shane stood between his spread legs, gaze roving over him.

It was so intense, Damian's blood couldn't decide if it wanted to rush into his face or head south and set up camp. Then Shane kneeled on the bed and hovered over him. He placed one hand flat on Damian's chest, pinning him down, and Damian's cock grew impossibly harder.

"We never, um." Shane bit his bottom lip. "I meant to ask you sooner."

"What?"

"When we talked about being gay, we didn't discuss our . . . preferences." Shane's face was scarlet, though whether it was from arousal or embarrassment was a coin toss.

Damian smirked and tilted his head up to meet Shane's gaze head on. "Are you asking if I'm a top or bottom?"

Shane was definitely blushing. "Yes."

"So long as this happens, I don't care." Damian rocked up until their groins met, and they groaned in unison. "Do you want to fuck me?"

The wide-eyed look on Shane's face would have been hilarious under other circumstances. "I was kinda hoping it'd be the other way around." He brushed their lips together, a featherlight touch that had no business feeling as potent as it did. "Think you can handle that?"

Damian knew a challenge when he heard one.

He had Shane under him in seconds, a hand on either side of muscled shoulders. He leaned down and kissed Shane—passionate and deep—before shifting into a kneeling position. Straddling Shane's hips, he peeled his shirt off in one fluid motion. He couldn't see himself, but Shane's wild, almost startled eyes said it all as they raked down Damian's torso. By the time they got back to his face, Shane's mouth was hanging open.

"*Fuck* yeah," he whispered, seemingly to himself.

"Clothes off," Damian ordered, already working Shane's fly. "Need to see all of you."

They stripped in record time, underwear flying, and when they were done, they were left panting, flushed, and openly staring at each other.

Damian's gaze dropped to Shane's dick and stuck there. "Wow."

Shane raised his head enough to follow his line of sight. "What?"

"I couldn't really see last night, and tired as I was, I didn't notice—Phew, glad I'm topping."

To his credit, Shane smothered it with a hand, but there was a particular self-satisfied grin on his face. "For now."

"Promise?" Damian swooped down and claimed Shane's mouth before he could respond. Being naked and on top of Shane—finally, finally—was so good, so right, Damian thought he might unravel. Or worse, finish before they could get started.

"Be right back." Damian licked a wet stripe up Shane's long neck. "Nightstand. Get comfortable."

Shane scooched onto the bed proper while Damian rooted around in the top drawer, pulling out lube and a conservative three condoms. They had the day off, after all.

He tossed them onto the sheets and crawled back to Shane lips-first. Shane met him halfway and yanked Damian on top of him with a growl. He bit Damian's bottom lip—with force—and Damian fumbled for the lube.

Shane knocked his hand away. "Let me."

Damian could only stare in a daze as Shane popped open the lid, slicked up two fingers, and slid them between his own thighs. His cock stuck straight out from his body, and it twitched when he penetrated himself.

As Damian watched, enraptured, Shane worked himself open, frowning at first, but then his eyes drifted closed. By the time he was slick enough to take a third digit, he was squirming and moaning. His hips moved in rhythm with his fingers, fucking himself on them.

Damian was in serious danger of passing out. Never in all his years of dating and sex had he seen anything this obscene and gorgeous: the flush painting Shane's cheeks, his golden hair sticky with sweat, and the way he threw his head back with every thrust in. Had sex been this good before? It couldn't have been; he would have noticed. Had to be Shane.

Shane let out a ragged breath and cracked an eye open. "Ready? Please be ready."

Damian nodded, reminding himself to breathe. Shane tore open a condom and moved to put it on him.

"No, wait. If you touch me, I'll come on the spot." Damian took it and rolled it onto his cock with as few strokes as possible. Lube came next, and he had to clench his entire body to keep from losing it. "Jesus, I'm so turned on, it hurts."

Shane ran his hands up and down Damian's thighs, fingers digging into the muscle. "Right there with you. Gonna *explode*."

Damian prodded Shane's knees wider apart and lined himself up. He inhaled, let it out, and pushed forward until the head of his dick nudged against Shane's hole. "Shane?"

Shane shivered, his entire body flushing, and looked at him with eyes that burned. "*Damian.*"

Damian thrust in, biting his lip to distract himself. It didn't work. *Fuck*, Shane felt good. Tight and velvety and hotter inside than out. He slid home and stilled, begging himself not to orgasm. There was a spring coiling deep inside him, and when it released, even he couldn't say how devastating it'd be.

Shane's eyes were clenched shut, his hands fisted in the sheets. Damian nosed his cheek, and when Shane whimpered in response and bucked his hips, he took that as permission to move. Damian set a punishing pace he couldn't hope to maintain. The pleasure was so intense he felt it in his teeth. He bit Shane's shoulder, trying to delay the inevitable, but it was too much, a tidal wave sweeping him away. He hit a hard and fast rhythm that had Shane writhing under him, moaning with abandon.

A particularly powerful thrust left Damian quivering. "Shane, I—"

"Me too." Shane rocked under Damian in time with his pace, driving his cock deeper, and *Christ*, Damian was going to remember this feeling for the rest of his fucking life. Shane murmured, "Can you . . . I can't."

Wordlessly, Damian wrapped a hand around the cock rubbing against his stomach. It was dripping with pre-come. Damian could barely focus while balls-deep in a gorgeous, sweaty man, but three graceless pumps later, Shane tensed and came with a shout.

Damian tried to stroke him through it, but as soon as Shane clenched, it was game over. He shoved in deep, to the root, and came so hard he saw spots. If he made any noise at all, it was drowned out by the small earthquake happening inside him. It crackled through his veins, into the tips of every finger and toe.

When it was over, he collapsed on top of Shane, boneless. Something grazed his waist—Shane's fingers—before pushing at his right shoulder. Taking the cue, he rolled off Shane and landed on his back next to him. They breathed in unison, chests rising and falling.

"Holy shit," Shane said, eyes still closed.

"I agree." Damian shivered and wrestled with the sheets. Shane grunted a protest but lifted his hips so Damian could yank them out from under him. They were damp with sweat, but they'd do. He tucked them both in before his shaking limbs failed him. He ended up on his side, panting.

Shane peeled one shoulder off the mattress only to groan and lower it. "I'm gonna stay like this if that's okay."

"Understandable." Despite having just seen him naked, Damian resisted the impulse to tug the sheet down Shane's body for another peek. "How are you feeling?"

"Sore."

Damian shot up, his abs screaming at him. "Did I hurt you?"

"Not at all." Shane waved him off. "Haven't done this in . . . You know what? I don't want to do the math."

Damian chuckled and lay back down. "Same. Feels good."

They fell silent, but it wasn't awkward. Personally, Damian could bask in this particular post-coital glow for the rest of his life.

Shane, it seemed, had other plans. "When did you realize you had feelings for me?"

Damian blinked. "Was there a segue in there somewhere?"

"Sorry, I was thinking about it earlier. I'm curious because I remember the exact moment I knew."

"Are you sure you want to talk right now? We could rest for a bit." A grin tugged at Damian's lips. "Maybe have sex again."

Shane grimaced and stretched his back. "Not for at least an hour. I'm a pool and you just ate. No entry or something's going to cramp."

"All right." Damian snuggled closer, throwing an arm over Shane's waist. "Let me think. I suppose it started the moment we met, if that's not too trite. Before we fought over Meatball, I was thinking about hitting on you."

"That's funny. I almost did the same thing." Shane considered the ceiling. "You didn't really answer my question, though. The physical attraction was there from the beginning, but when did it become something more?"

Heat flooded into Damian's face. "Well, Meatball adored you, and I take the opinions of cats very seriously."

Shane nodded. "As you should."

"If I had to pinpoint the exact instance, it was when you told me you weren't leaving. I wasn't kidding when I said I think about that often. Or when I said I believed you. We barely knew each other, but I already *trusted* you. That's a big deal for me. There were other things too. Little things. It was like I'd been dozing for the past few years, and you woke me up."

"That makes a weird amount of sense. I think you did the same for me." Shane grinned. "Man, we could have been dating this whole time. We were laying a foundation before we realized we'd picked up the stones."

"You said you already knew your moment. What was it?"

"The first time you answered the door shirtless comes to mind, and the second time. But in truth, it was when our parents met. Having you in my apartment made me realize I never wanted you to le— I mean, you were everything I—" Shane flushed. "I don't know how to say it."

His stomach filled with plane-sized butterflies, but if Shane was brave enough to put himself out there, Damian could join him on the limb. "I can't believe I'm bringing her up while in bed with a man, but my mom thinks we're in love."

Shane's head whipped over. "You love me?"

A wave of uncertainty washed over Damian, but he recalled his promise: he was done pushing Shane away, no matter how scary things got. "I thought it was too fast at the time, but something Mom said stuck with me. Sometimes, when two people are right for each other, a month is all it takes." He squeezed Shane's hand. "Do you think it's too soon? To love me?"

A brief pause followed, then words tumbled out of Shane's mouth. "Listen, I can't lie. I'm like halfway there already."

Damian had to restart his heart with a set of mental defibrillators. "You are? I am too, but I don't want to freak you out."

"You're not, promise. We went through more in the past month than some couples do in their first year. We know what we're like when we're stressed, and we certainly hammered out any communication issues. Let's go on that date we keep talking about, and then I expect you to declare your intentions like a gentleman." He smiled. "One step at a time, right?"

"Right." Damian rested his head on Shane's chest. "This is weird. Nice, but weird."

"What? Do I need to shower?"

"No, you smell amazing." Damian nosed Shane's collarbone to illustrate his point. "I meant talking to a guy about the future and actually knowing there will be one. It's been a long time. I'm exhilarated. And terrified."

"Hey, look at me."

Damian lifted his head, and Shane stroked a finger down his cheek. "I'm going to do my best impersonation of you. Prepare to be dazzled." He cleared his throat. "I can't promise I'll be around forever or that things will work out between us. But I can promise to do everything I can not to hurt you. Is that good enough for now?"

"It's perfect. Regardless of what happens, I'm glad we ended up here. I didn't let the past dictate the future, and you found your stability." A thought tapped him on the temple. "My sister is going to be so insufferable when she finds out about us. Mom too."

Shane opened his mouth but was interrupted by furious pawing. Damian raised up enough to glance at the door. Yup, Meatball was digging under it as if hunting for buried treasure. The floorboards wouldn't survive for long.

Damian sighed. "I guess we should let her majesty in."

"Her *meow*-jesty, remember?"

"I'm going to ignore that joke every time. Gird your loins."

Shane shielded himself, and Damian forced his unsteady legs to carry him to the door. The second he opened it, Meatball darted in, froze in place in the middle of the room with her back arched and her eyes round, and flung herself onto the bed. She landed claws-first on Shane's bare chest, and his yowl could have rivaled Meatball's.

Damian rushed to his side, knees wobbling. "Are you okay?"

But Shane was already giggling. He captured Meatball and held her up, declaring, "*Dat's a spicy meat'a'ball!*"

Damian laughed so hard he doubled over. "Hands down the worst Italian accent I've ever heard."

"I may be the guy with the bad fake accent, but you're the guy who's dating him. Who's the real loser here?"

A ray of sunlight spilled through the window and pooled on Shane and Meatball. She'd curled up in his lap, her fur fiery red in the light. Shane stroked her dainty paws, adoration brimming in his eyes.

Not a trace of stress, anxiety, or fear showed on his handsome face. As Damian studied the picturesque tableau, every beat of his heart told him something he should've realized from the start: this was what he'd been missing, and he'd never let it go.

"Not me." Damian leaned over and kissed Shane, channeling every considerable ounce of love he felt for the incredible man. When he pulled back, he winked. "Pretty sure I hit the jackpot."

epilogue

Six Years Later

"On your left," Shane called as he carried a tower of dirty plates to the sink and dumped them in. "Sorry about this, Gina. It's a madhouse out there."

The petite woman next to him shrugged and adjusted her dish gloves. "All in a day's work, Chef."

"You should be apologizing to me," Beatrix shouted from the grill. She waved a fuzzy pink fan at her face while her other hand gripped a metal spatula. Burgers and steaks sizzled away in preparation for the lunch rush. "'Come work at my new restaurant,' he said. 'It'll be *fun*,' he said. Meanwhile, there's a line of people out the door, and my hair smells like grease."

"I thought you always wanted to be head chef?"

She held up a limp curl that had escaped her pink scarf. "Yes, this is living the dream." She made it all the way to the end of the sentence before she cracked and giggled, twirling the spatula with practiced ease.

Shane stuck out his tongue at her. "If anything on that grill comes off even a hair over medium, I'm shipping you back to La Coccinelle. Channel 4 named us the best steak in town. We have to live up to our reputation now that we have one."

Beatrix grinned. "What do you think Antoine's face looked like when he heard the news? Describe it to me. I want to revel."

"Back to work please."

"Yes, Chef," she answered in a tone that sounded suspiciously like, *Fuck you.*

"Love you too."

Shane tugged his apron off and headed for the double doors. They swung open, revealing a bustling diner. *Shane's* diner: High Steaks. Serving breakfast, lunch, and dinner—classic American fare without all the frills, and the single best decision he'd ever made, with two exceptions.

The restaurant had been remodeled with the fifties in mind: black-and-white checkered floors, red vinyl booths, and a nice long service counter. Throngs of people dotted the swiveling stools, and there were stacks of pancakes as far as the eye could see. The gentle buzz of mingled voices and music from an antique jukebox was punctuated by Beatrix yelling, "Order up!" at regular intervals.

Shane breathed in deeply, smelling butter, maple syrup, and fried eggs. Heaven. And to think, three years ago he'd been stress-reading article after article about how most new restaurants close before their first birthday. The name High Steaks had been a grim joke at first, but it'd proved perfect.

Business hadn't always been this booming, but through perseverance and the popularity of Shane's Foodstagram—bolstered by one particularly photogenic cat—word had spread. If he ever figured out how to bottle this feeling, he'd be a millionaire.

He spotted a man sitting at the counter with a little girl in his lap. She had black hair tied with a white ribbon and was using a butter knife to cut a single pancake with surgeon-like precision. The man steadied her with a hand on her tiny wrist but otherwise let her work, watching with a content expression. The golden band on his ring finger glinted blue, reflecting the light of a nearby neon sign that declared the restaurant was open for business.

Shane tiptoed over and managed to subtly lean on the nearby counter without them noticing. He pitched his voice as high as it could go. "Can I top off your coffee, sug?"

"No, thanks, we're waiting for—" Damian glanced over and stopped short. "There you are. Your Beatrix impression is getting good."

"The key is finding the right balance between sarcasm and affection." Shane leaned over and kissed him, lingering for longer than was decent. "How was breakfast?"

"Delicious." Damian jiggled his legs, making the child in his lap giggle. "What'd you think, Dottie?"

Dorothy's big brown eyes peeked up at Shane, the butter knife still clenched in her chubby fist. "Hi, Dad."

"Hi, kitten. Did you like your eggs? I scrambled them myself."

She made her most serious face. "Needs seasoning."

"That's my girl." Shane gave her a smooch on the forehead before adjusting the collar of her lavender dress. "If you two are finished, should we get going?"

"Sure thing." Damian picked up Dorothy with a feigned groan and pretended to haltingly lower her to the ground while she squealed. Then he stood as well and smiled, as handsome as ever, regardless of his complaints about gray hairs that hadn't been there before. "How much do we owe you?"

"Very funny." Shane called through the walk-up window into the kitchen, "Beatrix, we're heading out. The restaurant's all yours. Try not to burn it down."

Beatrix shouted back, "But think of the insurance money!"

Chuckling, Shane offered a hand to his daughter. "Hold on tight. It's a bit of a walk."

Damian took her other hand. "I'll carry you if you get tired, okay?"

Dorothy nodded, and they exited. The streets downtown were busy, speckled with tourists enjoying the temperate seaside summer. A deep blue sky stretched overhead, and heat radiated from the pavement. As they strolled away from High Steaks, the aroma of salty fries was replaced by tilled earth and tree sap.

Shane glanced down at Dorothy. "Are you excited?"

"Yeah!" She squeezed Shane's hand with all her tiny might. "Lions and tigers and bears, oh my!"

"They don't have any bears where we're going," Damian said, "but I bet we can find you something with stripes."

A few minutes later, they stood outside a familiar building: the shelter that had changed their lives in so many ways, expected and not.

Damian whistled. "Brings back memories."

"Fond ones?" Shane asked.

"No way," Damian teased. "The last time I was here, this jerk tried to steal a kitten from me."

Dorothy peered up at the sound of her nickname. "Steal?"

Shane crouched down to eye level. "Daddy was just kidding. We're going to adopt a friend for Meatball, remember? Like we adopted you."

"New kitty, new kitty." Dorothy's knees trembled, and Shane almost reached out to steady her, but she was doing her excited dance. "Aunt Hollis says I was a rescue."

Damian stroked her hair. "Sweetheart, do me a favor and never listen to anything your aunt says."

Laughing, Shane held the door open for them. The shelter was the same as he remembered yet completely different. New families milled around, checking out a fresh batch of pets in need of homes. The smell hadn't changed—kibble, clean cat scent, and not-so-clean dog—same as the jolt of excitement that crackled through Shane. Somewhere in here, the next member of their clan was waiting for them.

A woman in a teal shirt approached, much like all those years ago. "Hi there. Do you know what you're looking for?"

"A cat," Shane and Damian said at the same time.

"You got it." She bent down and smiled at Dorothy. "What's your name, sweetheart?"

Dorothy twisted chubby fingers together, staring at her frilly socks. "Dottie."

"Aw, what a cutie. Right this way." She led them down a hallway Shane definitely remembered. Over her shoulder, she asked, "Have you been here before?"

"Multiple times," Damian answered.

"Only once," said Shane. "It was . . . I was going to say eventful, but fruitful might be more accurate."

Damian narrowed his eyes, and Shane smirked.

"Oh good," the employee said obliviously. She stopped in front of a room filled with crates. "If you've adopted from us before, then I'm sure you and your husband will have no issues. I'll be back to check on you in a bit." At the sound of frantic barking, she hurried off.

"Ah, I'll never get tired of this," Shane said.

"What?" Damian was already peering into the kennels with Dorothy bouncing at his side like a pogo stick. "Adoption? Because after this one, I think we're good for a while."

"No, being referred to as your husband. Three years, and it still makes me smile."

"Sap," Damian said, but he reached for Shane's hand. "Did you text your folks? Speaking of which, Mom can't make it. She says hi, and also that Linda is a much more modern name than Dorothy. Not to bring up our oldest argument."

"Second oldest." Shane waggled his eyebrows. "You're just mad I finally beat you at rock, paper, scissors."

"Yeah, yeah, I lost. I admit it." Damian grinned. "Should we wait for your parents before we look in earnest?"

"No need," said a deep voice behind them. "Sorry we're late. Dot thought we were supposed to meet at the diner."

"Grandma! Grandpa!" Dorothy bounded over and hugged the original Dorothy's leg.

"Come here, you." Mom—now Grandma—leaned down and gave her a kiss on each cheek. "How's my favorite granddaughter?"

Dorothy didn't answer in favor of flinging her arms up in Grandpa's direction, the classic pick-me-up pose. Grandpa did, and Shane suspected his groan wasn't feigned. "When did you get so big? I swear, a year ago you were knee-high to a grasshopper."

"Right?" Shane said. "Every time I blink, she's taller. And that beautiful dark hair." He nudged Damian with an elbow. "She gets that from you, adopted or not."

Damian slung an arm around his neck. "Let's hope she gets your cooking skills."

Dorothy glanced at her grandpa. "I wanna look at the kitties."

"Here, darling." Damian took her from Grandpa and balanced her on a hip. To Shane, he said, "I'll take her. You catch up with your folks."

"You're the best." He pecked him and turned to his parents. "So glad you two could make it."

Grandpa slapped him on the shoulder. "As if we'd miss the anniversary of our granddaughter's adoption. How's the restaurant?"

"Busy. We're adding a brunch menu next week, and it's going to be—" he glanced at his daughter "—h-e-l-l."

"I'm so proud of you." Grandpa pulled him into a rib-crushing hug. "My son, the successful business owner."

Grandma patted his cheek. "I can't believe my baby is thirty."

"Don't remind me," Shane wheezed, arms pinned to his sides. "Getting older is no joke."

Damian snorted from over by a row of cages. "Tell that to my lower back. It thinks it's *hilarious*."

Grandpa released him, and Shane took a deep, rattling breath. "It's funny, I didn't cross one item off my list of things I wanted to be when I grew up, and yet I couldn't be happier."

Grandma smiled. "We're so happy for you two. Or three. Or five, depending on how you're counting."

"See?" Grandpa elbowed Shane. "If you'd let us set you up with Linda's son in the first place, you might've gotten together sooner."

"Doesn't matter how much time it took," Shane said, his heart expanding like a balloon, "so long as we ended up here."

They were interrupted by a squeak, followed by, "This one, this one!"

"I think we have a winner," Damian announced. "And he's a panther to go with our tiger. Very energetic."

"Good." Shane craned his neck to see. Dorothy had her nose pressed up to the bars, blocking the view. "He can keep up with Meatball. Our little girl sure didn't stay little for long."

He almost warned Dorothy to watch out for claws, but Damian was already scooting her back to safety. "Everyone, come see."

They huddled around the cage. A sleek black cat was racing around the perimeter, trying to pay attention to all of them at once. His coat was so shiny, he almost had white patches when the light hit him a certain way. He pranced like he was on parade.

"What a charmer. He's perfect." Shane pumped a fist in the air before turning to Damian. "Halloween kitties! I've been rooting for this ever since you brought it up."

Damian frowned. "When did I do that?"

"A million years ago."

"Giant green eyes," Damian observed. "Beautiful. He and Meatball will be twins."

Dorothy wiggled a finger through the bars. "Pancake."

"What's that, kitten?" Damian kneeled next to her. "Pancake? You're not still hungry, are you?"

"That's his name," Dorothy said, stating a fact.

Shane and Damian exchanged a silent look before they both broke into grins.

"*Pancake*," Shane said. "Meatball and Pancake. I love it."

"Me too."

"We'll grab an employee," Grandma said, already tugging Grandpa along with her. "I don't think your particular brand of lightning will strike twice, but with a cat that outgoing, someone's bound to snap him up."

"Thanks. We'll be right here." Shane waited until they'd disappeared before planting a big kiss on Damian's cheek. "I love you."

Damian leaned down and kissed him properly on the mouth. "I love you so much, Shane. You okay?"

"Can't a man kiss his own husband?" Shane pulled him closer. "I'm excited is all. Everything's going so well, I don't know how we got so lucky."

"It wasn't luck, but I know exactly what you mean." He winked. "Don't worry. It'll be fine."

Shane's parents returned with a shelter employee in tow. She approached the cage and peered in. "This one?"

"Yup," Damian answered. "Our daughter already named him and everything."

"Ah, it's a black cat too. That's great. They don't get adopted as quickly."

Dorothy sniffled. "They don't?"

Damian scooped Dorothy up and whirled her around before she could break into proper tears. "That's why it's so wonderful you picked him. We'll take Pancake home and give him all the love he can handle. Okay?"

"Okay." She tucked her face into the crook of Damian's neck. "I'm sleepy, Daddy."

"As soon as we're done, we'll take a nap."

Grandma linked arms with her husband. "We'll get out of your hair. Thanks for letting us be here, and if you ever need a babysitter . . ."

Shane smiled. "You'll be the first one we call. Though you may have to fight Linda for it. She's almost spent more time at the new house than we have."

Grandma chuckled. "Bless her. It takes a village. Are you worried Meatball will be upset about Pancake?"

Shane's smile widened. "Maybe a little, but I did marry a cat expert. Whatever happens, we'll handle it together."

They said their goodbyes and after a final round of hugs, his parents left while the employee went to get their application.

Damian set Dorothy back down. "You guard the cat. Don't let anyone get close, unless they promise they're a dog person."

She giggled and plopped down in front of the kennel, eyes glued to it.

Shane seized the opportunity to pull Damian closer. "Did you ever think we'd end up here? Married with our own growing family?"

"I'm sure you're expecting me to say hell no." He peeked at Dorothy, but she was absorbed in playing with Pancake. "But yeah, around six months in, I knew you were the one."

"That soon, huh?" Shane squeezed his waist. "Yet you made me wait two years."

"You could have proposed yourself, you know."

"And miss the sight of you getting down on one knee, shaking so hard you almost dropped the ring? Perish the thought."

"Har-har," Damian said without any real venom. "But seriously, I've been meaning to send your father a gift basket for insisting you adopt a pet."

Shane tapped his chin. "You know, there's one thing about that day we never resolved."

"What?"

"Our oldest argument: Which of us saw Meatball first?"

In lieu of an answer, Damian kissed Shane with fervor. It was infused with so much warmth, love, and tenderness it left Shane breathless. Not for the first or last time.

When Damian pulled back, he was smiling, bright as the sun. "Does it matter?"

"No," Shane agreed. "Not even a little."

Dear Reader,

Thank you for reading Quinn Anderson's *Are You Kitten Me*!

We know your time is precious and you have many, many entertainment options, so it means a lot that you've chosen to spend your time reading. We really hope you enjoyed it.

We'd be honored if you'd consider posting a review—good or bad—on sites like **Amazon, Barnes & Noble, Kobo, Goodreads, Twitter, Facebook, Tumblr,** and your blog or website. We'd also be honored if you told your friends and family about this book. Word of mouth is a book's lifeblood!

For more information on upcoming releases, author interviews, blog tours, contests, giveaways, and more, please sign up for our weekly, spam-free newsletter and visit us around the web:

Newsletter: riptidepublishing.com/newsletter
Twitter: twitter.com/RiptideBooks
Facebook: facebook.com/RiptidePublishing
Goodreads: tinyurl.com/RiptideOnGoodreads
Tumblr: riptidepublishing.tumblr.com

Thank you so much for Reading the Rainbow!

RiptidePublishing.com

also by Quinn Anderson

Murmur Inc. series
Hotline
Action
Cam Boy

The Long Way Around
The Academy
New Heights
On Solid Ground
All of the Above
The Other Five Percent
Fourteen Summers

about the  Author

Quinn Anderson is an alumna of the University of Dublin in Ireland and has a master's degree in psychology. She wrote her dissertation on sexuality in popular literature and continues to explore evolving themes in erotica in her professional life.

A nerd extraordinaire, she was raised on an unhealthy diet of video games, anime, pop culture, and comics from infancy. She stays true to her nerd roots in writing and in life, and frequently draws inspiration from her many fandoms, which include *Yuri on Ice*, Star Wars, *Buffy*, and more. Growing up, while most of her friends were fighting evil by moonlight, Anderson was kamehameha-ing her way through all the shounen anime she could get her hands on. You will often find her interacting with fellow fans online and offline via conventions and Tumblr, and she is happy to talk about anything from nerd life to writing tips. She has attended conventions on three separate continents and now considers herself a career geek. She advises anyone who attends pop culture events in the UK to watch out for Weeping Angels, as they are everywhere. If you're at an event, and you see a 6'2" redhead wandering around with a vague look on her face, that's probably her.

Her favorite authors include Gail Carson Levine, Libba Bray, and Tamora Pierce. When she's not writing, she enjoys traveling, cooking, spending too much time on the internet, playing fetch with her cat, screwing the rules, watching Markiplier play games she's too scared to play herself, and catching 'em all.

Connect with Quinn:
Facebook: facebook.com/AuthorQuinnAnderson
Twitter: @QuinnAndersonXO
Tumblr: QuinnAndersonWrites.tumblr.com
Email: quinnandersonwrites@gmail.com